"I've alrea ▓▓▓▓▓▓
stitch on,"

Tessa said firmly.

To her surprise, a dull flush crept over Ross's lean cheeks, and he gripped the sheet about him all the more firmly. He was actually modest! she realized.

"I can't help last night," Ross muttered. "Since I wasn't able to give my consent, I hope you got a thrill—"

"As a matter of fact, I didn't," Tessa hurriedly lied. "I was too busy saving your life to bother looking at you."

The expression Ross trained on her was noticeably skeptical. "Shorts," he insisted.

"Oh, come on, Ross!" Tessa cried in exasperation. "As many times as you've been hospitalized, surely other women doctors have examined you."

"They weren't—" He bit back the retort. They weren't *you*, he added to himself.

Dear Reader,

In past months I've used this page to tell you what we editors are doing to live up to the name Silhouette **Special Edition**:

We've brought you the latest releases from authors you've made into stars; we've introduced new writers we hope you'll take to your heart. We've offered classic romantic plots; we've premiered innovative angles in storytelling. We've presented miniseries, sequels and spin-offs; we've reissued timeless favorites in Silhouette *Classics*. We've even updated our covers, striving to give you editions you can be proud to read, happy to own.

All these editorial efforts are aimed at making Silhouette **Special Edition** a consistently satisfying line of sophisticated, substantial, emotion-packed novels that will touch your heart and live on in your memory long after the last page is turned.

In coming months our authors will speak out from this page as well, sharing with you what's special to them about Silhouette **Special Edition**. I'd love to hear from *you*, too. In the past your letters have helped guide us in our editorial choices. How do you think we're doing now? Some time ago I made a promise on this page—that "each and every month, Silhouette **Special Edition** is dedicated to becoming more special than ever." Are we living up to that promise? What's special to *you* about Silhouette **Special Edition**? Share your feelings with us, and, who knows—maybe some day *your* name will appear on this page!

My very best wishes,

Leslie Kazanjian, Senior Editor
Silhouette Books
300 East 42nd Street
New York, N.Y. 10017

ANNE LACEY
A Charmed Life

Silhouette Special Edition

Published by Silhouette Books New York

America's Publisher of Contemporary Romance

SPECIAL THANKS to Bob Morse,
the first bird-watcher to see
the flame-colored tanager
in the United States (Coronado National Forest,
Portal, Arizona, April 11, 1985).
For taking me to see this beautiful bird, *gracias!*

SILHOUETTE BOOKS
300 East 42nd St., New York, N.Y. 10017

Copyright © 1988 by Anne Lacey

ISBN: 0-373-09498-1

First Silhouette Books printing December 1988

Printed in the U.S.A.

Books by Anne Lacey

ANNE LACEY

hails from Baton Rouge, Louisiana, an ideal jump-ing-off point for her ardent explorations of antebel-lum homes up and down the Mississippi River and her frequent visits to two favorite cities, Natchez and New Orleans. Having lived in Arkansas, Oklahoma, Arizona, Mississippi and several places in Texas, and having traveled extensively in the United States, Europe and Canada, she is admittedly a rolling stone. Even when she's busy writing, Anne keeps a bag packed at all times; after all, she never knows when a chance to travel might pop up.

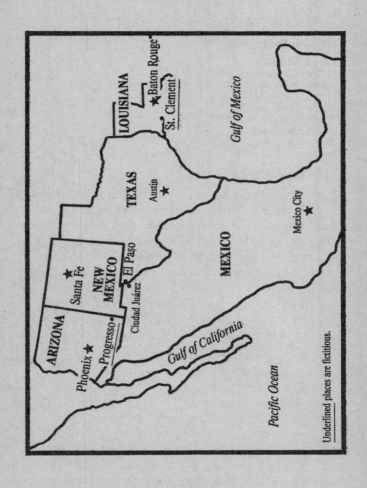

Underlined places are fictitious.

Prologue

The Atchafalaya Swamp—Southern Louisiana

Things were going just great until the snake dropped into the boat.

Oh, shoot, thought Ross Stanton in annoyance. But there was no point in getting upset, even though he could tell both from the serpent's color and the shape of its head that he was now sharing his motorboat with the notoriously ill-tempered cottonmouth moccasin. They grew large in the steaming swamplands; even so, this particular specimen was a real granddaddy.

The snake had landed with a soft splat, which obviously made it madder than hell because it hissed and then immediately headed straight for Ross's sandal-clad foot.

At that moment his finger, poised on the shutter of his camera, started sweating and he wondered why he'd worn casual thongs instead of his knee-high waders this morning. Hey, no big deal, Ross sought to reassure himself. You've seen hundreds of snakes before—even been bitten a couple of times. And it's not like this cottonmouth is hanging in your face or someplace where a bite can get serious. Why, the most he can chew on is a lousy toe.

For some reason, the logical voice in his mind didn't particularly cheer him up. Maybe it was because the snake, which Ross kept watching from the corner of his eye, looked like one mean, mad, ugly customer.

Still, Ross managed not to move or even sigh, since the bird he was after was hiding in the bush nearby. By God, he *knew* it was here. Maybe the rest of the world had written off the ivory-billed woodpecker as extinct and kaput, another species lost to mankind, but he and Émile Arceneaux damned well knew differently. And it wasn't because that crazy Cajun fisherman had been drinking too much of his own home brew, either! Émile's razor-sharp eyes could always be trusted, Ross knew, whether the guy was sober, drunk or hung over.

All the while the moccasin kept gliding closer and closer, until Ross observed that now time was doing a warp act. It always happened. When he was having fun—or sex—time accelerated. An hour fairly galloped by. But just let him be bored out of his skull or in imminent danger of some sort, and time promptly slowed down. Each second seemed to last an agonizing minute and every minute became an excruciating hour. And right now time was doing its very slowest crawl.

Ross swallowed hard and tried not to remember how sick he'd been the last time a snake had bitten him. Because now just wasn't the best time to go overboard into that deep, black, murky swamp water, he thought as he caught a glimpse of the alligators he'd seen earlier.

When Ross had first poled into this thicket today, dodging cypress stumps and overhanging limbs, those three big sleepy-looking creatures had been dozing on a sandbar. They'd looked for all the world like overfed executives, nodding off after lunch in the board room. But now that the alligators were swimming around again, they bore an entirely different appearance. They were alert, even predatory. Ross began to fear they might have missed lunch and were starting to feel just a tad hungry.

Still keeping his camera trained on the thicket concealing the ivory-billed woodpecker, Ross allowed himself a sigh. Some days nothing went right. Now he was going to have to make one of life's minor but irritating decisions. Come on, bird, he coaxed silently. Time's running out for ol' Ross. C'mon, sweetie, and get your picture snapped.

Then all at once it was too late, because the cottonmouth was right here, a scant inch away. And suddenly, in one of those wholly irrelevant flashbacks, Ross remembered the very last interview he'd had with a news reporter, after he'd won the Pulitzer Prize.

"Ross, what do you wear to go shooting in the swamp?" the fashion-conscious woman from a major wire service had inquired. "A wet suit?"

"Only in January," Ross had replied. "The rest of the year in Louisiana it's just too blame hot for clothes. Mostly I wear cotton shorts. No shirt. No skivvies, either."

But despite his deliberately coy revelation, the lady reporter just hadn't been interested. Maybe she had been married or something.

And thongs, Ross thought, eyeing the snake who now had his big cottony-white mouth open. Yeah, I really should have told that lady reporter that I usually just wear thong sandals, an unwise decision I am presently beginning to regret.

Do something! his mind screamed.

"You stupid bird," Ross railed aloud at the shy woodpecker, who was still hiding discreetly. Then he abruptly jumped out of the boat backwards. That way his camera still pointed aloft until the very last second. Maybe, just maybe, he could flush out the elusive bird.

Ross was a born optimist, but it wasn't a perfect plan.

He landed in the brackish water with a huge splash and came up thrashing just inches away from a prowling 'gator. Frantically Ross backstroked once, twice—and then went smack into the middle of a water bush where two close relatives of the cottonmouth in his boat lay sunning, strung out like strands of lights on a Christmas tree. At least they were strung out until Ross upended them. As he went back down again into the thick, inky water, Ross thought he felt something graze his thigh. Probably just a stick or thorn, of course.

How about a fang? his mind inquired pointedly.

He came up spluttering and by now, of course, the ivory-billed woodpecker, frightened by all the commotion, had indeed soared out of the thicket. Although Ross managed to grab one quick shot, he knew drearily that even if his reckless aim proved accurate, the stupid bird was flying too fast to be more than a mere blur on film.

Angrily Ross muttered a certain expletive that his gentle stepmother, Linda Hays-Stanton, had always called, "That awful, awful word!"

Ross's thigh had started to throb in earnest, and as he tipped up his motorboat to dump the original moccasin he added a few more awful words to the first. Another lost morning, Ross thought.

Wearily he crawled back into his boat and started poling himself out of the vast green swamp. I might need some medical help soon, he admitted to himself.

Five minutes later he arrived back at the fork, where adjacent bayous ran off like canals in two different directions. Here the water was deep enough so that Ross could use his outboard again and he pulled the cord that fired up the motor.

Ten minutes later he had put-putted through clusters of blooming water hyacinths to Émile's boat landing. He informed his beaming Cajun friend that maybe he'd gotten a little snakebite.

"'ey, you'd better come sit for a spell, Ross," Émile advised and thoughtfully served him a couple of cool home brews.

Since Ross wasn't dead or even unconscious by the time he'd finished drinking them, he told Émile that he thought he'd be all right. Surely it was safe now to shove off for home.

"'ere," said Émile kindly and sent Ross away with a half-gallon jug of potent red-eye to help him sweat out any left-over snake juice.

Back at the landing of the Bide-a-Bit Motel, which was owned by Émile's cousins, Jeannette and Claude Couvillion, Ross tied up his boat and opened the unlocked door to his cabin. His head was aching pretty badly by then, and his thigh had started swelling and turning several shades of purple.

Ross had just settled down for some serious medicinal treatment with the 180 proof whiskey when he noticed that his hostess had thoughtfully left him a telephone message. It was stuck under a votive candle at the shrine in the corner of the room.

Kindly Mrs. Couvillion had started the shrine for Ross about three years ago, after she'd gotten to know him really well. It had all begun quite humbly—one single inexpensive statue, one simple white candle. But as Mrs. Couvillion's concern and affection for Ross had mounted, the shrine had begun to expand.

Mrs. Couvillion had been particularly distressed after the hang gliding accident in the Rockies where Ross had photographed American eagles in flight. She had grown even more alarmed following the incident in the piranha-infested waters of French Guiana where Ross had grabbed rare shots of the cock of the rock in its gaudy mating plumage. By last year when he had been trapped in a pit with some buzzards in Cameroon, Mrs. Couvillion had become completely familiar with Ross's go-anywhere and to-hell-with-the-risks reputation and the simple shrine had swelled to the present elaborate monument.

Now it was completely encircled by medals and holy cards bearing the pictures of miracle-accredited saints. A big statue of the Madonna stood in the center, along with numerous candles, vials of blessed water from Lourdes and a holy relic from Rome.

Clearly Mrs. Couvillion considered Ross an absolutely desperate case.

Ross limped over to the shrine and saw that his father had phoned him earlier that morning from the headquarters of his animal rights organization in Richmond, Virginia. Boy, oh boy, Ross thought as he read the news. Immediately he forgot all about his recent injury.

According to Ross Stanton, Sr., a flame-colored tanager, the first ever sighted in the continental U.S., had just been positively identified in southern Arizona. The bird was out there somewhere squatting on a limb right now. Naturally every nature magazine in the western hemisphere wanted photographs by Ross.

"Well, well," Ross exclaimed and grabbed a handy bag and his camera case. His perennial chase after the ivory-billed woodpecker would just have to wait. What the hell, everybody in the world thinks it's dead, anyway, except Émile and me, he mused.

Ross packed quickly, taking all of his really important gear, then went out to his Bronco. When he passed the motel office he honked and blew a kiss to Mrs. Couvillion, who promptly waved back, then crossed herself.

An hour and a half later Ross pulled into the parking lot at New Orleans International Airport. Twenty minutes after that he dropped into the only seat still available on the first flight to Tucson. After takeoff, as the plane soared over the great Atchafalaya Swamp, the pilot called it to the passengers' attention and they all turned to the windows to peer down. All but Ross.

Stupid bird, he thought, then signaled to the flight attendant to bring him another drink.

With his thoughts fixed on ornithology, the last thing Ross Stanton expected—on this of all days—was that he would soon fall head over heels in love.

Of course, some days were like that.

Chapter One

The Chiricahua Mountains—Progresso, Arizona

It was hot enough to roast even a dust devil.

Heat waves shimmered in the still dry air. The white-hot sun blazed down, striking the sand of the desert floor and then bouncing back. As Tessa Fitzgerald pumped gas into Mrs. Alberta Sandoval's vintage Chrysler, a terrific wave of light and heat radiated off the car's shiny body.

Tessa squinted painfully against the glare—minus sunglasses, since she hadn't been able to find them anywhere. As for the heat, she felt like she was in a furnace.

And if I think it's hot, what about that poor guy pushing his car down the road? Tessa thought suddenly.

She could just barely see the man behind the disabled compact. Still, Tessa could tell that he was tall. He also had to be quite powerful to push the car unaided.

As she watched, the car halted once again and the man straightened up.

Poor dumb son of a gun, he probably didn't know enough about desert driving to keep his radiator filled, Tessa reflected. But why didn't the man simply abandon the car, walk down here to the Progresso general store and get out of the merciless sun?

She shrugged off the question, using her free hand to brush her dark hair off her perspiration-streaked forehead.

That stranded guy's hair must be soaked by now, too, Tessa mused. It was thick, a bit too long for current fashion and the most astonishing shade of blond. Why, it looked just exactly like ripe wheat, she thought wistfully, remembering a trip she'd made once to the Menninger Clinic in Topeka, Kansas. From her compartment on the train Tessa had watched a wheat field being harvested.

The memory still lingered sentimentally—a memory of the clinic, that is, *not* the wheat field. What she remembered fondly was the modern, state-of-the-art institution that absolutely reeked of civilization.

Mrs. Sandoval's gas tank gave a still-thirsty gurgle and Tessa concentrated on her work again. The old Chrysler had a voracious appetite for high octane. During the three weeks, five days and thirteen hours that Tessa had been stuck out here at what felt like the ends of the earth, she had filled up the car's gas tank with monotonous regularity.

Her brother, the glib liar, had sworn she would enjoy this visit. Glenn had vowed that it would be just like staying at a dude ranch, even though he knew perfectly well that Tessa always felt insecure without sidewalks, and the only wildlife she had ever liked were children. But after Aunt Fay had broken her leg, Glenn had waxed eloquent in extolling the virtues of up-to-date Progresso, Arizona.

Her brother's forked tongue hadn't uttered one word about stark high mountains, streams that abruptly cascaded over dangerous rapids or the lonely cactus-studded desert that was crawling with rattlesnakes, Gila monsters and tarantulas, Tessa remembered darkly. Perhaps the countryside might have been more attractive if the weather had been cool, but broiling under a late-May sun as it was now, Progresso was a veritable hellhole.

Mexico lay immediately to the south, right across that range of tall purplish mountains, and from the stories spun by the natives that Tessa had heard so far, there were paths through those mountains worn smooth by drug smugglers and illegal aliens.

Certainly Progresso could seem like the ends of the earth when one was more or less stuck here, as Tessa was, running the general store and caring for an injured elderly aunt who would probably never have sustained such an injury if she had just been properly cared for to begin with.

Nor did it help Tessa's feelings to be faced almost daily with large deliveries of supplies that had to be uncrated or a temperature that topped ninety degrees every afternoon by two.

Bzz...

Tessa jerked up quickly to swat at a stinging insect that had chosen her brief moment of reflection to attack.

Damn horseflies, she thought, taking another futile swing at it. Damn gas pumps, too. If she never saw another one for the rest of her life, that would suit her just fine. Why, a month like this was enough to turn anyone into a vocal fan of mass transit.

At least that poor man down the road had finally acquired some help, she noticed. A glance in his direction showed a black head alongside the bright blond one. Probably one of Mrs. Sandoval's numerous relatives was there helping the guy.

Tessa hoped that the man was enlightening Mr. Golden Hair as to the limited automotive facilities available at the Progresso general store. They were confined to gas, oil and booster cables. Period.

So just who was the tall man, anyway? Not a native, for sure. They drove around in pickup trucks, jeeps or even atop tractors.

Three weeks, five days and thirteen enormously boring hours gave one time to notice little details like that.

At least the tall blond guy with the compact probably wasn't a salesman, Tessa concluded. When one lived as Aunt Fay did in such a sparsely populated region, one was spared most sales calls. So either the man was someone's visiting relative or, possibly, a devout bird-watcher who had come to view the local Big Deal, the bird that had been spotted yesterday in the forest at the base of the Chiricahua Mountains.

The sighting had caused quite a stir. Since most of the natives had ornithological leanings, they went trooping out wearing binoculars like necklaces. It had been all that Tessa could do to restrain Aunt Fay from going off with her walker and leg cast to see the bird, too.

But to sight the unique whatchamacallit was apparently really something, judging by the way the party line had kept humming and by the dozens of people who had dashed to the store for film.

Audubon Society officials had arrived from Tucson this morning and made it official. The rare whatsis had actually invaded American airspace. So now there was a local celebrity to be interviewed, the retired gentleman who had made the first, near-miraculous sighting.

All it meant to Tessa was a lot more work. She didn't like birds, anyway, since several species could transmit diseases. And now there were more gas tanks to fill and more hamburgers to serve in the small dining area that adjoined the general store. Bird-watching folk, most of them wearing bifocals and health oxfords, had certainly been showing up in droves.

But that man with the shock of bright blond hair, who was strong enough to push his compact car, didn't look like one of the older set. Unless Tessa was badly mistaken, this man wouldn't have gray at his temples or an age-weathered face.

The car he pushed kept edging closer every minute. American made, two-door, about four years old, Tessa diagnosed through another squint. Those lemons always fall apart at that age. Three weeks and five days ago she hadn't known that. So who said massive boredom wasn't also educational?

Mrs. Sandoval's gas tank topped off so suddenly that Tessa was caught unawares. A hot stream of odorous gas splashed down and spilled over her sneakers before she could take her hand off the nozzle.

Tessa swore under her breath as she shut down the tank and shook gas off her shoes. "Okay, Mrs. Sandoval!" she yelled.

Mrs. Sandoval's bottle-black head came out of the door. Once, as Señor Sandoval could undoubtedly attest, she had had hair that was naturally raven black, as well as having a figure lighter by fifty pounds. But the shrewd knowledge of her flashing brown eyes had probably always been there.

"Thanks, honey. Just put it on my tab," Mrs. Sandoval yelled back to Tessa.

Honey? The word never ceased to send horrified chills zigzagging down Tessa's spine, although she supposed she should be getting used to it. If you performed chores at a filling station/general store/café, you automatically became "honey."

Okay, so maybe she'd needed to get back in touch with people again. Maybe, for the good of her soul, she'd even needed these humbling experiences. But deep in her indignant heart Tessa didn't believe a word of it. Back home in Washington, D.C.—how wistfully she now thought of home!—she had grown used to being treated with dignity and deference. "My research associate, Teresa Fitzgerald," Dr. Corman had always said by way of introduction. To certain awed subordinates she was just "Dr. Fitzgerald" or even "Yes, ma'am." She could sure do with a little of that respect now, Tessa thought, especially when Mrs. Sandoval leaned out of her door once more.

"Hey, honey, you want Juan or Luis to come help you when they get home from school?"

"Yes, please," Tessa cried fervently, thinking of all those boxes and crates waiting to be unpacked.

"Okay, I'll send one of 'em along."

Mrs. Sandoval's ancient car sped off and Tessa wearily raised her bare forearm to wipe sweat off her brow. Why bother to go inside for a dainty hankie? At that very instant the little navy compact was coming her way, pushed on its final uphill stretch by two grunting, heaving males.

A sturdy young Mexican man stood on the side closest to Tessa as the car glided to a stop before the gas pumps. Tessa took one look at his dark unfamiliar face and the bundle tied on his back and just knew he spoke only Spanish.

Illegal alien, she thought, seeing his wary eyes. Not that he had anything to fear from her. Tessa was too sympathetic toward someone who wanted a better life to call the border patrol.

Still, the young man's gaze shied away nervously as he turned to accept the payment that was now being offered by Mr. Golden Hair. *"Gracias,"* he murmured.

Tessa turned, too, and for the first time her eyes collided with the tall blond man's. Two sets of eyes locked—and neither could veer away.

Tingles ran through Tessa from the top of her head to her gasoline-soaked feet. Something about this very attractive man with the wheat-colored hair activated an immediate, primitive and wholly feminine sense of excitement.

Here was a bold, brash guy with whom a woman could easily fall in love, she knew with her very first glance. To a careful woman like Tessa the thought was absolutely frightening.

Abruptly she broke eye contact, as if to prove to herself that she could. Next, Tessa forced her gaze to turn coolly professional as she assessed the exhausted, sweaty man before her, viewing him as though he were a mere physical specimen. He had slumped against a gas pump now and was visibly gasping for breath.

Ectomorph, definitely. Over a tall, long-limbed skeleton lay just enough lean flesh to pad and protect his bones. A man blessed with this particular body build looked athletic, whether he was or not, and could eat with abandon and not gain an ounce. Ectomorphs had the model body structure for present-day society, Tessa reflected. This guy would look even better in swimming trunks—or in nothing at all. Her thought came unaccompanied by a blush, for she had seen too many nude males of all ages and sizes to find the human form embarrassing.

As her eyes ranged swiftly over him, Tessa took in a handsome, masculine face drawn into lines of exertion and weariness. The man's soaked clothes clung to him. The navy shirt, with most of its buttons open, was drenched while the khaki slacks enveloped his legs like a second skin. Since his body was wringing wet, his flushed face should have been, too, but wasn't, a fact that set off a small alarm within Tessa. The way he sagged against the broiling hot gas pump, as though he might be dizzy, rang yet another. But his eyes, still fastened on her in keen appreciation, didn't look dazed, and with all those prickles of feminine alarm rubbing like cactus along her spine, Tessa saw no point in predicting trouble.

As she studied the man's face more closely she saw that it was square-cut with high cheekbones and even features. His nose, long and perfectly straight, lay between clear, bright aquamarine eyes. A smear of dirty grease marked his strong, aggressive chin.

He had a glorious and spectacular tan, although no one with his fair coloring should get that deep a tan, Tessa thought, frowning with clinical disapproval. Thick blond eyebrows, one cleft by a small white scar, lay against the bronzed face. There was another smaller scar on his forehead and a much longer one on his neck.

This man looked outdoorsy, as if he could ride a horse or shoot a gun, and he seemed perfectly at home in these wild surroundings. But he also looked like he would be good with a woman, Tessa couldn't stop herself from thinking. That was stamped on his full, sultry lips. It was also written in his eyes, which were the color of the sea.

Abruptly Tessa drew herself up. She was being roasted alive beneath the Arizona sun while she stared at a man with her tongue practically hanging out. And he kept staring back at her with an equally interested gaze, Tessa noted, squaring her slim shoulders.

She didn't like to think of what this gorgeous hunk saw as she stood before him, hot and dirty and reeking, no doubt, of hamburger grease and *essence de pétrole*.

Why didn't he speak? For that matter, why didn't she?

"May I help you?" Tessa asked and noticed only then that his large but long-fingered hands were shaking slightly.

"Yeah. Hi! I'm Ross Stanton."

He spoke breezily, as if his name was at least as recognizable as that of the president of the United States. Actually it did sound vaguely familiar, although Tessa didn't even know whether he was someone she admired or deplored.

"Yes?" she said and heard impatience in her voice. It was blazing hot out here and Mr. Stanton, sweat-soaked as he was, should have realized it.

Why did his eyes keep staring at her so intently? That deep aqua gaze was unnerving, to say the very least, Tessa thought.

"I have to get to...to the Coro—Coronado National For-Forest." His voice was low and even-toned; it resonated pleasantly against her eardrums. But did he always stutter? Tessa wondered.

"Mus'...must find the tanager," he continued with visible difficulty.

Tessa's eyes narrowed. She looked at the handsome man steadily and seriously now. Was he sick from the sun? His speech seemed definitely headed toward the incoherent. Aloud she asked, "Tanager? Oh, you mean that bird."

"Yes...th' bird." Despite Mr. Stanton's obvious state of exhaustion, he spoke with a fine irony that wasn't lost on Tessa. "I'm a—a wildlife photographer. Expected to...file a report with pix soon's...possible." he stopped, still breathing with difficulty. "They're waiting in Washington."

Again a note rang like a bell in Tessa's head, but overpowering her medical instincts was her heart's sudden burst of homesickness. Right now Washington stood for all that Tessa held dear.

Futile yearnings sharpened her voice. "Well, we all have our little problems today. Right now too much sun is one we share."

"Th' tanager—"

"Will just have to wait for a few hours," Tessa finished calmly, turning to gaze at his disabled car.

"No." His voice was still low, and if Tessa hadn't been concerned about his physical well-being she might have enjoyed its melodic tones, drifting across the heat waves. But added to that voice now was a rigid note of total male implacability. This was a man who was determined not to yield one inch. Furthermore, he was obviously determined to take charge.

"You . . . rent cars?" he asked.

"No," she sighed.

"Borrow yours? I'll . . . pay well."

He kept blinking, his long thick lashes closing over those fantastic aquamarine eyes. Was he having any visual disturbance? Tessa wondered. Aloud she replied, "I don't have a personal car here in Arizona. Sorry."

"Mechanic?" He had straightened up from the gas pump and was towering over her, a tall, strong man for whom she was decidedly no match. Just humor him, Tessa decided.

"There's no mechanic in Progresso. I think the closest one lives in Ysletta," she replied.

"How far?" he asked.

"Forty-five miles."

"Fan belts?" His voice was beginning to sound desperate. "All that's wrong is . . . is a fan belt."

"We don't sell them," Tessa said with another sigh, wondering at her intense personal reaction to this man. Her heart kept racing, while her blood pounded through her veins. With every word he spoke her stomach fairly quivered in response. Such disgustingly immature symptoms had never happened to her before.

"Are you sure?" the man said, still focusing on her relentlessly.

His voice held such a note of entreaty that Tessa looked at him in some alarm. Had the sun made him crazy? A worse thought occurred to her: maybe he was crazy to begin with!

"Of course I'm sure we don't sell fan belts," she protested. Hadn't Aunt Fay been crystal clear on what the store did and did not have? Impatiently Tessa drew her forearm up over her forehead, removing collected drops of perspiration. She felt giddy, almost light-headed, and wondered if heat was really the cause.

His face still isn't sweating a drop! He's—

She didn't allow herself to finish the thought. Concern for this man's mental state now yielded to her renewed concern for his physical health. Weren't obstinacy and slurring of speech often indicative of heat-related disorders?

Tessa suspected now why he kept focusing on her so intently. It probably had nothing to do with her feminine charms, worse luck. Rather, it exhibited his stubborn determination to hang on to consciousness until he could see and photograph that silly bird.

"Look, I insist we go inside," Tessa said, an edge to her voice. Her co-workers would have recognized that inflexible note as characteristic of Dr. Fitzgerald at her most authoritative. "You may not think it's hot, but I'm about ready to drop."

"Ph—phone?" he croaked.

Aha, she finally had him. "Yes. Inside. Look, do you need any help?" she offered, automatically extending her arm.

Those surprising eyes of his filled with an expression of amusement. Slowly he shook his head, as if silently asking what help a little thing like Tessa could possibly provide.

Good Lord, the man was obstinate as a mule and probably a sexist to boot, Tessa thought in exasperation. Why, he would collapse on the hard hot sand of the desert and die before he ever owned up to a moment's weakness.

Tessa turned and led the way toward the store, her sneakers leaving gas prints in the sand. She walked up two steps onto the long, wide wooden porch and stopped in the doorway of the store to be sure Mr. Stanton was following her. He lurched grimly along behind.

A touch of respect stole unbidden into Tessa's heart. This man might be crazy as hell, but he certainly did have grit.

And rugged good looks, Dr. Fitzgerald. Let's not forget those rugged good looks.

Suddenly Tessa was distracted by a movement off to her right. She turned in that direction and there was the young Mexican man, now sprawled in the shady picnic area that lay a short distance from the gas pumps. He sat smiling and counting his money, examining each dollar bill with care and holding it up to the light for an even closer inspection.

Good, Tessa thought automatically. He, at least, knew how to take care of himself in a climate like this. Then she turned back to—what was his name?—Ross Stanton. That she remembered it so readily was another source of annoyance for Tessa.

He had maneuvered up the two steps onto the porch and was rocking back and forth. But at least he was still on his feet, and from the steely set of his handsome jaw he plainly intended to stay that way.

Lessons Tessa had learned as an intern and resident on the busy wards of a big city hospital in Baltimore returned unerringly. She wanted to urge him to sit down while she ran for electric fans, cold drinks and a wet cloth for his face. She hadn't forgotten her early training, even though she had been in medical research, rather than clinical medicine for the past four years.

Don't borrow trouble, she advised herself as she stepped inside the store. Its interior was so dark by comparison with the out-of-doors that, at first, she felt temporarily blinded. But it was also blessedly cool. As Tessa's eyes adjusted she glanced around and saw the place as this handsome stranger undoubtedly would: one big, heaping mess.

The store looked like something from a bygone era. It stocked everything from harnesses and saddles to dry goods and canned foods. A chewing tobacco display bumped noses with a freezer full of ice cream. Racks of garden seed bordered racks of spices. Hats from straws to sombreros hung from the ceiling rafters as did brooms, rakes and hoes. Postcards offered scenic vistas of places other than Progresso and well-thumbed magazines and ancient paperback books sagged in dusty trays.

A hand-lettered sign pointing to the rear of the store said Café. Below, in smaller print, the meager offerings were listed: hamburgers, hot dogs, French fries, eggs and enchiladas. Tessa could recommend none of them since all were laden with salt, cholesterol—or both. Available drinks, leaning heavily toward caffeine, of which she also disapproved, consisted of coffee, colas and tea.

Dusty and overcrowded, the vast one-room store was temperature-controlled by what Aunt Fay called a swamp cooler. This was a window box arrangement that recycled water in front of a madly spinning fan. Although the "swamp cooler" wasn't as efficient as refrigerated air, it still worked well enough here in the humidity-poor atmosphere of the desert.

Tessa turned to find Ross Stanton standing directly behind her and, with such close proximity, she could practically feel the heat emanating from his body. She also noticed an aroma that might have been alcohol. Good Lord, she certainly hoped he hadn't been drinking.

Sternly Tessa ordered her eyes to move upward since, for some reason, they wanted to linger on his broad chest, where she could almost see his heart pounding beneath the bronzed skin. She also saw a mat of gleaming gold inside his half-open shirt. Kindred golden hair ran up and down his arms and gleamed on the back of his long, capable-looking hands.

As Tessa's gaze skimmed over him, she found him staring down at her again. Unconsciously she tucked a wayward wisp of hair behind one ear and found herself wishing she looked just a little better. The picture Ross Stanton was seeing of her was distinctly unflattering. Tessa, a short, small-boned brunette with unruly curls, was usually branded "cute," a label she despised. However, if she expended a little effort, she could also look "smart."

Today, though, she doubted if even cute would hack it, since she wore no makeup and had on a less-than-chic outfit consisting of oversize shorts and a tank top that had been laundered a few hundred times too many. Of course, Tessa had dressed this morning to pump gasoline, flip hamburger patties and restock shelves—work that didn't exactly call for a designer outfit.

"The phone's over here," she offered and led the way toward the wall. She didn't mention that two comfortable rocking chairs were also in the immediate vicinity of the phone. They were rarely in use unless one of Aunt Fay's women friends dropped by for a visit.

If I can just get this crazy but beautiful guy to sit down before he passes out, she thought.

But she was too late to practice preventive medicine. As Ross Stanton weaved along after Tessa, one of the store's myriad items swam suddenly into his line of vision.

"You—you said . . ." Breathing stertorously he stopped beside a pyramid built from pints of motor oil.

Tessa swung back around and found herself wrapped in flame from aquamarine eyes. One of his hands rose, its first finger pointing toward the pyramid.

"What?" asked the mystified Tessa.

"F-fan belts!"

"Those? You mean that's what's in those packages?" Tessa bent down to read the label on one. *Well, I'll be damned,* she thought.

At just that moment the handsome blond man swayed. Then, like a tree being felled, he toppled slowly over into the aisle and landed with a loud and resounding crash.

A small shelf, two display racks and several giant-size boxes of laundry powder went with him. Tessa, who had sidestepped swiftly, now moved back into the melee. Quickly she rolled the unconscious man onto his back and bent down to check his pulse. It was very rapid, as she had feared.

Heat stroke? she wondered, then groaned aloud. For now she could definitely smell alcohol on his breath. That could only aggravate his condition. "Oh, Lord," Tessa suddenly heard herself praying.

She had to drop everything else immediately: store, gas pumps, café and clutter—even poor old Aunt Fay, in a manner of speaking, because this man had presented her with a real life-threatening emergency.

My God, what a vacation I'm having, Tessa thought and allowed herself one single second to wallow in self-pity.

Then she flew into action.

Chapter Two

He was absolutely gorgeous, even more so than she'd imagined. Why, he was so beautiful in his bare and natural state that he made Tessa's heart pound from excitement and her mouth fairly water. Even her hands, sponging off this Adonis, were trembling.

But what sort of abuse had this wonderful body been subjected to? she thought with concern. It was marked, laced and occasionally even crisscrossed with old scars and the signs of numerous injuries. Tessa suspected that one arm and several of his ribs had been broken, since they were all slightly out of alignment. Examining his nose made her sure it had also been broken at least once and, mystifyingly, he was missing one joint on the little toe of his left foot. But mostly there were just the thin white threads of healed scars—veritable yards of them. He must have marvelous recuperative powers at least, she reflected.

There was a more recent, festering wound on his thigh, the origin of which Tessa couldn't even begin to guess at. As she stared at the swollen, angry-looking flesh, she knew she wouldn't be surprised if the tissue didn't survive and had to be removed by surgery in a few days.

Still, scars and all, he was gorgeous. He was also helpless, unconscious and had a dangerously high temperature for an adult. Best concentrate on those facts, Tessa, she reminded herself sternly, and forget about the way he looks.

Ross Stanton lay sprawled on Tessa's own narrow bed in the guest room, right next to Aunt Fay's more spacious bedroom. At least, I have both patients in reasonable proximity to each other, thought Tessa.

Naked except for a hand towel that modestly covered his loins, the unconscious man dominated Tessa's small, feminine room. His breathing seemed to fill the empty spaces and his slender feet, limp as a puppet's, hung over the end of the standard-size bed.

From the window a room air conditioner hummed at full speed. Tessa had also scooped up several fans and these were all in motion, too, trained directly on Ross Stanton's body.

Tessa sponged him off carefully again and again, dipping a cloth into a large basin of cold water in which several ice cubes floated. As she worked, Tessa reviewed the probable medical causes of his condition, much as if she were writing it up for a professional journal.

Pushing the car was hard manual labor, performed under the blazing hot Arizona sun. Obviously this had tested Ross's body critically, causing it to sweat profusely. Since this meant loss of both water and salt, his overworked mechanism had finally just shut down.

Then his body, without its normal escape valve of perspiration, had suffered a rise of core body temperature until the poor man grew as hot, figuratively speaking, as an uncovered nuclear reactor. Dizziness and disorientation had set in and all of his symptoms had been aggravated by whatever amount of alcohol was in his system. On the whole, Mr. Stanton's spectacular swoon in the store aisle was not at all surprising.

Oh, God, he is so beautiful!

Tessa wrung out her cloth into a wastewater pail and dipped it into the icy water again. She automatically used her right hand, since that was the one she'd always favored, but suddenly she realized what her unguarded left was about.

Her hand had glided through the air until it hovered a scant two inches above the unconscious man's golden hair.

Good God, what was she doing? Trying to get herself drummed out of the medical profession by lasciviously taking advantage of a poor comatose patient? Was she that sex-starved, for heaven's sake?

Angrily Tessa snatched her hand back and dropped it firmly into her lap. But her gaze continued to move over the fantastic male form before her.

Take away the scars and that recent injury on his thigh and his body might have been a stylized drawing in an anatomy textbook. Its curving lines and flat planes were close to absolute perfection. Tessa drew an unsteady breath as her eyes moved upward over the narrow hipbones and the gentle indentation of his navel, then roamed avidly across his flat stomach and up to his broad chest, which was so thickly covered with golden curly hair.

In repose his face exhibited a vulnerability that Tessa hadn't expected. Because Ross had appeared so confident, she wasn't prepared for this trusting, little-boy look. Somehow it activated her every protective instinct.

He looked as if he were sleeping very deeply, and Tessa studied his face as though she were an art student, expected to reproduce it.

Aggressive chin. Sculpted mouth. Eyes rimmed with lashes that appeared almost ridiculously long now that she was close enough to observe their pale gold tips.

Then there were those charming, beguiling aquamarine eyes.

Yet for all his blatant male beauty there wasn't even the slightest trace of effeminacy. As a wildlife photographer he must be versatile, adventurous and, Tessa thought with a shudder, used to braving life in the wild, surrounded by untamed beasts. Looking down on Ross Stanton, Tessa felt certain that he was a man so utterly secure in his own masculinity that he could, with equal ease, remove and install fan belts or appreciate a rare and exotic bird.

His face still looked flushed. She wondered if, despite his tan, he had been burned beneath the Arizona sun.

Tessa wished the thought had occurred to her earlier. She jumped from her straight-backed chair and walked over to her black doctor's bag. Until this trip to Arizona, Tessa hadn't used the bag in years. Now, from within its depths, she drew out a tube of salve suitable for burns. Gently and carefully she began stroking it on Ross Stanton's fine-textured skin, trying to ignore the feel of his warm vibrant flesh. It was just coincidence, of course, that her fingers tingled and throbbed from their contact with him.

As she worked, her shoulder gave an occasional twinge, reminding Tessa of the difficulty that she and the young Mexican had had in lifting Mr. Stanton. Thank God, the boy had still been resting beneath the trees. Carrying Ross off to bed had been a neat trick for two much smaller people. Still, they had managed—barely.

And, in some fashion, Tessa had also managed everything that followed. She had hastily locked up the store, since she dared not leave it empty and unguarded. Fortunately Juan Sandoval had arrived five or ten minutes later. When he'd located Tessa in the cottage and learned about the tall, fair-haired Anglo who lay near death, he had promptly phoned that fount of wisdom, his mother.

Mrs. Alberta Sandoval had driven back over just as promptly, bringing along Luis as well as a jewel of a daughter named Consuela, who could match the best of fast-food chefs when it came to swinging a basket of fries out of hot grease and flipping hamburger patties. On the one brief break that Tessa had taken to make sure the store was staying intact while she tended "the blond dreamboat"—Aunt Fay's antiquated phrase—everything was going fine. So Tessa had returned to the cottage, leaving Juan manning the gas pumps, Luis unpacking all of the new merchandise and Consuela swinging the ample hips she'd inherited from her mother around the counter in the café.

Mama Alberta was even baby-sitting Aunt Fay.

Mrs. Sandoval, I love you, Tessa thought as she wrung out her washcloth for the umpteenth time.

She should check her new patient's temperature, pulse and blood pressure again. Ross scowled suddenly as Tessa performed these functions, alerting her to the fact that he might be closer to consciousness than he actually looked.

His pulse was still very rapid, his blood pressure quite low, but at least his temperature had dropped by two degrees. Just keep on keeping on, Tessa assured herself and wondered why she didn't find the nursing work boring and monotonous. Of course, this was a life-and-death situation. Still, given all the available facts, the prognosis for a young, strong man who was receiving expert medical attention was favorable.

Wring, sponge, sponge, sponge, wring. . . .

Abruptly and with absolutely no warning, the aquamarine eyes flew open. Confusion swam in their depths. Was he conscious? Could he respond to her at all?

There was no attention-getter like a patient's own name. "Mr. Stanton," Tessa said sharply. "Do you hear me, Mr. Stanton?"

There was a little response. He blinked and the tip of his tongue emerged to lightly touch his lower lip.

Tessa tried again. "Ross."

That did it. His head moved and his eyes focused, intelligence flaring back into them. Of the two names, Ross was obviously the one with which he was most deeply imprinted.

"Hi, Ross. I'm Tessa. Can you see me?" she asked eagerly.

His lips formed the word "Yes," but apparently he was still too weak to talk. Doubt moved through his glorious blue-green eyes, and he made a massive effort to speak. "You..."

He no longer looked straight at Tessa. Rather, he seemed to focus on something that lay just beyond her.

She turned to follow his gaze and understood. "Oh, you see my black bag? Man, I sure wish those doctor carryalls came in prettier colors. Basic black is such a drag, don't you think?"

Seemingly he understood that she was trying to reassure him with her flippant lightness, but he couldn't quite give credence to her new stature. "Doc?" he said hoarsely, his features stamped with disbelief. "You?"

"Yeah, that's me," she continued brightly. "Teresa Fitzgerald, M.D., Ph.D. I trained at the University of Maryland and Johns Hopkins Hospital. Bet you're sure surprised, aren't you, Ross?"

He managed a feeble nod, licked his lips and tried to speak again.

Tessa continued in the same light vein. "Yeah, I could tell what you thought of me in these stylish clothes. Had me pegged for a girl who quit school at fifteen 'cause she got pregnant. Right, Ross?''

His lips curved upward and his greenish eyes sparkled. Why, he has a sense of humor, too, Tessa thought in delight. Then she wondered why she hadn't particularly noticed the smile lines around his mouth and eyes before. She reached for a glass on the nightstand into which she had already put a straw. "Here, Ross. Take several long deep sips for me, if you can," Tessa directed.

He gave a nod to show that he understood and she lifted his head—to discover the delicious texture of his golden hair. Crisp and alive, it clung to her hand as if magnetized.

Ross took three deep and audible gulps before unpleasant surprise, even distaste, registered on his face. "Salty," he complained in a hoarse whisper.

"Well, I'm sorry it can't be a margarita. But, Ross, you've lost a lot of salt as well as liquid. I need to get both back inside you," Tessa confided. "Take another sip, if you think you can handle it. Stop if it's going to make you sick, though."

He grimaced, but swallowed noisily twice more. Suddenly anxiety tightened his features. "The car—"

Wouldn't it be great when he'd progressed beyond these simple one-word sentences, which made him sound like a rather dim-witted child? "Your car? The one you risked life and limb pushing?" Tessa asked. "You want me—"

She stopped abruptly. Ross's eyes had glazed over and rolled back in his head. His lids drooped and he was unconscious again. Tessa knew that their brief conversation must have completely exhausted him.

So what lay in his car to concern him so? Uncut rubies or diamonds? A cache of gold bars? Or, far more likely for this southwestern locale with its conflux of state and international borders, was it drugs? Although Ross didn't look like the drug-smuggling sort, one never really knew.

Tessa thought for a moment, then she stood up and began to methodically rifle his clothes, which were still damp with sweat.

There was a veritable fortune in the car, all right, but not of the sort that Tessa had half expected, even half feared to find. Rather, it came in the form of expensive, top-of-the-line equipment: a couple of 35-mm cameras, each equipped with a zoom lens, a big bag of film, two pairs of binoculars and sophisticated video and sound equipment. There was even a small portable computer.

Good Lord, all of this for one little bird that had unwittingly violated the U.S.-Mexico border. Tessa had always suspected that bird lovers were crazy, but now she knew for sure.

While Mrs. Sandoval baby-sat with Ross, Tessa rounded up the woman's two stalwart sons. She also looked for the young Mexican who had helped her earlier, but apparently he had melted away with the cooling temperatures of late dusk.

With Juan and Luis pushing Ross's car while Tessa steered it, they moved it down beneath the trees by Aunt Fay's cottage. Then Tessa sent the two young boys back to work while she unloaded the equipment packed inside. No wonder Ross hadn't dared to walk off and leave this treasure trove.

Tessa didn't want the Sandoval boys to know what was in the trunk of the car, not because she doubted their honesty, but because they were young, macho and anxious to impress their swaggering teenage friends. They might talk too much at school and, in a region as poor as this one, there were certainly others who were less scrupulous.

On Tessa's final trip between car and cottage she routinely flipped open both the glove compartment and ashtray. She hadn't really expected to find anything so she was surprised when the glove compartment yielded a contract with a Tucson car rental agency. Mr. Stanton, Tessa read with interest, had given an address in St. Clément, Louisiana—wherever in creation that was—and had paid by credit card.

In the ashtray she also found an expensive man's watch and a silver and turquoise ring. Of course it made sense that a man about to inspect the greasy innards of a broken-down car would have shed them.

No wedding ring. Unfortunately, not all married men wore them.

Tessa put Ross's jewelry into her black medical bag and locked it. Then she relieved Mrs. Sandoval, who announced her intention of going straight home and fixing supper, not only for her own large brood but for Tessa and Aunt Fay as well.

Tessa was too busy to protest. She knew that she and her aunt both needed something more nourishing than hamburgers and French fries, but she also knew she had more than enough to keep her busy. There was simply no time tonight to stop and cook a well-balanced meal.

To her distress her new patient's temperature had moved up a degree and a quarter. "You're not making this easy, Ross," Tessa muttered to him and returned to her sponge-and-wring routine. Another hour passed before she dared leave him again to go check on Aunt Fay.

She found her great-aunt seated in a leather recliner, watching TV. Her broken leg was elevated, just as Tessa had insisted it should be, for Aunt Fay was a very good patient. Although she was eighty and had bones that knit back together with excruciating slowness, she was determined to mend. Tessa knew that her aunt's positive attitude and independent nature—exasperating though the latter quality had often proved to be—were still the best things that Aunt Fay had going for her.

As she caught sight of Tessa, Aunt Fay used her remote control to turn down the evening news. "Come in," she called companionably to her niece. "The world's in its usual mess." Her blue Irish eyes twinkled with good humor.

Tessa sank onto a footstool and sighed wearily.

"Bet you never expected to be pulling duty on a patient ward again," Aunt Fay said, punctuating her words with a smile.

"No, I didn't," Tessa said frankly. "It wasn't exactly an experience I'd intended to repeat."

"That's what I figured," Aunt Fay chuckled. "A Florence Nightingale you're not."

Tessa felt a stab of remorse. "I hope you don't think I've been negligent, Aunt Fay."

"No, not at all," her aunt said briskly. "I just think you're a doctor, not a nurse. There is a difference."

"Well, I haven't really minded." Under the open skepticism of her aunt's gaze, Tessa went on weakly, "I mean, I've definitely enjoyed the opportunity to get to know you better."

"Same here. Now, tell me the truth for a change. How did Glenn ever talk you into coming way out here in the first place?" her aunt inquired.

"He conned me," Tessa admitted. "He even used Dad's affection for you as emotional blackmail. My brother is certainly his father's son."

"You can't ever trust those fast-talking politicians," Aunt Fay remarked.

"I know," Tessa reflected. "I guess I must have suffered temporary amnesia—"

"Wait a minute, Tessa. I want to see this," Aunt Fay interrupted abruptly as she turned the volume back up on the TV set.

While Aunt Fay listened to a news anchor from Tucson rave about the sighting of the tanager in the Chiricahua

Mountains near Progresso, Tessa remembered once again her brother Glenn's glib phrases.

"Best climate in the world, Tessa. It'll put some color in your cheeks, which, if you'll pardon my saying so, sure could use some. You've been stuck under that lab's fluorescent lights till you're positively green. And, of course, you could evaluate Aunt Fay's condition in a way that Evie and I just aren't qualified to do, even if we weren't going to be out stumping all summer with the twins.

"I mean, let's face it, a lot of folks Aunt Fay's age are, well, slipping. Definitely slipping. And since you know how Dad always felt about the old girl, now that he's gone I think we have a definite responsibility—I mean, if she's in a bad way, then the family ought to know about it.

"Say, did I ever tell you about that summer I spent in Arizona with Aunt Fay and Uncle Ben, back before he rode one bronc too many? Oh. Well, I didn't know if you'd remember. Anyway, it was lots of fun—the real Wild West and all that. Believe me, I have nothing but fond memories. And since you're kinda at loose ends, anyway—I mean, I'm sure not surprised about that guy, Cary, because I never did trust his looks. And I'm not surprised, either, that the college trustees kicked you and Dr. Corman out. Frankly, I always wondered how you could stand to handle all those rats and mice. I'm sorry Corman hasn't been able to find another place, but, hell, cutbacks are happening everywhere. Federal funds for medical research have all dried up.

"Anyway, since you are at loose ends, Tessa, why not help out the whole family by going to check on Aunt Fay? I know you're not hurting for money, but I'll gladly buy your ticket. No, I insist. It'll be like having a vacation at a dude ranch. Trust me."

Yes, she'd definitely been conned with a lot of blarney by that deft, high-powered Irish politico who was her brother, and the minute the miserable so-and-so finally quit campaigning and got around to phoning her again, Tessa intended to tell Glenn exactly what she thought both of him and of this so-called "vacation" in Arizona.

Of course, to give the devil his due, Glenn probably hadn't realized just how confined an eighty-year-old woman would be by a broken leg. Nor had Glenn known that Aunt Fay actually had far less help in running the general store than she'd led him to believe. No, Glenn probably hadn't even suspected that he was sending his tired, frustrated, and distinctly urban-oriented sister into a wholly chaotic situation where, to keep the store going, she would actually be frying hamburgers, stocking shelves and pumping gas.

But he certainly should have remembered what a hellhole Progresso could be in hot weather, Tessa thought bitterly.

Aunt Fay turned off her TV set, satisfied with the coverage of the local bird story, and turned back to Tessa. "So my slick great-niece, the physician, got conned by her even slicker brother, the next congressman from the great state of Maryland." Her eyes sparkled with amusement.

"Don't enjoy it so much," Tessa said crossly. "Actually, you're partially responsible for the whole mess, you know. You kept telling Glenn about all the leisure time you had to read and go bird-watching."

"Never could abide leisure time," Aunt Fay said, her lip curling distastefully.

"I can tell," Tessa retorted as she wearily got up from the hassock. "Now, I'd better go see about my other patient."

"Yes. You take good care of him." Aunt Fay paused significantly. Against Tessa's wishes, she had hobbled into the guest room with the help of her walker to inspect the unconscious man. "That's quite a likely-looking fellow you've fetched in here, my dear, and you aren't getting any younger, if you don't mind my saying so. Why, you're what? Thirty-four? In my day a woman of thirty was considered an old maid."

"I'm thirty-two. And I feel very fortunate not to have been born back in your day," Tessa replied, her voice sharp.

"Might be two ways of looking at that," Aunt Fay said reflectively. "Today it's nice that a woman doesn't feel like she has to marry. Lord knows that's all that ever led me to marry my sorry first husband. But it's also too bad that you modern things feel so all-fired self-sufficient with your jobs and salaries, your cars and apartments. At least the women of my age knew we needed someone. Yes, ma'am, we weren't ashamed to admit that we wanted love, caring and companionship. And don't go wrinkling up your nose at me, Miss Tessa. Maybe life has changed a lot, but human beings haven't. So you just cure up that nice-looking man and give Mother Nature a chance."

"I've already given Mother Nature a chance," Tessa retorted on her way to the door. "His name was Cary Steward, and it didn't work out."

"'Course not," her great-aunt said scornfully. "You were both so busy runnin' in two different directions, with no real commitment to your relationship or to each other. Why, I could never figure out when the two of you even *saw* one another, for all that you were living together."

Bingo, thought Tessa unwillingly. She had to admit that Sunday afternoons were about the only time when she and Cary, a busy doctor in private practice, had been relaxed and cozy together. Of course, there had also been evenings by the pool at their apartment complex, as well as occasional weekends at the beach. But overall, there just hadn't been enough that was shared and significant to sustain their relationship. When Cary had finally packed up and left, Tessa had felt little sense of loss. Rather, it was as if he'd been a pleasant houseguest, but she had always known he was just passing through.

But no relationship with the feverish man who was Ross Stanton would ever be like that, Tessa thought, her pulse quickening just from re-entering his room. Oh no! A woman would certainly want to know where this handsome man was each and every hour of the day.

Tessa checked his vital signs again. His blood pressure seemed to be stabilizing and his temperature had continued to stay down.

Tessa shut off one fan. Then she stopped sponging long enough to eat the heaping plate of mesquite-smoked beef, gazpacho, guacamole salad, corn pudding and flour tortillas that Mrs. Sandoval had passed in to her. Rarely had food tasted so delicious. Then, with her appetite stilled and her strength renewed, Tessa rechecked her patient thoroughly from head to toe. Yes, he definitely appeared to be improving, so she drew up the crisp sheet at the foot of the bed to Ross's waist. When he awoke next, Tessa expected him to be more cognizant of his surroundings and ready to exhibit concerns for his personal modesty.

What now? Oh yes, she had meant to look at his wallet again. At the height of the emergency she had glanced through it quickly to see if he carried a card warning her about chronic diseases or specific allergies. Since he hadn't, Tessa hadn't bothered to make a more detailed search. Now, though, she sought the names of people to notify in an emergency. A parent or sibling? A girlfriend or fiancée?

How about a wife? He's at least thirty-five or -six so, wedding ring or not, he's probably married, you know. Tessa sighed, finding her thoughts depressing.

Ross's leather wallet yielded a lot of items. There were several major credit cards, a Louisiana driver's license and a voter registration card. There were also membership cards for the Audubon Society and the Sierra Club. Then Tessa found an especially ornate card decorated with bird designs and wildlife sketches. In Grateful Recognition said a swirling script that preceded Ross's name, followed by the initials of the organization commending him: FLAC.

Oh no, Tessa thought warily, as a few floating bits and pieces of random information suddenly began to come together. Weren't those FLAC folk all a bunch of raving lunatics? The very same sort of animal rights activists that had cost Tessa and Dr. Corman their lab?

"Stealing my money, Doc?"

Ross spoke suddenly, startling Tessa so much that she almost dropped his wallet. Mechanically she flashed him a smile. "Yeah. You know what bloodsuckers we are when it comes to getting paid."

He tried to grin back, but Tessa's mind was racing too quickly for her to notice. There was also a sinking sensation in the pit of her stomach. Apparently this guy was mixed up with people that she considered to be real nuts.

Aloud she kept her voice light, not wanting to alarm Ross. "Any special reason you woke up?" she inquired.

"Couldn't resis' that d'licious cocktail you're serving," he replied, and mirth edged his aquamarine eyes.

"Less joking and more swallowing, Ross. Take three good sips," Tessa coaxed, holding the glass to his lips again while she cradled his head. Although she longed to start flinging philosophical questions at him, she knew she needed to restrict herself to bare essentials right now.

He swallowed obediently, then turned away from the glass with a shudder. Tessa sympathized, knowing the taste of the liquid was sickening.

"Ross, there's a recent injury on your right thigh," she asked casually. "What happened?"

Ross frowned as if trying to remember. "Oh, that. I think I got a snakebite this morning."

"What?" Tessa wasn't aware of leaping to her feet until she found herself looming over him. "My God! What was it, a rattlesnake?"

"A cottonmouth. I was deep in the . . . the swamp."

"Do you mean a water moccasin?" she demanded, then sheer logic prompted another panicky question. "There aren't any swamps in Arizona. Where in hell were you?"

"Louisiana, where I live. I was photographing in—in the Atchafalaya Swamp this morning. It's a wild place."

"Do you mean to tell me—" Tessa didn't even recognize her voice, it was shaking so from her sudden combination of anger and fear "—that you were pushing a car across the desert when you were full not only of alcohol but of snake venom, too?"

"Guess I shouldn't have, huh?" Ross gave her a lop-sided smile of apology. "Really, I only got a little snakebit."

"There's no such thing! Getting 'a little snakebit' is like being a little pregnant!" she wailed, but Ross had already closed his eyes again.

Oh dear God, Tessa thought frantically as she tried to remember everything she had learned years ago about medical treatment for snakebites. It was pitifully little—and stranded out here at the ends of the earth she also had no ready access to proper antivenin.

He's probably going to die, Tessa thought drearily.

No, I won't let him die. Think, blast you, think! she commanded herself.

Angry both with her patient and her own helplessness, Tessa paused just long enough to check his pulse again, then rushed for the telephone.

Chapter Three

Ross kept trying to wake up, but he didn't feel very good, although he couldn't remember why. His face burned. His head throbbed and so did his thigh. But those were minor particulars. The entire rest of his body ached, as though some sadist with a wicked knitting needle had entertained himself by punching big holes in it.

Nor could Ross remember just exactly where he was or what had actually happened. But obviously something had. Again. Usually he wasn't so puzzled by injury and disaster.

It was all quite baffling, so he lay very still with his eyelids squeezed down tight while he tried to make sense of things.

He began with the simplest of explanations: did I get drunk last night?

Ross didn't often drink to the point of unconsciousness, and such episodes had grown rarer with every passing year. Still, he'd occasionally acted stupidly and gotten blindsided. Like with that incredible stuff he'd thought was Tibetan yak milk, Ross reflected, or the downright lethal pineapple punch he'd been served by a black-haired charmer in Malaysia.

Ross had always had a weakness for pretty brunettes. It certainly wasn't an inherited characteristic since Stan, his father, had married all blondes, with Ross's late mother being the first and Linda the last. Sandwiched in between were three others with whom Ross, Stan and Linda were still quite friendly.

Since his tongue didn't feel especially furred, Ross thought he probably wasn't suffering from a hangover.

But thinking of women brought up his next logical question to himself. Did I meet some irresistible chick and get rolled? Ross wondered.

Possibly. He kept hearing some woman's voice right now—an authoritative brisk Northern voice that was talking to someone called Aunt Fay. Into his mind swam the memory of a particularly fresh and vibrant face. Ross also recalled that this particular brunette had thick dark curly hair and bright blue eyes. Big bright blue eyes, and an enchanting smile, as well. Abruptly Ross frowned. It wasn't fair that someone so sweet and innocent-looking had drugged him, rolled him, then dumped him.

Oh yes, he was starting to remember now just how the sly wench had plied him with an absolutely vile-tasting potion. What Ross couldn't understand was why on earth he had ever cooperated with her. But he had, he knew. He could still remember her hands—small, warm and competent—cradling his head while he had willingly sucked some awful swill through a straw.

"Ross?" The woman spoke suddenly, her voice holding a slightly irritable edge now. "Are you awake, Ross? Speak to me if you are."

Did bad girls stick around after they'd taken all of a guy's money? Aha, Ross thought triumphantly, I've got it now. I'm hallucinating!

"Open your eyes and talk to me if you're awake. Otherwise I'll have to give you another shot," the woman threatened.

"You're a snippy little witch," Ross thought and didn't realize that he'd spoken aloud until he heard a gasp.

"What did you call me?" she demanded.

Slowly, painfully, Ross opened one wary eye and there she was, the innocent-looking hoyden of the gas pumps and that turn-of-the-century general store. But she was mistress of the sinister black bag, too, he recalled, and of the salty, vile-tasting cocktail. He hoped she wasn't also into whips and leather, since that wasn't his kind of thing. Then Ross saw the stethoscope strung around her neck.

At the sight of her tight-lipped yet still lovely face it all came back to him in a flash. Oh, hell! He'd messed up somehow and injured himself again.

It had certainly happened plenty of times before.

"Hi, Doc." Ross sighed and opened the other eye. "So what's the damage?" Even as he asked, he cautiously began testing his arms and legs. Then he relaxed as he realized he still had them all.

The lady doctor regarded him with a very serious expression in her big blue eyes. She also appeared to resent his casual question. Ross had seen this before, too, and he stifled another sigh. Why did members of the medical profession always have to act so grave and altogether humorless?

"You have been dangerously ill, Mr. Stanton," she warned.

"But I surprised you and lived, right?" Ross said flippantly, taking in the room with a casual sweep. Since he wasn't in a hospital, this couldn't be too bad. For that matter, Ross never even worried about hospitals anymore unless he found himself in intensive care hooked up to twenty machines, with a man in a black suit reading aloud from a prayer book.

"Believe me, it's nothing to joke about," the pretty doctor said, growing more tight-lipped by the minute. "A bite by any one of the pit vipers can be very serious business. So can a sunstroke. The combination might easily have proved fatal."

Ross gave an elaborate yawn. Then he saw that this was a mistake since the lady doctor went from being moderately angry to wholly infuriated. Her deep blue eyes flashed fire.

Why? What had he done? Last night she had seemed so sweet, so friendly and caring. Of course, she'd thought then that he was probably going to die. Was she sorry he hadn't? Ross looked back at her anxiously and noticed for the first time that the lady doctor also looked very weary indeed.

"Listen, I'm really grateful," he said to her pleasantly. "But now I do have to get up and get on with things, like photographing the tanager." Anxiety pinched him. "I'm also worried about that car I was driving—rather, about losing the gear I was carrying in the car."

The woman stared down at Ross, her expression distinctly hostile. "It's all fine. That bird is still out there, chirping on some branch, and I moved the car myself. Your gear is stored safely here in the house."

"Wonderful! Thanks so much," Ross said, trying hard to act properly appreciative. But the fact that the tanager had waited for him only added to his determination. Why, the entire bird world waited! There were people panting to pay Ross thousands of dollars, just because any photograph he snapped was utterly unlike anyone else's. "Dramatic and unique," was the way they'd frequently been described.

"I'm still on assignment so I'll have to leave now," Ross explained, trying to ignore his numerous aches and pains, "so if you'd just bring me my clothes—"

"Relax, Mr. Stanton, you're not going anywhere," the lady doctor answered.

"Uh, I'm not?" Ross inquired dubiously. "Why not?"

A trace of satisfaction crossed her face. "First, you aren't going anywhere because you are simply not up to it. You're still weak, debilitated and dehydrated. There are also a couple of other medical problems I intend to discuss with you later."

"Pardon, ma'am, but I think I'll just have to check myself out A.M.A.—no offense, you understand," Ross added politely. He'd had lots of experience at leaving various citadels of healing "Against Medical Advice."

The satisfaction on her face deepened, revealing two downright cute dimples at either side of her thoroughly luscious mouth. Ross regarded their appearance warily. "Second, you aren't going anywhere," she repeated, "unless you don't mind being stark naked."

Ross raised his eyebrows at her. Then he raised the sheet at his waist with a hand that admittedly still felt quite weak. "Uh-oh," he sighed when a glance confirmed the truth of her words.

She nodded emphatically. "Uh-huh."

Actually she still looked kind of cute, even though she was obviously feeling frazzled and raggedy. Maybe I could get back to her after I've shot a few rolls of the bird, Ross thought.

"Hey, you don't really mean it about my clothes, do you, Doc?" he coaxed.

"Yes, I certainly do mean it." As he watched, the last traces of grim satisfaction left her face and she just looked tired. Tired and drained and plenty mean. She stalked over to the bed and punched Ross in the chest with a slim, indignant and surprisingly sharp finger.

"Ouch," he protested.

"You'll have more than that to complain about if you so much as move!" she shouted. "You are going to lie there and rest, and gradually you'll get your strength back. Then, and only then, will you be allowed up and out of bed, mister!"

With that, she stormed out of the bedroom and left Ross to ponder a much more immediate problem. How was he expected to get to the bathroom when he was stark naked and had just been ordered not to move?

Fortunately an old woman soon peeked in on Ross. She introduced herself by her full name of Fay Fitzgerald Dozier, then shrugged and added that he might as well call her Aunt Fay since her niece, Tessa, did.

Tessa, Ross decided, was the lady doc's nickname. "Tessa," he repeated softly, trying out the name on himself and liking it.

"What's her real name?" he asked Aunt Fay.

"Teresa Kathleen Fitzgerald."

"A real shame she's not Irish," Ross grinned.

"Unfortunately for you, fella, her Irish is way up, so you'd better watch out," Aunt Fay warned him bluntly.

Ross liked the old lady immediately. Aunt Fay was short, small and positively ancient, a white-haired woman with the same bright blue eyes as her niece. "You want to borrow my walker and visit the bathroom?" she asked Ross. He nodded gratefully and wound the top bed sheet around his waist.

Tessa was right in thinking that he was still very weak, Ross discovered. He had to sit on the edge of the bed for several minutes before he dared to stand up. Even though he took it slow and easy he still felt dizzy and moderately disoriented. Objects seemed either too close or too far away, and black spots swam before his eyes.

"Slower," Aunt Fay cautioned him.

Ross never could have made it without her walker. Just traveling the few steps down the hall and into the bathroom made his heart race and pound sickeningly, while a sheen of perspiration broke out all over him.

Someone had brought his brown leather kit of toiletries into the bathroom, he was glad to see. Still, Ross decided the shower and shampoo he wanted could wait till tomorrow. He settled instead for brushing his teeth and washing his face, then he hastily dragged a safety razor over the blond stubble that had sprouted on his cheeks and chin and above his upper lip. A glance in the mirror told him he looked like death warmed over. Maybe I had better go back and lie down, he thought, not even taking time to inspect his various wounds.

Aunt Fay was sitting on the foot of Ross's bed as he crept cautiously into the room, the sheet now wound around him toga-fashion. It was hard to realize that yesterday he'd felt strong enough to push a car. Silently he and Aunt Fay traded places and, as she reclaimed her walker, Ross eased his long body across the too-short mattress.

"Want me to leave you now?" Aunt Fay asked.

Ross shook his head even as he closed his eyes and began the first of several deep restorative breaths. Since he was going to have to be in bed for a while yet he might as well avail himself of company, he thought.

"Why is your niece so grouchy today?" he asked Aunt Fay plaintively. Until he spoke aloud Ross didn't realize he still had the dark-haired lady doctor on his mind or that he wanted to see more of her dimples and more of the sweet, caring expression that had warmed her blue eyes yesterday.

"Well, now, I guess Tessa's got her reasons for being all put out," Aunt Fay said equably.

"Why? Did I do or say something revolting?" Ross asked in concern.

"Not that I heard of," Aunt Fay replied, "and, knowing Tessa, if you'd done it, I'd have heard about it. She's not one to suffer in silence. But she sat up all night nursing you, so she's just plain worn out today. She's always cranky when she gets tired."

"I was really that sick?" Ross asked in near disbelief.

"Son, to hear my great-niece tell it, you were hovering between life and death for several hours there." Thoughtfully Aunt Fay added, "Tessa's not one to exaggerate. Anyway, sitting up with you is just for starters."

Uh-oh, Ross thought again. "What else happened?" he asked Aunt Fay cautiously.

"Well, she wasted 'most a gallon of good water sponging you down. Then when she found out that purple, swollen-up place on your leg was a snakebite, was she ever upset!"

"Oh, I've been snakebitten a couple of times before. By now venom doesn't affect me as much as the average person. Maybe I should have mentioned that," Ross said thoughtfully.

"Guess so. Anyway, the next I know Tessa's burning up the phone lines trying to track down some snake whatchamacallit. Antivenin, that's it. She finally found some over in El Paso, so then she had to get the highway patrol of three states, Texas, New Mexico and Arizona to rush it down here. Then she started administering it and monitoring you for a reaction."

Ross groaned. Well, at least he knew now why he felt so especially lousy. Snake antivenin really messed up one's system.

"So that kept Tessa hopping till about two this morning," Aunt Fay continued. "Then, since your condition was still critical and she wasn't sure you wouldn't just up and croak on her, she decided she'd better track down your next of kin.''

Ross groaned even louder since he feared what was coming.

''First, Tessa called over to someplace in Louisiana named San Clemente or something—''

''St. Clément,'' Ross moaned, using the Cajun pronunciation, ''Clay-mon.''

''Whatever. Anyway, Tessa talked to your landlady for a long time.''

''Oh God,'' Ross said feelingly.

''What's that woman's name again? Tessa said she was very excitable and talked a whole lot—some of it in French.''

''Yeah, Mrs. Couvillion does that when she gets upset,'' Ross whispered.

''Couvillion, that's the name. Tessa said she also cried a lot. Anyway, Mrs. C. said the only reason you're still alive is the result of prayers and divine intercession. Tessa said she was probably right about that. Anyway, Tessa finally got the poor lady calmed down enough to find out your folks' names and where they lived.''

''Oh, God,'' Ross said again. ''Tell me she didn't call them, please.''

''Tessa called them. And she said Stanley and Linda Stanton must both have heads full of fruit flies.''

''She talked to both of them?'' Ross asked in horror and at Aunt Fay's vigorous nod, he closed his eyes helplessly. That made things even worse than he'd thought. Poor Tessa.

Stan would have begun, sounding almost normal. He would have thanked Tessa for the news about his son and stated that he and Linda would be wishing for the best, ''as we always do.'' Then Stan would have added his personal and very low opinion of the medical profession: how it made use of unnecessary surgery, far too many prescription drugs and innocent animals sacrificed for heartless research. Stan also thought doctors only practiced their lucrative profession to get "the big bucks."

Ross's father had always claimed that he couldn't resist pricking doctors' pretensions, exposing their pomposity and letting them know that not everyone regarded them as God Almighty. As a result, Ross had never been treated by a doctor who, after a conversation with Stan, hadn't come away mad.

Linda wasn't quite as abrasive. Oh, she might have used the same words as Stan, saying that personally she always sought alternate health care, usually from a herbalist or nutritional counsellor. But since Linda spoke in a breathy little-girl whisper, people just naturally assumed she was a harmless flake.

"My folks are a little weird," Ross admitted to Aunt Fay.

"Well, I don't think my niece appreciated their opinions," Aunt Fay continued. "You see, Tessa is a researcher into juvenile diabetes—or she was until some anti-medical establishment types persuaded several trustees at the college where she worked to cancel all research projects if they involved animals. Tessa and her boss were using white rats and mice, so their projects got axed and they were both invited to leave."

Hearing that, Ross groaned again. Both his father and stepmother were active in animal rights causes. In fact, Stan had even founded FLAC as an umbrella organization for several such groups. A couple of them were downright militant in their determination to stop all medical research that utilized animals.

Aunt Fay, however, was more interested in other aspects of Stan and Linda's life-style. "Are your folks really vegetarians?" she asked Ross curiously.

"They sure are," he said feelingly. "There's nothing like spending a weekend with them to get totally sick of tofu."

"I don't eat meat much myself," Aunt Fay volunteered. "Just don't like the taste. Anyway, vegetarians live longer, I've read. At my age longevity starts to be a concern."

"I'll ask Linda to send you her recipes for soybean burgers and total protein stew," Ross offered. "The stew has beans, brown rice, nonpasteurized whey and lots of sprouts."

"You like it?" Aunt Fay asked him curiously.

"I detest it!"

"Good. 'Cause I don't have any of that kind of stuff around here to feed you. Speaking of food, I guess you're getting hungry."

Ross hadn't really thought about it, but now that he did he was aware of his stomach rumbling emptily. He had missed a couple of meals and his ill, overworked and stressed-out body certainly knew it. Still, he could hardly let an old woman with a broken leg cook for him. Regretfully he shook his head, adding with real hope, "I'm sure your niece will be back to check on me before long."

"I don't know about that," Aunt Fay said thoughtfully. "Since Tessa never went to bed at all last night, she's crashed now on the living-room sofa. No telling when she'll wake up. Anyway, I'd better tell you the worst right now and get it over with: she's no cook."

"I'm really sorry she's so tired," Ross said with heartfelt sincerity and sent the silent message to his stomach that he regretted the news, but apparently this was another no-food day.

Maybe the wistfulness he felt showed on his face. "Look, Ross, I wasn't planning to fix you anything fancy," Aunt Fay assured him. "Just a glass of orange juice and a couple of pastries I could drop in the toaster."

Now his empty stomach actually rumbled aloud. "That would sure taste good, Aunt Fay," Ross breathed and added winningly, "Say, could you toast four of 'em?"

The sofa felt lumpy. The window blinds, although drawn against the bright Arizona sun, still allowed one single ray inside. It, of course, beamed directly into Tessa's weary eyes. Furthermore there were voices to distract her—several voices coming from happy, lighthearted people who kept chattering away and then laughing.

What in hell is going on? thought Tessa irritably as she shoved herself off the lumpy mattress on the ancient sofa bed. The cottage didn't sound at all the way a home with two sick people ought to sound. Rather, it sounded like someone was giving a party.

All that stopped Tessa from heading in the direction of the frivolity, snarling and spitting fire, was the distracting odor of fresh rich coffee and hot rolls that actually smelled homemade.

She glanced at her wristwatch as she stumbled in the direction of Aunt Fay's small kitchen. Ten-thirty. It was midmorning now, so she'd slept for a little over three hours.

It didn't feel like nearly enough, Tessa thought, yawning. She snatched up a mug and filled it with dark, strong coffee. Of course, she wasn't as young as she'd once been, as Aunt Fay had so kindly reminded her.

Since Tessa usually drank only decaffeinated coffee, several jolts of the real thing woke her up immediately. Once her eyes became more than mere slits, she looked around and followed her nose.

Fat fluffy rolls, topped with rich orange icing and dotted with pecan halves, stood on the counter. Tessa recognized the gifted hand of Mrs. Sandoval as she pounced eagerly on one and wolfed it down, then gulped a second. Why, she hadn't eaten in this fashion since she'd been an intern, but today she felt every bit as bone weary as she had then. With the first sharp edges taken off an unusually ravenous appetite, she went into the bathroom and threw cold water on her face.

Tessa noticed that Ross's leather kit was unzipped and reached inside it, to discover his still-damp toothbrush. So he'd managed to drag himself out of bed and obviously had survived it since he wasn't sprawled out dead on the floor. Tessa forced herself to shrug off her sharp concern over Ross and when she couldn't immediately locate her own toothpaste she borrowed some of his.

Then, yawning once again, she went lurching toward his room—that pleasant room that had once been hers—just as another gale of lively feminine laughter sounded.

"Where did you take this one of the pagoda, Ross?" she heard Aunt Fay ask.

"Oh, that was Bangkok in 1980."

"Mama, just look at these ugly ol' crocodiles."

"Yes, Consuela, I see them," Mrs. Sandoval replied fondly.

"Actually those are alligators," Ross cut in, explaining. "They live in the Louisiana swamp where I usually stay when I'm not off traveling somewhere."

My God, it really is a party, Tessa thought as she came charging through the door. And just what is this, show-and-tell? As four sets of eyes swung warily to her she immediately felt discomfited. She tried to tell herself that it was the women's scrutiny of her appearance that bothered her most. After all, they looked clean and morning-fresh. Mrs. Sandoval was stately in a purple dress, size eighteen or twenty, with Consuela rosy and radiant in baby pink, either a ten or twelve. Even Aunt Fay looked her eighty-year-old best, wearing a pristine blue duster in a petite size.

Tessa, by contrast, still wore her oldest clothes, which now looked even worse for having been slept in. Her hair was a mess, kinked and dull-looking, with various tendrils standing straight up. She hadn't applied makeup in days and this morning her face looked distinctly gray with fatigue, while her eyes were surrounded by dark circles. Although she couldn't do anything about her tired-looking face, Tessa did wish she'd paused to brush her hair and bathe and dress in something a bit more becoming.

It was especially disconcerting to look so awful and know it, then glance across the room at eighteen-year-old Consuela, who was blooming with youth. The girl's off-the-shoulder blouse also displayed a considerable expanse of smooth olive skin as well as highlighting a large firm bosom. Tessa, who had been slightly shortchanged in that department, couldn't help feeling a trifle envious of any woman who had cleavage.

At the sight of Tessa the group fell silent like guilty children caught whispering in class when they should have been studying. A large coffee-table book of photographs lay open on Ross's bed. Obviously it was one of Aunt Fay's prized possessions, to judge by the careful way in which she reached over to close it and lift it off the sick man's lap.

"Okay, everyone, out," Tessa commanded. "I need to examine my patient."

Aunt Fay and Mrs. Sandoval were sitting on the room's two chairs while Consuela had perched at the foot of Ross's bed. As the pretty young girl arose with a swing of her generous hips Tessa felt a stab of savage jealousy. It was followed by immediate chagrin.

What in the world is wrong with me? she wondered. How could I possibly be interested in a man like this one? Why, he's a perpetual accident just waiting to happen! And even if all those wild stories his landlady told me weren't enough, his relatives are clearly crazy!

As the women filed out to the rhythmic clomp of Aunt Fay's walker, Tessa took the chair just vacated by Mrs. Sandoval and reached for the thermometer.

"Hi, Doc," her patient said softly and flashed her a winning smile.

She couldn't help noticing that he looked like a young Caesar with the sheet wrapped around one of his broad shoulders.

"Hi, yourself," Tessa replied brusquely. She wasn't about to let Ross see what his slow lazy grin did to her heart. Why, it was actually hammering and pounding in a thoroughly adolescent fashion. "How are you feeling, Ross?"

"I've had better days—and expect to have a lot more."

He flashed another smile in Tessa's direction, this one earnest and replete with the sight of even, pristine-white teeth. My God, wouldn't you think Mother Nature could have omitted at least one lousy weapon? Tessa thought incredulously. The man could serve as a model for male perfection.

"I sure want to thank you for everything you did for me last night," Ross said with an even greater appearance of earnestness. "I'm sorry I was so much trouble, Dr. Fitzgerald."

I am immune to this man's charm, Tessa vowed, her twanging nerve ends telling her just the opposite. In fact, I am not susceptible to any man's charm, for I am in full control of my life and my emotions. The positive affirmation, which Tessa had read once in a self-help book, had sounded better then than it did just now.

She considered this man's wholly annoying effect on her with bewilderment. She had never been a sucker, a pushover or a patsy for any man. She had always prided herself on her level head and cool judgment. But now she was feeling positively tremulous, all because those fabulous aquamarine eyes were fixed on her, making a leisurely, relaxed perusal of her face and figure. Well, she'd better take charge again and quickly, before he had her eating out of his hand.

"Open up, Ross," Tessa said aloud, and when he parted his lips obediently she popped the thermometer in, then reached for her stethoscope. "Now stay quiet and stay still."

He winked at her, with a merry and good-natured expression that was yet another demonstration of his striking appeal. Oh Lord, must I be subjected to an entire repertoire of masculine charms? Tessa wondered.

How warm his skin felt today, she noticed as she wrapped the blood pressure cuff around one brawny arm. Not at all clammy, as it had been last night. Then she felt so angry with herself for making such an observation that she pumped up the cuff until Ross winced. Slowly Tessa relaxed the pressure, watched the silver mercury drop and listened for his heartbeat.

"Your blood pressure is back to normal," Tessa announced matter-of-factly, removing the cuff from Ross's arm and then drawing the thermometer from his mouth. "Hmm..."

"What's that?" Ross said interestedly. "Good or bad?"

"Normal," Tessa said curtly, frowning.

"Hey, why are you so mad at me?" Ross asked her. "Oh, I know you're tired and you probably got insulted by my folks—"

"All right, I'll tell you," Tessa flared, knowing that the sooner she killed that expression of interest in his eyes and wiped the warmth off his oh-so-handsome face, the safer she would be.

"Please do," Ross invited.

"I don't like daredevils! I have utterly no use for careless, thrill-seeking fools with a death wish! People like you, who live on the razor's edge, not only endanger themselves but probably others as well. As a doctor I've spent a lot of time trying to save lives. That includes patching up lamebrains like you, but there's nothing that says I have to like people who deliberately place themselves in jeopardy. In fact I resent the waste of my valuable time!'' Tessa stopped, her breasts fairly heaving with suppressed rage.

"Whoa." Ross held up a hand, amazement written all over his face. "I think we have a major misunderstand—''

"There's no misunderstanding." Since Tessa was wound up and going strong she had no intention of stopping. "Your landlady filled me in on your more recent escapades. It seems you got your ribs broken in a wrestling match with a python. Then you lost that joint on your toe to piranha fish."

Ross sighed. "South America was rather unusual—''

"Not to hear Mrs. Couvillion tell it. What about that cave in West Texas? Isn't that where you got dive-bombed by hibernating bats after you woke them up? Or the hang gliding accident over the Rockies? I believe you languished in Montana Memorial about three weeks following that one. Well, have I missed anything that's happened recently?''

"Not unless Mrs. C. failed to mention when I got hit by the dogsled—''

"Yes, she did neglect to mention that incident, Ross." Tessa leaned back in her chair, her arms crossed over her chest. "So tell me what happened. I'm waiting with bated breath."

"Well, it was just a minor accident near Fairbanks. I, for one, have never blamed the lead dog, because it naturally got blinded with all that snow in its eyes—oh, let's skip it." Ross turned his golden head on the pillow, presenting Tessa with an all-too-attractive view of his strong profile.

"No, let's not skip it," Tessa argued. "I'm fascinated in a horrible sort of way. What in the world is wrong with someone like you, Ross Stanton? That's what I'd like to know."

When Ross remained thoughtfully silent, Tessa stood up and began looking for the bottle of antiseptic she'd used last night. When she found it, she smacked the bottle down on Ross's nightstand, then grabbed the sheet he'd wound over his shoulder and around his waist. "Hey," he yelped in surprise, even outrage. "What are you doing?"

"What do you think?" Tessa cried in exasperation.

He cocked one thick golden eyebrow at her. "Seducing me? Not that it isn't a great idea, but I'm sorta wiped out after the sunstroke and the snakebite—"

"I am not seducing you. I am trying to examine your leg wound." With amazement Tessa heard her voice escalate shrilly—she who was never provoked into shouting! "Now, will you let go?"

"No," Ross said stubbornly. Suddenly they were in a tug-of-war over the sheet and somehow Tessa's hands had gotten all entangled with his.

"Are you crazy, Ross Stanton?" Tessa demanded, trying to free her fingers. His thumb brushed the back of her hand and electric thrills shot through her.

"You don't examine me until I get a pair of shorts to wear," he insisted, his voice sounding as stubborn as his face looked.

"You really are crazy," Tessa sighed, sinking back into her straight chair and finally jerking her hand from his. "Look, Ross, I'm a doctor. I've seen plenty of people in the raw and their equipment is nothing new to me. Why, I've already seen you without a stitch on . . ."

To her surprise a dull flush crept over his lean cheeks, but he only gripped the sheet about him all the more firmly. Why, he's actually modest, she thought in surprise.

"I can't help last night," Ross muttered. "Since I wasn't able to give my consent, I hope you got a thrill—"

"As a matter of fact I didn't," Tessa lied. "I was too busy working to bother with looking at you."

The expression Ross trained on her was noticeably skeptical. "Shorts," he insisted.

"Oh, come on, Ross," Tessa cried in exasperation. "Surely other women doctors have examined you, as many times as you've been hospitalized."

"They weren't beautiful young women," he retorted.

For some reason another ridiculous thrill shot through Tessa. Does he actually think I'm young and beautiful? she thought, momentarily awash in sudden, blinding happiness.

Then sanity returned to taunt her. What a snow job. Why, Ross Stanton could probably convince most women that it was sleigh time right now—but not Tessa Fitzgerald! Determinedly she reached out again for his improvised toga.

"Not on your life," Ross spat out through gritted teeth.

"Oh, for—" Tessa had to bite her lip to stop the flow of words that would have otherwise erupted. That was another strange thing. She rarely swore. But he was surely the most infuriating man she had ever met.

Ross won their battle. Annoyed, Tessa went to find his canvas clothes pack, which she'd hidden in Aunt Fay's storeroom. She opened it and extracted a pair of khaki shorts, then stalked back to Ross, tossed them onto his bed and closed the door. A couple of minutes later he invited her to return. Then Tessa exacted her revenge by slapping antiseptic on his snakebite and relishing his howl of pain.

The bite looked much better today, she thought on inspecting it closely. He really did have marvelous recuperative powers. What a shame that a little of his superb immune system couldn't be transferred to the young diabetics Tessa sought to help or to cancer patients who'd be more appreciative and careful. Tessa felt her mouth tighten grimly as she rebandaged Ross's wound.

"You're wrong about me, you know," he said quietly as Tessa deftly tore tape between her fingers.

She sniffed in disbelief.

"I don't have a death wish at all. Why, I've been to a hundred places and taken a thousand photographs when nothing at all went wrong."

"According to your father you've always lacked a sense of danger," Tessa shot back. "He said when you were just a little boy you used to dive out of trees or sail off the roof of the house. And that later, when you played football, you'd hurl yourself straight up and over the line—and never mind how hard you'd get hit. He thinks you're amazing. But, as I told him, I thought your brain had probably gotten scrambled."

To Tessa's surprise Ross burst into hearty laughter. "Maybe it has, at that," he agreed with such pleasant good humor that, once again, she found herself almost totally disarmed.

"Actually, the possibility of getting hurt just never occurs to me—at least not until I'm suddenly face-to-face with danger. You see, I'm always trying to snap a certain photograph in a very particular way and I'm thinking about that."

Ross smiled charmingly at Tessa, obviously intent on trying to coax her into a better mood, but she let her skeptical expression tell him it wasn't working.

"Dramatic and unique photographs don't come easily," he continued, "but I've snapped some great pictures over the years. Birds are my specialty."

"So I've heard," she replied grudgingly. Mrs. Couvillion had just happened to mention Ross's Pulitzer Prize; Stan and Linda had described the Associated Press awards and the Photographers' Hall of Fame induction. They'd also talked about Ross's longtime association with *American Geographic*, a famous magazine widely admired for its combination of nature and wildlife photographs taken in unusual or exotic locales.

Tessa glanced up at Ross as she slapped on another piece of adhesive tape. He met her gaze, managing a negligent shrug. But Tessa wasn't fooled by his further display of modesty.

"You know something, Ross Stanton? None of it means zip to me because I don't give a hoot about wildlife and I especially dislike birds. I think anyone's crazy to risk their life for a photograph. A lot of good all your honors and awards will do you when you're dead. And anybody who manages a snakebite and a sunstroke on the very same day is not merely practicing a high-risk career, he's living like a damned fool, as well!"

Rising, Tessa slapped Ross's leg emphatically to press down her neat new bandage and listened with considerable satisfaction as he uttered another yelp.

"So don't give me any more trouble," she threatened him softly, "or I'll make you sorry you were ever born."

Tessa had reached the door before Ross recovered enough to reply. "You're doing a pretty good job already," he said glumly.

Chapter Four

During the next couple of days Tessa had to admit that Ross caused her the minimum amount of trouble. He proved to be a quiet, thoughtful patient, adept at entertaining himself yet apparently pleased whenever any visitors appeared. Tessa should have felt gratified by his behavior, but she didn't. She should have been mollified since he was so nondemanding, but she wasn't. The man was simply too attractive and too distracting for Tessa to feel comfortable with him—or to trust him one inch.

Still, she kept finding out more and more things about Ross, just because it would have been, well, churlish not to exchange a few words when she checked him over morning, noon and night. So far his recuperation had provided her with few surprises, except that within twenty-four hours a great many packages began arriving for him. They had all been flown express to Tucson, then sent by special truck to

Progresso and they contained get-well gifts from women who had names like Kiki and Tammie, Bambi and Deby.

"Kiki sent me a chocolate torte," Ross exclaimed happily, showing the elaborate confection to Tessa. "Looks tasty, doesn't it?"

"Who's Kiki?" Tessa asked darkly, pumping away almost savagely on the blood pressure cuff.

"My stepmother."

"I thought Linda was your stepmother," Tessa retorted.

"I guess I should say Kiki is my ex-stepmother, but she's still a close and dear friend of the family. Kiki was Stan's second wife. She's a dedicated feminist now. Swears she won't ever remarry, but she's been living with this guy named Edgar for about ten years."

"Oh." Tessa wouldn't admit, even to herself, that it felt good to know Kiki was safely tucked away in bed with Edgar. "So who sent you the cheese wheel?" she couldn't resist asking.

"Deby. She's another of my ex-stepmothers. The third one, Bambi, sent the Colombian coffee. Hey, why don't we have a party this afternoon? I'll serve cheese, crackers, cold drinks and coffee. We can cut the torte, of course."

"And those pajamas sent by Tammie?" Tessa asked, hating the edge to her voice. She loomed over Ross, thermometer in hand. "Another of Stan's ex-wives or old flames?"

Ross laughed. "No, Tammie is one of mine. An old flame, that is."

For the first time in her life Tessa feared that she might actually jam a thermometer down a patient's throat. "Oh?" she inquired icily. "When did you and Tammie break up?"

"I was thirteen, I think. She was twelve. Eight years later she married Thad."

Tessa exhaled with something that felt strangely like relief. "You've never been married?" she couldn't resist asking Ross.

"I've never even come close." He looked up at her with an expression of such wistful interest that Tessa wondered how on earth he expected her to believe him. Surely if Ross had ever looked at any other woman in just the way he was looking at her now, that woman would still be draped across his body and clinging to his neck.

"Now I guess you'll tell me I'm secretly afraid of matrimony," Ross teased Tessa. "Maybe I've been extracautious because of Stan's example. I don't want three divorces."

"Oh, I don't think there's anything wrong in being cautious," Tessa said quietly. "I've never been married, either."

"The real reason I haven't is that I've just never met that special person," Ross said, shifting onto one elbow.

"I haven't either," Tessa heard herself whispering while her runaway heart began a whole series of erratic thuds. What a really glorious-looking man he was, with his bare chest covered thickly with golden ringlets and those aquamarine eyes looking up at her from beneath a heavy fringe of stubby lashes.

Tessa jerked herself back to reality, realizing that the forgotten thermometer still dangled from her hand. "Open up, Ross," she said automatically and slipped the thermometer under his tongue.

Ross's temperature continued to be normal. Still, Tessa confiscated both the torte and the cheese wheel. Both had entirely too much sodium and cholesterol for a recuperating man. Ross's impromptu party—with Consuela in attendance, no doubt—would just have to wait.

The lady doc wasn't really his type at all, Ross kept assuring himself. He knew about doctors and they were all dull and smug. Still, this one was not only beautiful but appealing, as well. There was an elusive something else about her, maybe a touch of hidden sadness that made him want to reach out and hug her. Since Ross couldn't quite define this little-girl-lost quality and since such unusual emotions left him feeling distinctly uncomfortable, it helped him to concentrate on Tessa's various deficiencies, several of which he had already identified.

For starters, Tessa Fitzgerald was much too serious. Sometimes she was even downright grim. Ross liked his women light and bright, witty and laughing. Oh, not that he wanted some smiling idiot, of course. Dumb women were certainly not stimulating. But whenever Ross stopped to relax in the company of the opposite sex he liked to be entertained.

Tessa was *not* entertaining.

Of course, Ross had to admit that right now she was beset with various problems. Not that she'd discussed them with him, but he wasn't blind or deaf. Tessa was caring for both him and Aunt Fay. She was overseeing the store, the café, the gas pumps, the Sandovals and various tourists, more of whom were turning up each day. She was also living uncomfortably in limbo, since that brother of hers still hadn't called to discuss their elderly aunt and Tessa was—understandably—growing upset over that. "Has Glenn called yet?" she asked Aunt Fay each evening, just as soon as she came back to the cottage. When Aunt Fay replied in the negative, Ross had heard Tessa's anxious sighs. She also inquired almost as regularly and hopefully about a Dr. Corman. Apparently he had been Tessa's boss, Ross gathered, but now they were both unemployed. It was bound to be worrisome.

So Ross found himself sympathizing with Lady Doc, even when he didn't always like what he saw and heard of her.

"I feel just fine now," he told her rather impatiently on his third evening in Arizona. At least it was almost true.

"Well, you're not," she replied so emphatically that Ross started to grow irritated.

"Look, just how much longer do you plan to hold me captive?" he asked, quirking an eyebrow at her to show that he was at least half joking.

But apparently she just didn't understand humor. A real shame, too, since she looked cute as a button today in simple white shorts topped with a bright blue shirt. Blue was definitely her color, just as it was Aunt Fay's, Ross observed. It deepened the color of Tessa's eyes and turned her delicately tinted cheeks and lips rosy. Also, her dark curls had been washed and brushed to a high gloss, making him long to reach out and touch them.

Although Ross would have liked to think Tessa was primping for him, he wasn't conceited enough to believe she'd given him more than a fleeting thought. No, her interest in him was strictly professional, although her nearness, her touch, her natural womanly scent were starting to cause plenty of healthy reactions in his body. That was one reason Ross knew he was ninety percent recovered.

Meanwhile Tessa Fitzgerald was seriously considering his question. "You can get up for a few hours on Friday, if you take it easy till then," she said at last.

As she bent to aim the ever-present thermometer at him, one small sweet breast brushed his arm, arousing Ross so quickly that he was startled.

"Friday! That's two whole days away," he complained to cover his extreme reaction to her. "The tanager—"

"Has shown no interest in going anywhere else, as I of all people certainly know," Tessa sighed. "I keep praying that wretched bird will fly away forever or, barring that, drop dead swinging on its perch."

Ross winced. As a bird lover he felt that that was a downright awful thing to say. "If you don't let me up you're going to sink my career, trash my reputation as a guy who always delivers—"

Tessa shrugged off his complaints, an earnest look creeping back into her pretty blue eyes. "Now that you're feeling better, Ross, there's a pertinent health matter that we need to discuss."

"Oh, hell," he grumbled, feeling frustrated for more reasons than one. "Can't it wait?"

"Well, pardon me," she said, her voice turning sarcastic. "I didn't realize what vitally important things you were doing sacked out here."

"As a matter of fact I'm staying pretty busy observing the squirrels," Ross informed her. He'd already devised at least three or four new ways to photograph them.

"Squirrels?" Tessa echoed as if she'd never even heard the word before.

"Yes. Look out the window." Ross held back the starched white curtain nearest his bed and gestured with his free hand. "See? There are probably twenty gray squirrels scampering up and down the trees."

"Oh," Tessa said with crashing indifference. "Those."

"Six of them are still quite young. So they're not only frisky but very clumsy and very funny. Why, one of them..." Ross stopped, seeing the expression on Tessa's face. Wryly he added, "A real animal lover, aren't you?"

She shrugged. "Squirrels are just rodents, aren't they? Pests."

"Rodents?" Ross was absolutely outraged. "Pests?"

"I've done a lot of work with rodents. Frankly, as companions I always found them a crashing bore," Tessa said with another impatient shrug.

"Did you ever watch a lively gray squirrel even once in your life?" Ross demanded heatedly. "They have personality and cunning. They race down tree trunks headfirst, like kamikaze pilots. They chatter and scold each other and sometimes fight over nuts. They use their big bushy tails a dozen ways—thumping to indicate danger, slapping each other silly when they're angry. Yes, I've been letting them entertain me—''

"A meeting of kindred minds, no doubt."

"—so I could stay out of *your* hair," he finished, glowering at her.

"So I'm not turned on by squirrels," Tessa said, giving another shrug. "Did you know that they can transmit rabies? Why, sometimes, out here in the west, they can transmit plague."

"Plague?" Ross couldn't believe his ears. "As in the Black Death that once wiped out a third of Europe?"

"Yes, indeed." She regarded him with amused superiority.

"Hey, you're just putting me on about the plague, right? I mean, my God, rabies is bad enough." Ross stared at Tessa, unable to believe that someone who looked at a cute, frisky, clever squirrel could immediately equate them with disease.

"No, I am not putting you on. Several cases of bubonic plague are diagnosed every year in New Mexico and Arizona. I'm deadly serious about that, Ross, just as I am deadly serious about what I want us to discuss."

"Aren't you always? Deadly serious, I mean," he sighed. "Okay, fire away."

"Not if you're just going to lie there with that bored and indifferent look on your face!" Tessa said angrily.

"I guess I get as excited about diseases as you get about squirrels."

"Oh!" She leaped out of her chair so suddenly that it almost tipped over. In a towering rage she headed for the door, affording Ross a suddenly distracting and wholly delightful view of her shapely slender legs and trim, delicate ankles. She was acquiring a nice tan, too, he observed.

"Look, I'm sorry, Dr. Fitzgerald—" Ross began.

Tessa swung back around in time to catch him focusing his gaze on her derriere. "No, you're not. You—why, you're staring at me!"

"Hell, I told you I was feeling better," Ross blurted out. "And I have an artist's eye. Can I help it if I notice a woman's figure? I even noticed how very nice you look today, Tessa. But I suppose I'm committing another crime to mention that."

To his amazement she colored and looked disconcerted for a moment. "No. I just want you to listen when I have something important to say. I don't exactly think you're a typical male chauvinist, Ross, but I also don't think you're in the habit of paying much attention to a woman's mind, or to her observations and thoughts."

Despite himself he was startled. Sobered, he propped himself up on one elbow to listen to her attentively. "You might have a point," he conceded, adding thoughtfully, "I didn't used to be that way. I always listened to my mother. We used to talk about everything. Then after she died I missed her tremendously. That's why, when all my stepmothers turned out to be friendly, I got close to them, too. Why, Kiki, Deby and Bambi used to talk up a storm. If you're right, I wonder when I stopped listening. I wonder *why* I stopped listening."

Tessa started to smile, and she really had quite a lovely smile, Ross couldn't help noticing. "Don't forget Tammie," she prompted.

"Oh, sure." Ross started to say that he hadn't talked to Tammie nearly as often as he'd kissed her. But something warned him not to add that bit of information. He pushed a pillow behind his back and sat up in bed. "Come talk to me," he invited Tessa. "I'll listen and I'll take you seriously, I promise."

For a minute she regarded him warily, then she returned to her chair. "Ross, you're recovering quite well, but a sunstroke is no small thing. From now on you're going to be more susceptible to heat-related disorders than the average person. You'll especially need to avoid being out all alone in high temperatures. And you should stop spending a lot of time outside between ten and two when the sun is at its highest."

"But—" Ross started.

"You should also begin—*immediately*—to wear sunscreen on your face and a straw hat on your head whenever you're out of doors," Tessa interrupted, quietly yet firmly. "Because if you don't, and you ever have another sunstroke, you may not live through the next one."

Sunscreen? A straw hat? Avoid going outside! Ross bit his lip to keep himself from laughing. He could just imagine poling through the Atchafalaya Swamp in his ongoing search for the ivory-billed woodpecker, wearing the accoutrements Tessa had just suggested. Or being accompanied by some keeper so he wouldn't be alone.

"Does something I've said strike you as funny?" Tessa asked, her voice cooling rapidly once again.

A revealing twitch of his lips told Ross he wasn't concealing his mirth as well as he'd wanted to. "Look, Tessa, I know you mean well," he said gently. "But what you're suggesting just won't fit into my life-style at all."

"I knew it," she exclaimed in exasperation, jumping to her feet again. "Oh, I'd really hoped I was wrong about you and that there did exist a single spark of sanity in your brain. But I wasn't wrong. You're the very personification of the headstrong, reckless male. I know your type. You eat and drink anything, smoke two packs a day, never exercise, burn your skin to leather in the sun and generally scoff at all forms of preventive medicine. Do you know what doctors like me expect for people like you? A massive coronary at the age of thirty-eight!''

Despite himself Ross felt momentarily jolted. "Hey, I get plenty of exercise," he protested, "and I've never smoked."

"But you'd flunk everything else on my high-risk profile, wouldn't you?" she gibed. "Just how long do you think you can get away with it?"

Ross couldn't resist firing right back, "Look, I know you're a well-meaning woman and a good doctor, but you definitely carry caution to the extreme. Just because *you* think that danger lurks everywhere—"

"As it does," Tessa cut in, her face turning an attractive shade of pink from wrath and her breasts rising and falling in a way that Ross found difficult not to watch.

"—doesn't mean that I happen to agree with you. And I don't," he went on testily. "Why, basically, this is a friendly universe—"

"It's as friendly as a war zone!" she shouted.

"—filled with beautiful plants and interesting animals and birds who sing for joy—" Ross's voice had also risen to a roar.

"And poisonous plants, dangerous animals and pathological microbes and bacteria," Tessa responded without missing a beat. "Not to mention a multitude of viruses and fungi!"

Ross stopped, simply staring at her. "My God!" This woman was a sadder case than even he had suspected.

He'd met her type before, not too often, fortunately. The Nervous Nellies, Ross called them. Worrywarts, killjoys and spoilsports who tiptoed through life. *If it tastes good, it's bad for you. If it feels good, it's dangerous. If you're having fun, you'll regret it. The only thing you can ever count on is that you are going to get sick and die.* Nervous Nellies always worked at dull, boring jobs, because change or challenges of any sort frightened them.

"No wonder you're a researcher in some cold sterile lab where you study little animals," Ross heard himself scoff. "Since people like you are scared to really live life, all you can do is watch it."

"How dare you!" Tessa gasped, then swung on her heel. She went through the door, slamming it decisively and Ross sank back angrily against his pillows.

What a shame, he thought, fuming. What a waste! She was damned pretty, too. But undoubtedly the only reason he'd ever been attracted to the foul-tempered wench was the tendency of the sick male to fall in love with his primary care giver, who was usually a nurse.

Furthermore, Ross thought resentfully as he pummeled his pillows, he had let his admiration for and attraction to that caution addict who was Dr. Teresa Fitzgerald keep him idle for a ridiculous length of time. Why, he felt fine now, just a little weak, but that was what came of lolling around in bed. He'd get his strength back as soon as he really started pushing himself again. Yet that rigid extremist—or was aggravating perfectionist the better term?—still wanted him grounded for another forty-eight hours. Well, the hell with that! The hell with *her*! If people like Tessa had their way, all of civilization would be cowering in concrete bunkers instead of being out in the fresh air and sunshine with the birds and beasts.

Ross was still so angry that it took a moment before he even heard the gentle knock at his door. "Yes?" he barked when the sound finally penetrated.

His door eased open a cautious few inches, then Aunt Fay's wrinkled yet merry face swung around it. "Ross? Sounds like you and Tessa were going a few rounds. She slammed all three doors on her way back to the store."

"She's gone?" Ross asked, forcing himself to wipe the scowl off his face and smile for Aunt Fay. A new thought struck him then and he began to grin, tentatively at first. Then he felt his smile spread, growing broader.

"What is it, Ross?" Aunt Fay asked, clomping into the room on her walker. "I can tell you've got some kind of devilment in mind."

Ross exhaled, letting the last of his anger and tension ebb away as the picture of outwitting Dr. Know-It-All filled his imagination, giving him a feeling of immense pleasure.

"Aunt Fay, how would you like to go see the flame-colored tanager?" he offered.

Was something wrong? Tessa wondered, awakening gradually on her lumpy bed in the living room. Everything was so still, so quiet. She raised her head off the mattress, pushed her hair out of her eyes and stared at the watch that never left her wrist except when she showered. Six-thirty. Usually both Ross and Aunt Fay were stirring by now.

Tessa herself was normally up no later than six since her inner clock, set to Eastern Time, still recognized that as 8:00 a.m.

Tessa listened for sounds of running water. Or footfalls. Or the clink of metal on stoneware as coffee was poured and stirred. She sniffed the air for its welcome smell—unfortunately she was getting addicted to caffeine again—and thought she detected a fresh but faint aroma.

Tessa sighed, stretched and began slowly peeling herself off the ancient mattress. At least there was one good thing to anticipate about Ross's eventual departure, she consoled herself. Never mind that he was handsome and eligible or that he constantly raised her hormone levels to earth-shattering highs. Once the man had gone she could reclaim a considerably more comfortable bed.

Tessa no longer had high hopes for getting out of here soon herself. Late last night she had finally heard from Glenn, or rather his instructions had been relayed via his officious longtime male secretary. Tessa was to please stay put and the future congressman would get back to her just as soon as he possibly could. After all, she didn't really have anything else to attend to now, did she?

"Your brother knows you will understand, Dr. Fitzgerald, and he promises he will make it all worth your while," the man had said soothingly.

"I don't understand and you can tell Glenn, that jerk—" Tessa had begun heatedly, only to find herself being cut off.

"Sorry, Dr. Fitzgerald, but the press is arriving now."

"Come back here, you coward," Tessa had yelled, but it was too late.

Tessa had hung up, promising herself ruthless retribution: blackmail, murder, blood and guts! Oh, one day she would make Glenn pay dearly for all of this.

Now, thrusting the whole situation from her mind, Tessa looked around for the others. "Aunt Fay," she called. "Ross?"

There was no answer as she made her way to the coffeepot in the kitchen.

She got her first clue as to what was going on when she discovered that the coffeepot was practically empty, and the scant half cup remaining was barely warm. Obviously the pot had been turned off at least an hour ago.

Clutching her lukewarm eye-opener, Tessa hurried down the hall. "Ross! Aunt Fay!" she called again. Why didn't they answer? she wondered, her skin prickling with alarm.

There was still no reply. Astounded, yet disbelieving, Tessa flung open both their bedroom doors before the truth finally dawned on her. Then she sagged against the doorjamb, almost blinded by fury. Both of her patients had absconded.

How dare they? Oh, how dare they? Tessa asked herself a short time later as she began to throw on her clothes after taking a hasty one-minute shower. First she cursed the ungrateful Ross and Aunt Fay aloud, then did it again silently through tightly clenched lips.

She knew, of course, where those two wretches had gone. She knew even before she had checked the storage cabinet where she had so carefully deposited Ross's expensive cameras and other costly gear. Yes, Ross and Aunt Fay had gone off into the nearby forest to see the tanager, and Ross would probably have another sunstroke and die while Aunt Fay would fall down, break her other leg and be an invalid for the rest of her life. Then Glenn would blame Tessa for not controlling their aunt!

Ross and Aunt Fay each deserved their miserable fates, of course. Furthermore, Tessa didn't even care what happened to either of them any longer, or so she assured herself as she dressed rapidly in attire suitable for crossing the Australian outback alone and on foot.

Tessa pulled on a sleeveless tank top and a long-sleeved gingham shirt. Then she put on new jeans, the denim so stiff it could have deflected arrows. She snatched up a lightweight jacket, although even at this early hour the temperature was heating up rapidly. But its deep pockets were convenient carryalls for Tessa's emergency assortment of needles and vials, insect repellent and antiseptic. She also stuffed candy and granola bars for quick energy into both pockets.

Boots that were heavy and hot went on over thick socks, but Tessa intended to take no chances with rattlesnakes. Finally, she snatched up a lightweight hat that she crammed into a pocket, and looked around in vain for the keys to Aunt Fay's elderly, asthmatic Buick. They were missing, so she went stomping outside in temporary defeat.

Just as Tessa had expected, Ross's navy-blue rental car—the same car that she had so carefully driven down and parked beneath the squirrel-infested trees—was gone. So she was stuck with pursuing the two miserable malefactors on foot. The unfairness and sheer outrage of it all set her heart banging against her ribs.

Surely some bird lover will be along soon and I can hitch a ride, Tessa thought, waiting impatiently beside the gas pumps.

She was in luck. Two minutes later a large van came lumbering down the road. Its driver, a bald and elderly man accompanied by his chattery silver-haired wife, told Tessa that they were heading straight to Coronado National Forest in hopes of glimpsing the tanager.

"We'll be glad to give you a ride," the driver said to Tessa kindly. "You can come back with us, too."

"Thanks," she said grimly, hunching down in the back seat. "But I'll probably be riding in an ambulance on my return trip."

"Oh, my!" they clucked in unison, then asked so many questions that Tessa was sorry she'd ever mentioned anything connected with the two runaway scamps.

She really wasn't surprised about Ross. That he would take advantage of her work, her worry, the vast trouble and inconvenience he'd caused her and then flee like a thief in the night—oh, she had already figured out that that was exactly the sort of thing his type of man might do. But Tessa had truly thought Aunt Fay, at least, had better sense. Since she clearly didn't, the old woman must definitely be growing senile. Tessa intended to recommend to Glenn—if and when that wretched, self-important windbag ever got around to phoning her—that Aunt Fay be placed immediately in a secure nursing home—yes, even one where guards patrolled the grounds!

The van left the paved road and lurched along a rocky dirt trail. White dust from earlier traffic hung heavily in the air and Tessa, staring morosely out the window, watched as the arid cactus-studded desert gradually gave way to grass, trees and towering rugged cliffs.

"Gonna be another nice day," the old man said cheerfully, veering to the left to avoid hitting a quail.

"Sure is," his wife chirped.

No, it's not, Tessa thought, sunk in silent gloom. She felt put-upon, deceived and emotionally abused. Everyone dumped on her. Everyone took advantage of her kindness and solicitous concern. Just look what her two ornery ex-patients had pulled, after all she had done for them.

The elderly bird-watcher pulled his van into a parking area in the forest, then turned to look at Tessa. "This is where folks park who come to bird-watch," he announced. "See, Mother, there's Mel and Molly's pickup—"

"That's Reuben Neel's Jeep, too," his small wife added.

"Do you see the car your folks were driving?" the old man asked Tessa. She shook her head. Although three vehicles were parked in the clearing, none of them were the navy compact she sought.

"I wonder where they could be," Tessa fretted aloud.

"'Course if that guy—what did you call him, Ross—if he's kinda adventurous, he might have tried to drive down closer to the trail."

"Oh, he would have tried it," Tessa said grimly, "especially since my aunt—that demented lady I mentioned—has to use a walker."

"Okay, I'll tell you just what you do," the bird-watcher advised Tessa. "You follow the main trail until it splits, then take the right fork and keep on bearing to the right. Ross or whatever his name is won't be able to drive more than another half mile and he'll be parked there."

"Just as a matter of curiosity, what happens if I go to the left?" Tessa asked, reaching for the door handle.

"You'll wind up smack-dab in the middle of a creek that's backed up to a big cliff, isn't that right, Mother? We've been bird-watching here lots of times, so we know the terrain pretty well. I 'spect Mother and I will wait till our friends come back 'cause we don't want to miss them. We haven't seen Mel and Molly since Big Bend National Park."

"Thanks a lot," Tessa said, leaping out of the van. She hurried down the path, turning back once to wave to the helpful elderly couple, who were alighting more slowly. Then Tessa alternately walked and ran. Despite being in a darker, cooler world beneath the tall thick trees she soon grew heated. She shed her jacket, tying it around her waist to make sure its precious contents stayed upright and intact.

She certainly didn't like being out here in the wilderness all alone. Indeed, Tessa felt small and vulnerable, the hair rising on the back of her neck while her heart moved up into her throat. Every rustle of wind in the grass made her think, snake, and she felt sure that hidden animal eyes tracked her relentlessly through the forested mountains.

Her clothes only added to her misery. Her boots grew hotter by the minute and the new denim jeans scraped her thighs. But uncomfortable though Tessa was in the out-of-doors, she was too cold-bloodedly angry now to even think about turning back. She was going to catch those culprits—or else.

She rounded a curve in the trail and came into another, smaller clearing. It held what Tessa's eyes wanted most to see: the navy compact, neatly parked, but covered now with a coat of dust.

"Aha," Tessa cried in triumph. She stopped beside the deserted car long enough to dry her damp flushed face on one of her gingham sleeves. Then she started off again, following a dusty trail that bore the obvious imprint of a metal walker.

Chapter Five

It can't be much farther,'' Ross said encouragingly to Aunt Fay.

"It isn't,'' she agreed, sounding winded. "But I'd better stop for a minute and catch my breath.''

"Sure,'' Ross said cheerfully. Eager as he was to see the tanager, he still didn't want to rush Aunt Fay. "You want to sit down on one of these boulders?''

"Might better,'' Aunt Fay admitted.

Gently Ross lowered her to the sun-warmed rock, then moved the walker so that it didn't impede Aunt Fay's view, but at the same time remained within her grasp.

"Ross, I'm an old ninny who's just slowing you up,'' Aunt Fay said apologetically.

"Nonsense,'' he scoffed, dropping down beside her.

"You better run on and find the tanager. Photographing that bird is the reason you came to Arizona in the first place, and you've already been delayed long enough.''

"I'm not leaving you," Ross said stoutly. "Anyway, we're in this together, aren't we?"

Aunt Fay's blue eyes twinkled up at him. "What you really mean is you're not leaving me to face Tessa alone."

"Maybe *I'm* scared to face her alone." Ross laughed, then looked down thoughtfully at Aunt Fay. This morning he'd been remembering all the nice things that Tessa had done for him and by now was having second thoughts about the wisdom of this outing. "You really think she'll come after us?"

"You bet she will. Why, the minute Tessa wakes up and finds us gone she's gonna be mad as a spitting cat. She doesn't like anybody to usurp her authority. Haven't you figured that out yet, Ross?"

"You're not making Tessa sound very attractive," Ross reproved gently, "and she is, you know."

"Humph. If you ask me, she's getting too big for her britches. Oh, that's not to say a good man couldn't still soften her up and gentle her down. In fact, having someone who really cares about her is what's missing in Tessa's life. It's always been missing, in my opinion."

"What do you mean?" Ross asked Aunt Fay curiously.

"Oh, Tessa's arrival in the world was a major surprise. She came along fifteen years after her brother, Glenn. By then her parents had figured they were out of the baby business and they had both gotten occupied with a lot of other things. Nobody had much time for Tessa, and to make matters worse she was a sickly, spindly-looking little thing. I used to go back to Boston to visit relatives every couple of years, and that neglected little niece always worried me. She had all the material things a child needs, but she just didn't get much attention or supervision. Still, she turned out well in spite of it."

"I'll say," Ross said enthusiastically. "Are her parents still alive?"

Aunt Fay shook her head. "My nephew, Big Glenn we called him since he was fifty pounds overweight, was one of those bluff, hearty, extroverted politicians. He always liked rich food, good liquor, big black cigars and lots of parties. He was laughing his head off at one of 'em the night he suddenly dropped dead. That was the same year Tessa finished medical school."

"And Tessa's mother?" Ross inquired.

"The original clinging vine," Aunt Fay said with a disapproving sniff. "Mary started every sentence with 'Glenn thinks' or 'Glenn says.' After he was gone, she just withered away. Sat in her room and wouldn't eat. Washed down tranquilizers with wine. She didn't listen to Tessa about how to take care of herself any more than Big Glenn had done. Within a couple of years she was dead, too. It really hurt Tessa, losing them both that way."

"She isn't very close to her brother, either," Ross observed. "Too much of an age gap, I guess."

"Yes. When Tessa was just six or seven, young Glenn married Evie and within a year they had twin boys. So Tessa's always been on the outside, looking in. I think she needs to find a man like my late Fred."

"What was he like?" Ross asked. Since Aunt Fay and her niece seemed so similar, both high-spirited and independent, he wanted to know what kind of man was successful with that type of woman.

"Most of all, Fred was sweet. Not weak, you understand. I never had any use for weak men. Why, I'd mow 'em right down like a steamroller, though I guess you'd find that hard to believe," Aunt Fay explained.

Ross managed to conceal his smile. "No, not really."

"I was about Tessa's age when I met Fred, and I guess I was like her in some other ways, too. Feisty and independent, that's what Fred always called me. But he was strong enough, so he could afford to be gentle and gradually that just melted me right down." A faraway look lay in Aunt Fay's blue eyes. "I was a city girl, too. Never knew a thing about the out-of-doors, never even cared. Then all of a sudden Fred's got me sleeping with him in a bedroll under the stars. Cooking beans and beef jerky over a camp fire. Going to rodeos instead of symphonies. And you know what? I loved every minute of it. Why, I even got interested in watching birds, after Fred gave me my first pair of binoculars."

Ross found himself wondering if Tessa could ever warm up to his world and his way of life. It seemed unlikely. Anyone who disliked birds and squirrels was surely a hopeless cause.

"Yes, Tessa needs a man who's sweet but strong," Aunt Fay mused. "You know what I mean, Ross?"

"Yes. Well, at least, I think so," he answered more honestly.

"There's something about you, Ross, something I see every time I look in your eyes, that puts me in mind of Fred. You know who and what you are. And you act content, not driven like so many modern men are. I guess it's a kind of peaceful quality."

"Why, thanks," Ross said, startled. "I do feel peaceful most of the time, even though my life's usually anything but."

"I know, 'cause Fred's was the same way. He busted broncos for a living and rode in rodeos for a hobby. But it's an inner peace I'm talking about." Aunt Fay leaned her arms across her walker and looked up at Ross speculatively.

Ross didn't want to talk about himself; he still wanted to talk about Tessa, since she was preying on his mind. "Hasn't that niece of yours ever gotten serious about a man?" he asked.

"Not really. Oh, I think she thought she was serious about Cary Steward, but I knew right away he wasn't the fella for her. Even though I never met him personally, my nephew Glenn said he was slick as bear grease."

"What did Cary do?" Ross asked, fascinated.

"He was a doctor like Tessa—an internist, I think Glenn said. Cary specialized in treating society women."

Cary. Just the name sounded suave and urbane. Ross glanced down at his own jeans-clad legs. Of course, since he personally was not the right kind of man for Tessa—Aunt Fay's wishful thinking to the contrary—he wondered why he was even puzzling over what the attractive lady doctor might like and find appealing in the male sex.

"Don't let's talk about Cary," Aunt Fay said, pushing herself up off the boulder. "He was hardly a ripple in Tessa's nice, neat life."

"You're sure?" Ross asked in concern.

"'Course I'm sure," Aunt Fay snorted. Then, abruptly, she stopped, her farsighted eyes fixed on the path just beyond Ross's shoulder. "Uh-oh. We've been found."

He turned to look, too. There came the object of their discussion, Tessa herself, her pretty face pink with anger and her blue eyes flashing pure fire. What a beautiful woman she is, Ross thought, then felt a rush of confusion.

Because she wasn't really beautiful, he realized. She was basically a cute little spitfire. And she abhorred nature, was entirely too bossy and had a tedious gloom-and-doom philosophy. Such a woman should have been anathema to him. And he ought to be glad she wasn't interested in him, either—in fact, he ought to be running for his life in case she changed her mind.

Instead a perverse gladness and warmth kept springing up inside him every time he saw her, like a healing spring bubbling through stone. Abruptly Ross found himself wondering what Tessa's fire would be like if it were redirected toward love and affection—oh hell, toward passion. What would she be like in bed with him? Spontaneously Ross smiled at her, only to receive a bitter glower in return.

"So here you two are," Tessa said coldly, accusingly.

Those worthless wretches didn't even have the good taste to look guilty, Tessa thought in complete exasperation. Rather, they kept right on having fun. Why, both Ross and Aunt Fay acted like this was a jolly field trip and wasn't Tessa fortunate to have joined them? Oh, they were absolutely infuriating!

Faced with their total lack of remorse, Tessa became tight-lipped and tagged after them with an air of silent reproach. Even she recognized the absolute futility of turning them back at this point. Aunt Fay was positively aglow. As for Ross, his eyes sparkled with delight each time they met Tessa's, yet he didn't really appear to be gloating. He just acted as if he was genuinely glad she was there.

Of course it wasn't right that Ross and Aunt Fay were having such a good time, Tessa thought darkly. They certainly deserved worse, after scaring her half to death. But life—as Tessa had learned long ago—simply was not fair.

Still, as she trudged along resentfully, even Tessa had to admit that neither of her patients looked the worse for their exertion and exposure. Ross, fully dressed again for the first time since the day he'd arrived, was so handsome in a blue-checked shirt, faded jeans and scuffed boots, that Tessa had trouble keeping her eyes off him. She noted that both binoculars and a camera were strung around his neck.

As they strolled along, Ross tried to interest Tessa in the flora and fauna. "You'll see a wide variety of plants and trees here in the Chiricahuas," he pointed out. "Piñons, pines and firs grow on the upper slopes. Cottonwoods and wildflowers grow along streams. You can find yucca and many different varieties of cactus out in the desert."

"Hey, Tessa, take a look over here," Aunt Fay exclaimed exuberantly and pushed her binoculars into her niece's hands. "Third tree from the left. Just follow the trunk up to the fifth branch."

"Good heavens!" Tessa blurted out, having followed her aunt's instructions. "Is that a—yes, of course, it's a woodpecker."

Perversely she felt thrilled both by the sight of the live bird boring its grayish bill into the tree trunk, as well as by her recognition of it. An hour ago Tessa would have bet that she couldn't even recognize a sparrow, but maybe she knew a bit more about birds than she thought.

Not, of course, that she would ever like chasing over hill and dale just to peer up at them. Still, she supposed the activity might appeal to a certain woodsy sort of person.

"There's something even better over here," Ross called softly and Tessa turned to him instinctively, as if she were a sunflower and Ross the sun.

Where they had stopped, dappled light seeped through the thick foliage of the trees. Off in the distance Tessa could hear the faint trickle of a running brook.

She took Ross's binoculars and focused where he told her to. Then, despite herself, Tessa gasped aloud. "Oh my, that's a beautiful bird! Why, he's so many different colors, red and black, white and gray!"

"That's a coppery-tailed trogon," Ross explained. "Showy fellow, isn't he?"

"How do you know that's a male bird?" Tessa asked and the other two chuckled together at her ignorance.

"Male birds are generally the more colorful ones," Ross explained. "Nature makes them handsome and appealing to interest the ladies, although sometimes the male still has to do a mating dance to win the female's heart. That's what I was photographing in French Guiana, the dance of the cock-of-the-rock. Another reason for the male's bright colors is so he can lure predators away from the nest where the young are. Birds make very good fathers, actually."

"Oh." Tessa reined in her enthusiasm. Ross's explanations were interesting, she had to admit. Still, she saw no point in going into raptures over a small creature whose droppings might land on her head at any moment.

Now, as Tessa continued to focus on the trogon, the binoculars held to her eyes, she became keenly aware of Ross at her elbow. Aware of the clean smells of soap, sunshine and sheer masculinity that he exuded. Slowly she lowered the binoculars to note again the striking appeal of his golden hair, tanned face and bold aquamarine eyes. Nature hasn't done poorly by him, either, she couldn't resist thinking. He's a showy fellow, too. But it doesn't pay to forget that I'm rather plain and ordinary, more like a sparrow or a little brown wren.

"Uh-oh," Aunt Fay exclaimed suddenly. "Is that water I hear running?"

Aunt Fay was growing slightly deaf with age, as Tessa had discovered through listening to the boom of her aunt's TV set.

"Yes, I heard it some time ago," she said as she handed Ross's binoculars back to him.

"Oh, shucks. I was afraid the creek might still be too high for me to get across," she lamented.

"Maybe not," Ross said hopefully.

But as they made their way down to the stream, Aunt Fay was proven right. "That's my Waterloo," she said matter-of-factly.

To Tessa, the rushing crystal stream looked so wide and treacherous that she was more inclined to characterize it as a river than a minor creek. But she thought that the others would laugh at her if she voiced her opinion aloud.

"The only way across when the river is this high is to jump from one boulder to another," Aunt Fay sighed. She pointed out to Tessa a natural path formed by six moss-covered boulders jutting up through the nearly knee-high water.

"Maybe I can wade through it and carry you across," Ross offered hopefully, but for once, Tessa and Aunt Fay reacted in unison.

"Oh no, you don't," they cried in unison.

Dire warnings of injury, torn stitches and pneumonia were bubbling on Tessa's lips when she saw the resigned yet philosophical look on her aunt's face. Wisely she waited to let Fay explain.

"Ross, I don't want to chance it. That water is melted snow from the high country and cold enough to paralyze both your feet. Even if Tessa would let you risk catching cold, which she won't, I don't want to risk your maybe slipping in the streambed and dropping me. I sure don't want to break my leg all over again—"

"Or the other one, either," Tessa chimed in.

Ross didn't argue, as Tessa had feared he would. He actually looked relieved, she thought.

"I'm sure that's wiser," he agreed, though not without regret. "Let me help you back to the car, Aunt Fay, and I promise to take lots of pictures of the tanager for you—if I can find him, that is."

"Don't bother about me," Aunt Fay said firmly. "I know you're dying to see that bird, Ross Stanton, so you and Tessa just go along and hunt up the fellow before mobs of folks arrive and scare him away. I'll sit and wait for you here. Maybe, if some neighbors of mine happen along, I'll hitch a ride back home with them."

"I'll stay here with you," Tessa offered and saw a gratifying flash of disappointment in Ross's clear eyes. So he actually did want her along. Suddenly Tessa wanted to be with him, too, even though it meant crossing that wide icy stream.

"You'll do no such thing, Tessa Fitzgerald," Aunt Fay commanded. "Now that you're finally in the woods for the first time in your life—"

"It's not exactly the first time, Aunt Fay—" Tessa began, only to have her aunt interrupt heatedly.

"I want you and Ross to go on together. Why, you'd just sit here and lecture me and I don't want to hear it. So scat! Shoo!"

Aunt Fay could be quite forceful, but Tessa still found herself hesitating. "I'm not sure it's safe to leave her here," Tessa said in an undertone to Ross.

But Aunt Fay won the argument, after all, when three bird-watching friends of hers suddenly materialized on the opposite side of the creek bank.

"Hello, Fay. Good to see you up again," they called to her, then nodded to Tessa and Ross.

Tessa watched them jump from one lichen-coated boulder to another with more than academic interest. These people, twenty years older than herself at least, must be part frog or else they had done this many, many times before.

"Hey, Fay," one older man called. "I've got a picture of the tanager to show you."

"I can ride back home with Reuben," Aunt Fay murmured to Tessa. "I want to talk to him, anyway, since he's the one who first spotted the bird. Now, will you go?" Impatiently she wrenched the binoculars over her head and passed them to Tessa.

Tessa glanced at Ross, then they both gave shrugs of good-natured acceptance.

As soon as Aunt Fay had started back to the parking area assisted by her friends, Ross leaped onto the first boulder in the stream, then swiftly to the second.

How agile he was, Tessa thought admiringly, watching the skillful movements of his long legs and the balancing act he

did atop the slick rock. Then Ross stretched out his hand
toward Tessa and she gave an involuntary shudder.

"Come on. I won't let you fall," he promised.

Tessa hated to admit she was scared silly, but her pulse
was racing so hard that she felt positively light-headed.
"You're slithering all over that boulder," she called to Ross.
"How are you going to keep me from falling?"

"I will. Come on, it's going to be worth it," he coaxed.

Tessa wasn't at all sure of that. Still, she heard herself
muttering, "Oh, all right." Then she drew a breath and
jumped. To her vast surprise she landed uneventfully.

"See," Ross said approvingly. "I knew you could do it."
He leaped toward boulder number three, steadied himself
and then nodded to Tessa. She drew another breath and held
it as she jumped toward the stone he had just vacated.

Although Tessa found the experience downright hair-
raising, she was all right until she landed on the very last
boulder. Suddenly, terrifyingly, she felt her feet skidding out
from under her and closed her eyes in terror. Surely this was
the moment when she would wind up flat on her back in icy
water.

But Ross's strong arms were there as he instantly reached
from the bank to break her fall. Gasping with relief, Tessa
felt her head drop to safety against his broad chest. Then,
with her hands still linked securely in his much larger ones,
she made the final jump onto the far bank.

There Ross beamed down on her approvingly and Tessa
found, to her surprise, that the experience had been as ex-
hilarating as it was scary. Oh, not that she'd want to jump
the stream every day, but it was fun for an occasional outing.

She found that her hands were still entwined in Ross's.
Their eyes met and clung warmly. "My, that was something," she exclaimed and suddenly they were both laughing from the pure joy of being alive and together.

"Forgive me?" Ross asked her, sobering abruptly.

"For what?" Tessa said, even though she knew the answer to her question.

"For those nasty cracks I made yesterday."

"Oh, patients always act bad-tempered when they start getting well," she replied airily. "Doctors expect it."

"Do you also forgive me for being a royal pain in the butt and causing you a lot of extra work?" he probed.

Tessa smiled. "I guess you're worth it."

"For going off and leaving you this morning?"

"Don't push it!" she yelled and Ross burst out laughing.

"C'mon," he said, squeezing her hand.

They walked on, going deeper into the thick, deep green forest and Tessa found that her senses seemed acutely attuned to Ross, as well as to these new and unusual surroundings. The woods weren't spooky now that she was with him and she had to admit that she actually enjoyed the clean pure air that was scented faintly with the essence of fir trees and wildflowers.

There wasn't a path on this side of the stream, Tessa noticed. Yet Ross's stride, shortened just enough to accommodate her steps, continued steadily onward. "How do you know which direction to go?" she asked and told herself that her breathlessness was purely the result of exercise and had nothing to do with the fact that she was now quite alone with him. It was still too early in the morning for anyone except local residents to be here, and Tessa enjoyed sharing the wilderness solitude with Ross.

"See where the grass has been flattened," he said, his hand still curled warmly over Tessa's.

"Yes."

"Footprints, too," Ross added and stopped long enough to point out one that was half-visible.

"Besides, Aunt Fay gave me explicit instructions," he admitted. "So I think that just about... yes, here!" Ross stopped to survey the ground, which Tessa could see was well trampled. Then after giving her hand a parting squeeze, he dropped it and lifted his binoculars.

Ross muttered to himself as he scanned the limbs of the nearby trees. "Nope, not there . . . or there."

Tessa peered through her binoculars, too, then thought she might do better if she knew exactly what she was looking for. "Say, what color is this bird?" she asked Ross.

"The tanager is orange and black—oh, God, there he is! Beautiful! With such brilliant markings, too. Look, Tessa."

She felt Ross's arms sweeping around her in an excited, exuberant hug, then he turned her so she could see the flame-colored tanager for herself. Thrills shot through Tessa that had nothing whatever to do with any winged creature. How snug and safe she felt in Ross's arms. How wonderful the smooth brush of his skin felt on hers. Tessa's heart went haywire, pounding as if it were completely deranged.

She hadn't failed to realize, either, that Ross's first reaction had not been to grab for his camera, but rather, to share this moment that was so important to him with her.

Swinging the binoculars up to her eyes, Tessa rapidly scanned the tree he'd indicated. Really, hunting for a bird in a tree wasn't very different from hunting an elusive bacteria on a glass slide set beneath a microscope, she thought with something like astonishment. Then, at the far end of a branch, she saw the tanager.

"Yes, there he is!" Incredibly she heard herself squealing like an excited teenager at a rock concert. "I see him! Why, his head and neck are very orange, aren't they, Ross? Is the rest of him solid black? He's hidden in the leaves, so I can't tell."

"He has white bars on his wings. Can you see those?" Ross asked.

"No, yes, now I do! Oh, Ross, take his picture quick before he flies away! Ugh! He's eating breakfast. There's a worm in his mouth,'' Tessa exclaimed, fairly hopping up and down. ''Or is that his beak?''

''His bill,'' Ross corrected and now he did reach up for the camera dangling from his neck.

''I don't like to watch him eat. Ross, what's that? A zoom lens?''

''Yes,'' he said softly, laughing a little at Tessa's excitement, although he was plainly feeling the same way himself. Then Ross focused on the tree and began snapping one shot after another. He stretched high on tiptoe, then he dropped to one knee. He turned and began to slowly, cautiously, circle the tree while Tessa padded right after him.

''I guess we'd better shut up, right? I wouldn't want us to scare him off.'' Tessa found that her hand kept touching Ross's broad back, as if by instinct.

''Just keep your voice low,'' he suggested, continuing to move.

''I'm going to look at the tanager again. Maybe he's through eating that worm.'' Tessa was still feeling tingly and excited as she swung the binoculars back up to her face. She relocated the bird and watched him fixedly for a minute. He was definitely another showy fellow. Then Tessa realized that Ross had gone some distance without her, so she ran to catch up with him.

He let his camera drop back around his neck as she approached, turning to smile at her. The extent of his pleasure was evident by the radiant, happy glow that filled his wonderful eyes, leaving them crinkled up so attractively. The same joy wreathed his face into something more than a grin. As he looked down at Tessa, she recognized an incredible tenderness behind his smile.

His expression made Tessa's heart swell with a pleasure so acute it was close to pain. Her heart began doing flip-flops as she gazed back at Ross. He was exciting at any time, but on this occasion, he was dangerously more so.

Then Tessa reminded herself of the obvious cause of his happiness—and it had nothing whatever to do with her. "I guess, unless you're a birder, you can't really appreciate how wonderful this is, right?" she asked him a bit wistfully.

"You appreciate it, Tessa, at least a little bit," Ross replied generously, "because you so obviously appreciate what I feel right now." After a minute he added, "It's always a thrill to see an animal or bird that I've never glimpsed before. But I have seen other tanagers. So I think the reason this one is special is because you're here."

Slow down, Tessa warned herself. You can't go into ecstatic leaps and bounds because Ross is being so kind. Not that warning herself did any earthly good. Her heart just kept hurtling along like a runaway train.

"I enjoyed seeing the tanager, too," she admitted. "I just didn't know it would—what?"

She looked up, startled, as Ross came steadily closer until he reached out and removed the binoculars from around her neck. The leather strap tangled briefly over one of Tessa's ears before he swung it free.

"What?" she said again as he set down her binoculars, then reached matter-of-factly for his own and his camera as well. He deposited them all quickly yet carefully on a dry, clean-looking boulder.

"You know, I always thought you had certain possibilities," Ross told her, his smile widening. Then an intense glint shone in his eyes. Before Tessa could say, "What?" for a third time he caught her close, bending his shining golden head down to her smaller, darker one.

It happened very quickly, and yet it didn't, for Tessa's mind was busy memorizing each moment of the scene. She noticed all of the dialogue, and every one of Ross's easy, casual movements. It was so important that she mentally recorded each single microsecond.

First she felt Ross's hands on her shoulders, their warmth radiating through her clothes in a grip that was gentle but compelling.

Then, for the first time, Tessa felt the press of his magnificent and perfectly proportioned body on hers. The feeling, even through their layers of clothes, was heady, even exciting. Tessa looked up at Ross in startled wonder as her insides quivered, both from the delights already experienced and her anticipation of those to come.

Did Ross drop his own hands momentarily, encouraging her to touch his back? Or did she manage that one all by herself? Probably the latter, Tessa thought, since it happened so spontaneously that she wasn't quite sure when she first felt those hard muscles beneath her fingertips.

But as they rippled in response to her touch, Tessa visualized Ross's back in all its masculine perfection, just as she'd seen it when she examined him. Her mind envisioned his wide smooth shoulders, the golden tufts of hair under his arms, and the gradual narrowing of bone, muscle and skin down to his waist. Again she saw the indentation in his back just below his belt line—the gentle scooped-out hollow that led down toward the lean buttocks. Mechanically Tessa's hands followed the delightful picture she was visualizing.

Then Ross's face moved down over hers, his eyes suddenly a bright bold blue—as blue as the sky overhead—and brimming with desire. Yes, his expression was obviously passionate, just as much as the lilting bird song she suddenly heard filling the placid morning.

"Is that the tanager singing?" Tessa whispered as Ross's lips moved inexorably closer to her own.

"Probably," he answered lightly. "I don't think it's a song I've ever heard before."

"Shouldn't you be, uh, recording it or..." It was suddenly very hard for Tessa to think, much less speak, since

Ross's lips were brushing the corner of her mouth. It felt like she was being touched by delicate angel wings.

"Probably I should record it," he agreed, then his lips pressed tenderly against the soft skin of her cheek.

"I mean it must be important, or you wouldn't have brought all that..." Oh, how could she possibly finish a sentence when those warm, tender lips were gliding first a half inch in one direction, then a half inch in the other?

"It's important," he agreed. "I'll get around to it sooner or later."

His lips were warm, his breath sweet, and all the feelings he engendered deep inside Tessa were as unique as they were ecstatic. She felt safe and sheltered. At the same time, she felt herself being gradually, erotically aroused. She should run away from him, but she wanted to close her eyes and sink down in complete and total surrender. She wanted to cry and she wanted to laugh.

But more than anything on earth Tessa wanted the kiss that she knew was coming next.

Slowly, gently, Ross's lips moved, parted, then hovered over hers. When his mouth finally moved to capture Tessa's, the kiss was as urgent as it was tender.

She felt her head drop back, as she made her lips more accessible to his. Their kiss deepened as their mouths merged, meshed, melted. Suddenly Ross caught Tessa possessively to his chest and a new and softly sensual explosion began. Yet the only added ingredient of which Tessa was aware was the sweet swirling of his tongue deep in her mouth as Ross sought for, then tasted her.

Tessa clung to him, meeting that avid kiss with a response just as intense. Silently she invited a wealth of further kisses. Silently she urged him to continue feasting on her lips and mouth and tongue, sharing his own essence at the same time.

Long, long minutes passed before the first semblance of sanity returned to her. Then Tessa realized that they were still standing locked together—kissing, clinging and caressing in a way she'd never done with any man except Cary and even then that shared affection had been only a pale imitation of this raw, hungry and wholly mutual passion.

Cary and what he represented was like a faded watercolor done in tepid pastels. Ross, by contrast, was a vibrant canvas splashed with living oils in every possible color combination and hue.

We have to stop this before it gets out of hand, Tessa thought but already Ross was nudging her down to the forest floor beneath the canopy of trees.

A carpet, springy with grass and the season's last wildflowers, supported them as they turned breathlessly, moving even closer into each other's arms. Another hungry kiss followed, then just one more...

Finally, at almost the same moment that Tessa began to pull back, she felt Ross lift his head. He lay half across her, their bodies crushed together, and Tessa reached up to caress his cheek. As her hand dropped, he bent to brush her throat and chin, her eyelids, temples and hairline with light, tender kisses like angels' wings, kisses so incredibly gentle they made her want to cry.

Then Tessa felt herself trembling—at least she thought the small movements shaking her were her own until she saw the strong arms still linked about her were also trembling just a little. So Ross wasn't unaffected, either! She wondered if his system had been as happily surprised as her own.

"Who would have thought it?" Tessa asked in an awed whisper as they turned on their sides, simply gazing at each other.

"Me!" Ross laughed, but his arms were slow and reluctant to withdraw from around her. "I kept suspecting that all that fire of yours would make us magic together. From the first moment I saw you I just wanted to reach for you.''

''If you'd reached then I'd have slugged you.'' The languor in Tessa's voice sounded to her own ears like a verbal caress.

''Would you really?'' Ross moved again, rolling to lie on his back in the grass, his left hand still touching Tessa's elbow.

''Yes.'' Now she propped herself up, the better to study his handsome face. Every time she looked at him she always found something absolutely fascinating. Today it was a small freckle on Ross's earlobe, the ear that had faced the wall while he lay unconscious in Tessa's bed. She also admired his thick gold-dusted lashes that were now lazily half-closed.

Then her heart, only just slowed from his kisses, began to pound ominously with a brand-new realization.

Chapter Six

Ross, you're tired, aren't you?" Tessa asked and reached for his wrist to count his pulse.

His hand stopped her. "Me? Nonsense!" he blustered.

"Ross," Tessa said threateningly.

"Maybe a little bit," he conceded. "A man's strength wanes when he lies around in bed for four days. Say—" he flashed her an engaging smile "—just how did you happen to become a doctor, anyway?"

"What is this, story of my life time?" Tessa demanded. Her voice was less breathless now, but she still remained keenly aware of his nearness.

"I've wondered," Ross said earnestly, "and I'd really like to know."

"Okay, okay," Tessa conceded. Talking about herself usually made her feel uncomfortable, although Ross's interested gaze gave her some reassurance. But she was more influenced by the acute weariness she saw etched on his face than by a desire to discuss herself or her profession. She wanted him to lie still and rest.

"Well, when I was a little girl—" she began.

"Probably the cutest little girl in Baltimore," he interjected.

"How did you know I was born in Baltimore? Oh, of course, Aunt Fay told you," Tessa said, but couldn't restrain a smile. Aunt Fay didn't volunteer information any more than Tessa herself, so Ross must have asked.

"Yes, Aunt Fay told me. I was curious about you," Ross confirmed. "She also told me you were sick a lot as a little kid. Was that what turned you toward medicine?"

"Definitely," Tessa answered, continuing to watch Ross's face, which looked much too pale. "I had a lot of earaches, sore throats, colds and flu to make me feel miserable. I was also a skinny little thing, so everybody worried about me. The doctor was always coming up our walk."

One thick golden eyebrow shot up over Ross's lazily half-closed eyes. "You rated house calls?"

"I sure did. My pediatrician—a woman, by the way—was also a neighbor. She once told me she spent the first five years of my life dropping by every evening to take my temperature. All I knew was that she was warm and reassuring—a lot of fun, too. She had to put tubes in my ears, but she convinced me and everyone else that I'd grow out of all the illnesses and she was right, I did. I was never sick after the age of seven. But I guess I'd gotten used to playing doctor to my dolls. When I got older it never occurred to me to be anything but a physician. Later, in medical school, I got interested in the special problems certain diseases like diabetes pose for children. After I became acquainted with Michael Corman and his work, I knew I definitely wanted to be on his team. He's a brilliant endocrinologist as well as a splendid research scientist."

"How old a man is Dr. Corman?" Ross asked.

"Fifty-seven, no, fifty-eight. Why?" Tessa inquired.

Ross drew one of his lean warm fingers teasingly down the side of Tessa's nose. "Because, with all the admiration for Dr. Corman that I heard in your voice, I was starting to get jealous."

"Don't be silly! Why, he's a happily married grandfather," Tessa chided, but she couldn't help coloring with pleasure. "Now it's your turn, Ross."

"Mine?" he asked in surprise, his hand gliding down to lazily stroke Tessa's chin.

"Yes. How did you ever get to be such a crazy, risk-taking adventurer?" she inquired, unaware that she was automatically frowning until she felt Ross's fingers smoothing out the lines in her forehead.

"First, I don't consider myself a crazy, risk-taking adventurer," he said, chiding her in turn.

"Pardon me. How did you get to be such a crazy, risk-taking Pulitzer Prize winning photographer, as well as twice taking the World Press Photo of the Year?" she amended politely.

He paused to study her face. "My business really bothers you, doesn't it?"

Tessa saw no reason to pretend. "Yes, it does. Dangerous activities of any sort bother me."

"Oh, hell," Ross sighed. "I never started off planning on anything dangerous at all. I was just a kid, like you when you got interested in being a doctor. The year my mother died I was almost nine. Stan and I lived in California and he bought me a small camera, more to distract me, I think, than for any other reason. So I shot up about twenty rolls of film, and when some of my pictures actually came out, Stan told me they were great. So I entered the best ones in a kiddie photo contest and lo and behold, I won first prize! I got twenty-five dollars and a bus trip with the prizewinners from other cities to visit Sequoia National Park and photograph the trees there.''

Tessa laughed. "I can tell this was a big deal."

"Lady, this was an actual and decisive revolution in my young life. Just consider it from a nine-year-old's point of view: I got local glory, a lot of money and a whiz-bang trip where I saw the biggest trees in the world. That did it. I was hooked. After that, I ran around taking photos of everything, especially after Stan built me a darkroom.''

"When did danger enter this happy picture?" Tessa inquired quietly.

"Oh hell, I don't know." Ross sighed resignedly. "I think when I didn't win any more contests with my predictable puppy and kitty pictures. Also, about that time Stan and I first heard the raccoon—"

"The what?" Tessa asked and yielded to the desire to rub a strand of his golden hair between her fingers. Silken sunshine, she marveled.

"Raccoon," Ross repeated patiently. "See, we lived about five miles from town and there were woods close by. A raccoon used to forage for scraps in our garbage can every night. They're nocturnal creatures. So Stan helped me bait the can with chicken scraps and corn on the cob, things that raccoons find very tasty. That night I hid behind a tree and, being a kid, I promptly fell asleep, of course. When the raccoon woke me up rattling the garbage can I was still half asleep. I grabbed my camera and crept closer and closer— too close, really, because when I finally fired off the flash the raccoon charged me—snapping, biting and clawing. I screamed and Stan came running out to scare him off, but by then I was a mess. He had to drive me straight to the emergency room.''

"You should have learned a lesson from that," Tessa said thoughtfully and watched Ross's hair curl over her fingers.

"Yeah, I did. You see, that shot I got right before the raccoon leaped in my face was a real dandy," Ross recalled, smiling at the memory. "It sold for one hundred dollars while I was still walking around bandaged up like a mummy. That's when I learned that to be the best you have to take a few risks."

"That wasn't really the lesson I meant," Tessa sighed and released the strand of Ross's hair.

"I know." He twinkled up at her, his aquamarine eyes mischievous.

The man was incorrigible. She hadn't a prayer in the world of changing him, Tessa knew, since he had absolutely no intention of reforming. He was going to continue to go banging and slamming through life until someday, like almost every other daredevil who flirted with fate and frail human mortality, he lost his high-stakes gamble.

Tessa remembered the experiences as an intern in the emergency room. The race car driver. The stunt pilot. The window washer. The snake charmer. The teenagers who got drunk and went for a spin over a winding mountain road. The college boy who tried to climb into a third-floor window of a sorority house. Tessa had seen all of their broken bodies. She had closed their eyes and drawn sheets up over their faces. Then she had had to give their next of kin the news.

She remembered her own parents, too, and the way they'd shrugged off her repeated warnings.

As the memories poured over her, Tessa determinedly pushed herself away from Ross and up off the grass. "I've got to get back," she said, glancing at her wristwatch. Then she looked down at the handsome man with the light-hearted manner and irresistible charm who was still sprawled, relaxed, in the grass. "Any chance you'll come back to Progresso with me, Ross, and have a long rest?"

Regretfully he shook his head. "No way. I'm here now and so's the bird. But I'll be glad to drive you back to the store. I need to get something from the car, anyway."

"I know. All your bird gear," she said evenly. "I don't suppose you'll listen to me if I tell you that you really need to take it easy?"

"So what's this?" Ross said expansively. "I'm lying flat on my back."

"Yes, and you won't stay that way nearly long enough," Tessa said in a resigned voice. "You've also probably forgotten everything I ever told you about preventing another sunstroke."

"I haven't forgotten," he argued gently. "But this is early morning. It's still nice and cool."

"But for how long?" Tessa inquired, throwing a look at the blue cloudless sky. By the time she looked back at Ross, he was already on his feet.

They walked back to the car in silence, not even speaking when they crossed the stream again. Although Tessa felt unbelievably discouraged, Ross was exhilarated enough for both of them.

After all, he was back doing work he clearly enjoyed. He even started whistling as he drove Tessa to the store until her withering glance halted his merry song.

As he eased his car to a stop by the gas pumps, Tessa reached for the door handle.

Ross's hand shot out, restraining her. "Tessa, I do appreciate your opinion and I really care about what you think. I promise to do one thing, at least, that I know you'll approve of."

She looked at him hopefully.

Ross smiled at her, his grin as devastating as it was devilish. "I intend to watch out for snakes."

Tessa whirled out of the car and slammed the door with all of her strength.

What could possibly come of all this? Tessa thought bleakly when she was tending Aunt Fay's store again, filling gas tanks and selling hamburgers and film to tourists. As the mundane chores she so disliked drained away the last of her excitement from the morning, Tessa promised herself that she'd be hanged if she'd worry about Ross any longer.

No, indeed. The man was impossible. He was terminally danger-prone. And she was through.

Stronger than her temporary anger was Tessa's feeling, coming from the deepest recesses of her heart, that a romance between Ross and herself was impossible. They were completely and wholly incompatible. He was reckless, daring and unconventional; she was careful, deliberate and precise. While Ross was usually relaxed, Tessa knew she was basically uptight. And that was just for starters. Tessa had yet to seriously consider Ross's father's and stepmother's beliefs and actions. Of course, she also had yet to inform Ross about her own ultraconventional family members back in Washington and Baltimore, headed by Glenn and Evie. Heck, why even bother to discuss relatives when too many deep, fundamental differences already lay between the two of them?

It was midafternoon before Ross limped in, his face the color of a dingy dishcloth. He came into the store to use the pay phone so he wouldn't have to disturb Aunt Fay, who was napping in the cottage.

Tessa didn't actually hear Ross place the call, but she overheard a part of it, just because he was shouting. "I know I'm several days late checking in, Leo. Well, that's just tough! Didn't Stan call you? Yes, I *did* have a snakebite and a sunstroke—yes, it's true they both happened the same day. I know with me it's always something. Look, Leo, if you don't believe it, I think I can arrange for you to talk to my doctor since she thinks I nearly croaked—"

Ross listened for a minute, then his voice roared again. "If you don't want the pictures, Leo, that's fine! I'll sell 'em to somebody else, 'cause the tanager's here and I'm here and back on my feet again and the hell with—"

Ross's tirade stopped. He appeared to be listening to some compromise solution, for Tessa watched his face change, then calm. "Of course, I'll get them shot as fast as I can. Don't I always?"

Ross hung up and by then Tessa was standing not far from his elbow, too concerned to be anywhere else. Okay, so my resolutions don't last very long where he's concerned, she admitted to herself.

Ross gave her a weak grin. "Editors," he muttered.

"What else does he want you to do besides kill yourself?" Tessa inquired sarcastically. "You're not even well enough yet to work!"

"Oh, Leo's okay. He just gets bent out of shape when photographers miss deadlines."

Tessa shot him an incredulous look, then brushed past him without further comment.

It was her busiest time of day, because it was still too early for the helpful Sandoval brothers to be out of school. As Tessa made change for tourists she tried to ignore Ross, who was obviously weary. Consuela was hard at work in the café, which was doing a brisk business, and from the corner of her eye Tessa watched Ross sprawled on a counter seat in front of the girl. Consuela set a tall drink before him, then smiled sweetly, as only a pretty teenager can.

I don't care! Tessa assured herself. Let them fall in love, get married, and have eleven kids! But I probably ought to warn Consuela that Ross is liable to commit suicide taking photographs and meeting deadlines.

Then she ran outside to pump more gas. By the time Tessa had finished with that car and another that drove up and returned to the cool darkness of the store, Ross was nowhere to be seen.

Tessa was too proud to ask Consuela where he had gone. When the Sandoval brothers arrived to relieve Tessa of her duties, she withdrew to the cottage to check on Aunt Fay, and there was Ross. He lay facedown across his narrow bed, sound asleep. His boots had been tossed into a corner of the room and his stockinged feet and long lean legs hung off the end of the bed.

Tessa couldn't prevent a small smile from forming on her lips as she looked down at him. Like a small headstrong child, Ross had simply worn himself out. Now he slept deeply in childlike fashion, too, his tired body so relaxed it looked almost boneless. How could he manage to look so vulnerable and trusting while being so tall and strong at the same time?

Tessa tiptoed back out, closing the door noiselessly behind her. Then, since Aunt Fay was up from her nap and watching television, Tessa dropped down on the footstool where she usually sat and gave her aunt a brief rundown on the day's events. "Now that Ross is back at work, I suppose he'll be leaving soon," she said with feigned indifference. I don't care. I really don't care, Tessa kept assuring herself. Aloud she continued, "I rather expected he would drive off this afternoon, but I guess he's too tired. It's a disappointment for me. I was looking forward to sleeping in a real bed again."

"Uh, Tessa," Aunt Fay began hesitantly.

Tessa realized immediately that something was about to be sprung on her, and, her hackles already rising, she jumped up from the stool. "What?" she demanded, looming over the hapless Aunt Fay. "What?"

"Ross needs to stay on with us for another three or four days. He'll be shooting an extensive photo essay on the tanager—"

"Don't tell me you agreed? My God, Aunt Fay, don't you think I already have enough to do? Now we're opening the cottage to boarders who'll need clean towels and sheets and, I suppose, three meals a day."

Aunt Fay defended herself stoutly. "I told Ross he could stay because he's a famous bird photographer. As a loyal birder myself, I didn't feel like I could do anything else. Besides, he's a pleasant man and *I* happen to like him. But I didn't promise him anything about towels or meals."

"How about beds?" Tessa shot back.

"We didn't discuss it. But I'll tell him when he wakes up that he'll have to sleep on the sofa from now on. You're right—you're doing all the work, and you certainly deserve a good night's sleep."

Tessa ran a weary hand through her thick hair, which needed to be trimmed and styled rather badly. God, what she wouldn't give for a beauty parlor and a glimpse of civilization again. Her mouth positively watered whenever she thought of things like city traffic and skyscrapers, restaurants and shops.

"You're not fooling me, Aunt Fay," she informed her aunt coolly. "You're having fun trying to match me up with Ross Stanton, but it won't work. We're completely incompatible. Why, I can't think of a single thing we agree on."

"I know. Cupid always likes a good laugh," Aunt Fay said, her blue eyes twinkling. "But you two are physically attracted to each other, any fool can see that. So why don't you just start there?"

We already have, Tessa thought unwillingly. But a few kisses, achingly sweet and passionate though they might have been, still weren't going to bridge their basic differences.

Ruefully Tessa started for the door, only to turn back. "Don't change the sleeping arrangements," she told her aunt curtly. "As long as Ross stays here, he'd better sleep in the bed. He's not well enough to be bunking on the sofa."

"Tessa." Aunt Fay spoke her name in gentle apology, but Tessa felt too disheartened to listen to anything else. Each day had found her thinking more and more of Ross and feeling increasingly drawn toward him. Having him hang around for several additional days was certainly no way to get over him.

She walked out of the cottage. Then, needing a place of peace and quiet to help knit her ragged edges back together, she continued on to the deserted picnic area beneath the trees. There Tessa wearily sat down on a bench, then batted her eyes furiously, wondering why weak, ridiculous tears threatened all of a sudden. Maybe she was simply due for a personal pity party. But before she could start to indulge herself, a squirrel leaped down from a nearby tree and scampered across the table. Then, spotting Tessa seated at the far end, he sank back on his haunches and began to scold her sharply.

Ross knew something was wrong with Tessa, but he just didn't know what it was. Nor did he know what to do to solve it. She had been unnaturally quiet for the last several days. Quiet, thoughtful and sad. Yes, most of all, Ross thought she was simply sad and he wished she could be happy.

He probably should never have kissed Tessa in the forest. It had been an impulsive move that resulted in shared excitement and joy. But now Ross was regretting those kisses, because they had turned into something quite different from what he'd expected. Now he dreamed of them at night and thought again of them during the day, each time that he happened to pass Tessa. Nor, apparently, could he control his gaze, which was drawn back to her mouth again and again. He couldn't forget its taste, its texture and tenderness.

Still, there was just no future for him with the pretty lady doc. Ross couldn't kid himself about that any more than Tessa could. They both knew that the attraction between them—irresistible as it sometimes appeared to be—wasn't the start of a match made in heaven. They were both old and wise enough to appreciate the difficulties of trying to mix oil and water.

"Ross, do you support your father's organization, FLAC, and their stand on animal rights?" Aunt Fay asked him at supper that night.

As Ross watched, Tessa's head jerked up sharply. "What does FLAC stand for, anyway?" she demanded. "Flak?"

"No, though it was certainly designed to cause plenty of uproar," Ross replied candidly. "It's an organization that links several animal rights groups. That's why it's named The Friends of Laboratory Animals Coalition." Then he turned back to Aunt Fay. "Yes, I'm basically in sympathy with FLAC. I agree that too much medical research is being conducted on animals. I also think too many medical experiments are being needlessly duplicated and that far too much of animal experimentation is for the benefit of the cosmetic industry. While I don't take to the streets in protest or break into labs to let animals out of cages, like some of Stan's friends do, I sign plenty of petitions and help support FLAC and similar groups with financial contributions."

Aunt Fay glanced over at Tessa, her eyes twinkling at the prospect of mediating a good rousing argument. "You want to defend the medical profession, Miss Tessa?"

"No, I don't," Tessa said flatly. "I never answer fanatics." With that she pushed away from the table and stalked outside.

How righteous she sounded, and what an establishment crank she really was. Ross couldn't even begin to imagine the monotony of her life, a life Tessa apparently missed so much. Imagine going to the very same place, day after day. He repressed a shudder as he thought of glaring fluorescent lights in white labs full of antiseptic. He visualized cold clinical machines that measured life forces and printed out computerized results.

A research scientist. Ross didn't even want to think about what Stan and Linda would say if they knew about Tessa. Why, if he ever got mixed up with someone like her, they'd probably never speak to him again.

They would never understand how Ross could possibly be attracted to a woman like that. As a matter of fact, Ross wondered about that himself, though he was equally sure that Tessa had never exploited animals or been deliberately cruel to anything or anyone in her life.

Still, all three of the Stantons had long been concerned with the natural order and rhythm of life. All of them sought to protect birds, animals and the environment. To people like them, Tessa was practically as alien as a creature from another planet.

Yet Ross knew she was also lovely, warm and desirable, and lately she was hurting, too. Somehow she seemed all the more gallant to Ross for trying to hide that hurt.

He certainly wasn't swelled-headed enough to think he was the sole cause of her pain. She had too many other concerns—her medical career, her negligent brother and Aunt Fay. But Ross also knew that he hadn't helped matters for Tessa by brushing off her warnings and failing to take her recommendations seriously. She had probably saved his life, and Ross thoroughly enjoyed living—whatever a psychologist who reviewed his accident record might say to the contrary. Yes, Ross knew he would be eternally grateful to Dr. Fitzgerald and knew, too, that such a pretty lady shouldn't be so lonely or, for that matter, so utterly alone.

Ross also knew he ought to get out of her hair—and out of her bed as well—that bed she still stubbornly refused to reclaim, insisting that he needed it for his continued recuperation. Yes, the very best thing he could do for the lady doc would be to climb into his rental car and drive away without a single backward look.

And he could do it, too. Today Ross had finished his various assignments involving the flame-colored tanager. He'd taken a lot of photos for Leo at *American Geographic*, as well as all those desired by AP, the Audubon Society and a lavish encyclopedia that was in the process of updating its bird files. Ross had also finished recording the tanager's own particular song for Stan, who collected and studied nature tunes. Ross had even done a few quick sketches to send to Linda, who would paint the tanager for posterity. Linda had acquired a reputation for doing some of the best bird paintings since Audubon, though Ross still thought she was underrated.

That very day Ross had gone to Tucson and shipped off his packages of exposed film, sketches and recordings. By tomorrow Leo ought to be a very happy man and should be busy wiring money into Ross's bank account.

Now, with his work finished, Ross had no further reason to stick around. And if he ever made the consummate mistake of kissing Tessa again he just might not stop until he'd bedded or wedded her, or done something equally permanent, serious and stupid.

So it made absolutely no sense for Ross to find himself glancing out the window to watch for Tessa or to contemplate walking to the picnic area where she'd been for the past several evenings. She hadn't invited him to join her, had she?

But instead of doing what he knew he ought to, Ross swung around impulsively. "Hey, Aunt Fay," he called. "I think it's time you and I hatched a nice surprise for Tessa."

Squirrels might merely be rodents, but Tessa had to admit they did have a lot more personality than she'd ever suspected. Tonight a couple of them had chased each other round and round the picnic tables, then shot up the trunk of the nearest tree. Now, as Tessa watched, another one whipped its broad hairy tail into its mate's face in an eloquent gesture.

Yes, squirrels were cute, frisky and playful, and she was glad Ross had opened her eyes to their charms. Tessa just wished he hadn't also opened her eyes to a lot of other feelings, as well.

His consummate tenderness when he had kissed her in the forest was proving to be the hardest thing of all for her to forget.

Not that she had stopped thinking about any one of his kisses, beginning with that impulsive and exuberant one when he'd swung her around, joyfully, making her laugh and her heart sing. Or those passionate ones when he'd awakened her whole body to a strange, new hunger, making her breasts tighten and desire burn through her.

But it was still Ross's tenderness that she remembered best of all. The gentle sensation of his lips moving over her face. The protective clasp with which he'd held her, as though she was someone infinitely precious. Even after she'd forgotten the rest—in twenty years or so—Tessa suspected that she would always remember Ross's tenderness.

Thank heavens, he would be leaving soon. Physically he'd kept improving steadily, and Tessa realized when Ross drove into Tucson to express his film to the eastern seaboard that his work was finished. He'd be moving on now. Wasn't that what adventurers always did, blithely leaving behind all the people who really cared about them?

Tessa heard the cottage door slam and glanced over her shoulder to see Ross step outside. His tall frame, bathed in twilight shadows and silhouetted against the purple mountains, looked so attractive he made her heart lurch. Even in the dusk his bright hair still glowed.

"Hi," he called to her.

"Hi," Tessa called back, but heard a certain dispirited note in her voice. She wasn't exactly sure when it had crept in there.

Ross strolled over. Just the faint sound of his footsteps crunching on leaves, twigs and sand made anticipation fill Tessa and yearning, too. They had consciously, deliberately, avoided each other for days. But now Tessa realized just how much she really wanted to talk to Ross.

Her heart, banging away against her breastbone, told Tessa something else, as well. It told her how afraid she was that Ross had come outside to say goodbye.

He stopped before her, a tall rangy-looking figure. Even in his faded jeans and loose pullover shirt he was still the most handsome man she had ever seen. His hands were behind his back, fingers hooked into the pockets of his jeans, Tessa suspected, since she'd noticed that he often stood that way. He wore his old scuffed boots and rocked back and forth in them, as if he felt a trifle uncertain, too.

"What's going on?" Tessa asked him. She had a feeling she wasn't going to like it, so that was all the more reason to go ahead and get it over with.

"Not much," Ross said obliquely. "I did have a chat with Aunt Fay."

"Oh?" Tessa steadied herself as she broached the most urgent question of all. "Are you leaving us, Ross?"

"Yeah." In the gathering shadows she saw the start of his smile, but Tessa herself suddenly felt dizzy, as though she'd been in an elevator that had just dropped twenty floors.

"Aunt Fay's working out the details now," Ross continued. "But she thinks she can get everything set with the Sandovals. Tomorrow I'm off to El Paso and Juárez for several days of R and R—and, Tessa, I want you to come with me."

Outside the wind rushed past the car, delighting Tessa with its eager, restless sound. A black-tailed jackrabbit went dashing off through the bush and she smiled, entertained by its antics. She was finally on the move again.

Outside Ross's air-conditioned car Highway 10 ran wide and straight across the southwestern desert, and although the stark landscape was not usually Tessa's favorite, right now she liked watching its changing array of early-morning light and color.

She felt like a pardoned prisoner, just set free. She really shouldn't have come along, of course, but her strength of will had been eroding steadily since she'd met Ross Stanton. When he'd offered her a chance to get out of town and be all alone with him for several days, she had simply lacked the moral fiber to say no. Because she might never see Ross again after he returned to Louisiana, Tessa felt she had to seize every opportunity that fate offered to her.

And surely he was the world's best guide to this new adventure. As Ross drove he constantly pointed out things to her, things Tessa would have missed otherwise. Until now the desert had seemed to her little more than red earth, baked sand and tall stark mountains.

But Ross exclaimed over everything, even the wide and seemingly limitless bowl of blue sky. He told Tessa that sometimes in the desert, you could watch entire storms go scudding across the sky.

Ross also praised the quality of the sunlight, declaring that it was even purer and more golden here than in either Florida or California. Especially in the afternoon, when it highlighted the ridges and far mountains, he added.

"It does?" said Tessa dubiously, admiring Ross's profile even as she struggled to admire the sunshine. To her the sun was simply hot. Period. But Ross's eyes allowed her to see so much more.

"This land we're crossing now was once called the New Mexico Territory," Ross added. "It was chiefly the Indians' land. There were Navajo, who were nomads, as well as the Apache, who went on raids. The Pueblo and Hopi lived near here, as did the Zuni and Papago, Pima and Yuma. There are still a lot of places out here on the desert where you can find ruins of their stone or adobe houses."

"I didn't know that," Tessa said politely while images of Indians flooded her mind.

"I wish we had time to stop and—you know, we could swing up by Silver City." Ross turned enthusiastic eyes toward Tessa and she managed a shrug.

"Whatever you want," she said with a game smile.

"No." Ross reined in his enthusiasm. "I might like to see Silver City but you, dear Dr. Tessa, will enjoy El Paso much more. What do you want to see first when we get there?"

Tessa hesitated and just then a strand of overlong hair that she thought she'd securely pinned plopped down over one eye. She pushed it back grimly and resolved to be completely honest with Ross. "Promise you won't laugh?" she asked and he solemnly crossed his heart.

"Ross, more than anything on earth right now I just want to see a shopping center!"

Chapter Seven

A large shopping mall appeared west of El Paso, looking to Tessa like an oasis in the desert. It was modern and bright with flowers, fountains and skylights. When Tessa sank into a chair in its very plush beauty salon she finally began feeling less like an escapee from a desert caravan.

Ross had said he could entertain himself for a couple of hours at the book and photography shops in the mall. If he exhausted both of those, then Tessa could find him at the computer store.

So she relaxed and ordered all that the beauty shop provided: a shampoo and haircut, plus a facial and manicure. She regretted that a pedicure, waxing and total body massage weren't also available, but to do all of that would probably have taken too long. After all, she wanted to spend most of her time with Ross, even if it was an irrational thing to do.

Two and a half hours later Tessa emerged feeling like a brand-new woman. She slipped down the mall to discover that Ross was still at the bookstore, completely engrossed in the latest best-sellers. Without interrupting him Tessa turned back and entered a shop whose windows featured a lot of stylish-looking clothes designed especially for the Southwest.

Recklessly Tessa decided to buy any garments that fitted and looked good and not to worry about their cost. As a result she had rung up in less than an hour, purchases in an amount that made her young salesclerk gasp. But Tessa herself didn't even flinch as she handed over a credit card. She knew that the two new pairs of slacks with coordinating tops transformed her. Knew, too, that the sleeveless emerald-green dress that virtually bared her smooth back, displayed her waist and rippled not quite to her knees with a flirty, swirly skirt was perhaps the most attractive garment she'd ever owned.

Tessa debated only over a short peach satin nightgown with matching peignoir. The color was reflected on her high cheekbones and appeared to turn her lips to a light apricot shade. Flattering, yes, she thought, but totally impractical, since she certainly didn't expect to make love with Ross or even to sleep in the same room with him. In fact, Tessa had already determined that she definitely wasn't going to do anything like that, since lovemaking could only make their inevitable parting in a few days even more painful.

She simply wasn't the kind of person who could spend a couple of passionate nights with a man who fired her very heart and soul, then emerge later, still independent and intact. Why, she had even found parting from Cary extremely painful, and he had scarcely set her ablaze. But from the time she had nursed Ross through those first long, dangerous hours, Tessa had sensed that he was the exception to every reasonable rule she had ever imposed on herself. He was the man she had always hoped, yet feared to meet.

She wasn't sorry she'd met him, Tessa reflected, changing into attractive new slacks and a matching tunic while the store validated her credit card number. No, now that she actually knew Ross, she realized that she wouldn't have missed meeting him for anything in the world.

At the same time there was no need to go overboard, no need to wholly jeopardize her emotions and hang herself up over an unsuitable partner. Since she was not a rash, reckless type she would definitely sleep in her own hotel room, Tessa assured herself, and if Ross Stanton had made different plans or had dared reserve only one room, then he could just sleep in a chair in the lobby.

"We've approved your credit card," the young clerk announced, her smile wide enough to reflect the commission she would earn. "Have you decided about the nightgown and peignoir?"

I don't need them. Take them back.

The words trembled on Tessa's lips, then died unspoken. *Oh, what in the world is the matter with me?* she thought, aghast.

As if she didn't know. That man had made an absolute mush of her wary brain and left chaos in her careful heart.

Meanwhile the salesclerk waited. "I'll take them, too," Tessa said recklessly, "and I'm wearing these."

Five minutes later she strolled confidently down the mall with the rest of her purchases in a large box under her arm, her old clothes on their way to the Salvation Army.

Ross was at the computer shop by now, earnestly discussing a new program with one of the clerks. He glanced up casually when Tessa entered the store, then stopped and stared openmouthed. Breathless, she waited as admiration began to flare in his marvelous eyes and he smiled at her warmly.

Tessa knew she looked her best. Her hair was neatly trimmed, its usually unruly curls momentarily subdued. Her clothes were chic. Also, for the first time since she and Ross had met, she wore a modest amount of makeup.

"You're beautiful, Tessa," Ross said, crossing swiftly to her side and looking down at her searchingly.

She could read his heartfelt sincerity in the blue depths of his eyes and suddenly she felt absolutely beautiful, too, for one of the first times in her life.

Tessa clutched the box that held her other new clothes, feeling happier than she had in weeks. No, make that months. She had never felt quite so feminine as she did now under Ross's admiring gaze. "I was hoping you'd say that," she teased. "Now I'm ready to go see El Paso and Juárez."

"Let's have lunch first," Ross urged. "There's a restaurant here that specializes in lunch food. Sandwiches, salads, quiche. We don't want to eat too much since we'll be having a fairly elaborate dinner."

"Lead on," Tessa said enthusiastically.

They came down through the Franklin Mountains and stopped at an overlook on winding Scenic Drive. Below lay a spectacular vista of the glitter and bustle of El Paso and the Rio Grande River, which was just a narrow silver thread when seen at this distance. Beyond the international border of the river lay the nearby Mexican sister city, Ciudad Juárez.

"Oh, Ross, it looks wonderful!" Tessa exclaimed.

"Let's go see it at closer range," he suggested, amused by Tessa's delight in the urban sprawl below.

They spent the afternoon doing just that, enjoying the gaudy city that was El Paso. They drove around the picturesque university campus and visited the outskirts of a major military installation. They also strolled through Placita Santa Fe, El Paso's old town, and Tessa learned that the buildings that now housed interesting shops and galleries had once been frequented by bandits, smugglers and prostitutes.

In the heart of the busy downtown area they wandered across tree-shaded San Jacinto Plaza. "Alligators were kept in the pond here until the 1960s," Ross noted in passing. "I saw them once when I was a little kid."

"Is there anyplace you haven't been?" Tessa inquired, and Ross flashed her a smile.

"There are fewer every year," he replied. "But I still enjoy visiting favorite cities like El Paso with favorite people."

Once again Tessa's heart gave a leap and a bound, threatening to fly far away. She appeared to have completely lost all control over her emotions.

They crossed into Juárez over the Bridge of the Americas. It led them through a once disputed swath of land called El Chamizal. Ross pointed out the Chamizal National Memorial, which commemorated the peaceful ending of the century-old dispute over the boundary between the U.S. and Mexico.

Large shops and stores soon appeared, catering primarily to tourists, but there were newer and more characteristically Spanish buildings at the Pronaf Center, which represented the Mexican Government's attempt to spruce up the border. Ross and Tessa looked through a museum that depicted the history and archaeology of Mexico, then they visited an arts and crafts center that sold Mexican handicrafts. Tessa couldn't resist buying Aunt Fay a vase copied from one of the pre-Columbian era as well as a small leather wallet for herself.

As they strolled through the airy buildings, Ross frequently let his hand cup Tessa's elbow or touch her arm until, at some point, his hand simply dropped down and captured one of hers securely.

Tessa debated whether to pull free. Teenagers held hands, not adults their age. But the warm strength of Ross's fingers linked through hers, with their message of masculine vigor, was too pleasurable for Tessa to deny.

After all, it's a foreign country, Tessa argued with herself. Who knows us here? Who *cares*?

They got back in the car and drove into the heart of Juárez, passing a large bullring with signs that identified it as the Plaza de Toros Monumental. Tessa barely repressed a shudder, thinking of various bullfight movies she'd seen and stark Hemingway novels she'd read.

Ross squeezed her hand, and Tessa knew her reaction hadn't escaped him. "Most Latin Americans love the bullfight the way North Americans love football. But I'm glad I won't have to take you to a bullfight on Sunday afternoon."

"I couldn't stand it," Tessa said simply, repressing another shudder. "I'd be afraid the whole time that the matador would get killed."

"Matador, hell," Ross replied explosively. "I'm always pulling for the poor bull!"

"Well, yes, I can see how you would," Tessa agreed. "After all, the bull didn't choose to be there."

"Exactly." Ross slanted a surprised look in Tessa's direction.

For just a few minutes, they actually understood each other. But, of course, it was all too good to last.

Dusk found them at the elegant Juárez restaurant where Ross had promised to take Tessa, and soon her hands were wrapped securely around an icy glass containing a fresh strawberry daiquiri. As Tessa sipped she thought she'd never tasted anything quite so good.

Civilization. She felt almost misty-eyed with gratitude and nostalgia as she looked around at snowy tablecloths, sparkling china and crystal, and deferential, low-voiced waiters. Tessa touched a sterling silver fork almost reverently. Her joy at being back in her own territory was complete.

Ross was drinking a supersize margarita and threatened to have the waiter bring Tessa the bill for his drink. "After all, you practically promised me one," he teased her. "Maybe I was close to paradise, but I still remember hearing you mention that margarita."

"Oh, all right," Tessa pretended to grumble. "If I have to pay up, I will." Actually, though, she was too busy admiring the suave figure Ross cut in his dark evening slacks topped with a baby-blue, heavily embroidered Guayabera shirt to be irritated.

Tessa knew Ross's clothes, like her own, were new since an errant price tag on the shirt had escaped him and Tessa had removed it in the car. That Ross had cared enough about her to buy clothes at a shop in their overpriced hotel and dress up for dinner meant something quite exciting, and provocative as well.

"Have you noticed the bullfight pictures?" Ross asked, directing Tessa's attention away from himself and toward a number of ornate silver frames displaying a variety of matadors and bulls.

"No, I hadn't seen them," Tessa acknowledged and leaned back in her chair for a perusal of the paintings hanging close to their table. In the Southwest one grew so jaded from seeing tacky, iridescent bullfighters on cheap black velvet that Tessa had neglected to notice that these were the real thing, actual original oils signed by the artist.

She had realized the restaurant's proximity to the bullring, of course. It had still been daylight when she and Ross drove here after showering and changing in their respective hotel rooms. Much as she disliked the sport that these oil paintings celebrated, she could still admire their artistry.

The waiter appeared at their table. "*Señor, señorita*. Are you ready to order now?" he asked, switching smoothly into English.

Ross cocked one golden eyebrow. "Tessa?"

"I'm ready," she said, setting down her overlarge glass. It was time to eat. Another strawberry daiquiri of this size and Tessa knew she would be absolutely crocked. "You order for me, Ross." This wasn't the right time to test her few Spanish phrases, not when she wanted something very good to eat.

"Gladly." Ross flashed her his irresistible smile, then turned back to confer with the waiter. "The last time I was here I ordered tacos *al carbón*. The steak was cooked over mesquite wood. Is that dish still available?"

"*Sí, señor*, and always cooked over mesquite."

"Good. We'll have that as our entrée. Gulf shrimp for an appetizer, if they are very fresh."

The waiter promised Ross the freshest shrimp in all Mexico. Then as the two men pored over the wine list, Tessa drained the last of her daiquiri. She smiled at the way Ross's left hand continually rested on his camera case.

She had learned today that the camera went everywhere with him. Oh, not that he'd been engaged in very much picture-taking while he was trying to show Tessa a good time. In fact, the only shots he'd grabbed today had been of her. But he carried his camera as a policeman carried his gun; it was practically a part of him, always at hand and always ready for use.

The waiter took Ross's order and sped away, obviously pleased by the size of the forthcoming bill and determined to provide the sort of service that would guarantee him a good tip.

...be tempted!

See inside for special
4 FREE BOOKS offer

Silhouette Special Edition ®

Discover deliciously different romance with 4 Free Novels from

Silhouette Special Edition ®

Sit back and enjoy four exciting romances—yours **FREE** from Silhouette Books! But wait . . . there's *even more* to this great offer! You'll also get . . .

A USEFUL, PRACTICAL DIGITAL CLOCK/ CALENDAR—FREE! As a free gift simply to thank you for accepting four free books we'll send you a stylish digital quartz clock/calendar—a handsome addition to any decor! The changeable, month-at-a-glance calendar pops out, and may be replaced with a favorite photograph.

PLUS A FREE MYSTERY GIFT—A surprise bonus that will delight you!

You can get all this just for trying Silhouette Special Edition® !

MONEY-SAVING HOME DELIVERY!

Once you receive your 4 FREE books and gifts, you'll be able to preview more great romance reading in the convenience of your own home. Every month we'll deliver 6 brand-new Silhouette Special Edition® novels right to your door months before they appear at retail. If you decide to keep them, they'll be yours for only $2.49 each!* That's 26¢ less per book than the retail price—with no additional charges for home delivery!

SPECIAL EXTRAS—FREE

You'll also get our monthly newsletter, packed with news of your favorite authors and upcoming books—FREE! And as a valued reader, when you join our Reader Service, we'll be sending you additional free gifts from time to time—as a token of our appreciation.

BE TEMPTED! COMPLETE, DETACH AND MAIL YOUR POSTPAID ORDER CARD TODAY AND RECEIVE 4 FREE BOOKS, A DIGITAL CLOCK/CALENDAR AND A MYSTERY GIFT—PLUS LOTS MORE WHEN YOU JOIN OUR READER SERVICE!

* Terms and prices subject to change.

A FREE
DIGITAL CLOCK/
CALENDAR
and Mystery Gift await you, too!

↳Clip and mail this postpaid card today!↲

Silhouette Special Edition®

Silhouette Books®
901 Fuhrmann Blvd., P.O. Box 1867, Buffalo, NY 14240-9952

☐ **YES!** Please rush me my four Silhouette Special Edition® novels with my FREE Digital Clock/Calendar and Mystery Gift, as explained on the opposite page. I understand that I am under no obligation to purchase any books. The free books and gifts remain mine to keep. If I choose to continue in the Reader Service, I'll receive 6 books each month as explained on the opposite page. I can cancel at any time by dropping you a line or returning a shipment at your cost.

235 CIL R1XP

NAME _____
(please print)

ADDRESS _____ APT. _____

CITY _____ STATE _____ ZIP _____

Offer limited to one per household and not valid to current Silhouette Special Edition subscribers.
Prices subject to change.

SILHOUETTE "NO-RISK" GUARANTEE

- There's no obligation to buy—and the free books and gifts remain yours to keep.
- You enjoy the convenience of home delivery and receive books before they appear in stores.
- You may end your subscription at any time—by just dropping us a line or returning a shipment of books at our cost.

If offer card is missing, write to: Silhouette Books, 901 Fuhrmann Blvd., P.O. Box 1867, Buffalo, NY 14269-1867

✓ Clip and mail this postpaid card today!✓

BUSINESS REPLY CARD

First Class   Permit No. 717   Buffalo, NY

Postage will be paid by addressee

SILHOUETTE BOOKS
901 Fuhrmann Blvd.
P.O. Box 1867
Buffalo, NY 14240-9952

NO POSTAGE
NECESSARY
IF MAILED
IN THE
UNITED STATES

Ross turned back to Tessa and now, when their eyes met, a sort of stillness fell over her, a stillness and peace that she felt deep down inside. Every other thought flew out of her busy mind; every other person in the world disappeared.

"Did you enjoy today?" Ross inquired.

"Oh, yes! Couldn't you tell?"

"Good. I want you to be happy and enjoy yourself. What would you like to do after dinner?"

Tessa wondered if she was imagining it, or if there was something more than politeness gleaming in Ross's eyes and resonating in his voice.

"Oh, I don't care. Truly." With him she was alive, minute after precious minute, and Tessa savored them all. Tonight she was not going to look either backward or forward.

"Would you enjoy seeing the greyhound races?"

"Not particularly," Tessa said truthfully.

"Or the horse races?"

"No, not unless you—"

"No, I don't, either. Well, let's see. There are several chic, hot night spots with exotic strippers, both men and women—"

Tessa felt a pang of disappointment that Ross could suggest such a thing.

"—or so I've been told," he finished.

She raised a worldly-wise eyebrow in his direction. "Oh, all right," Ross laughed. "I did see them all—once. I was eighteen and here with a crowd of other guys the same age."

"You can skip the rest," Tessa offered.

He laughed again and for a minute his hand actually left his camera case. In fact, both his hands glided across the snowy-white tablecloth to capture Tessa's with warm sinewy strength.

"So much for the ordinary tourist attractions," Ross said, dismissing them while his gaze moved over Tessa like a slow-speed scanner. He studied her hair and brow, then her eyes.

When his gaze dropped to her mouth, she shivered a little with anticipation. "What I'd like to do is take you back to our hotel for some dancing on the patio."

"Yes," Tessa agreed, thinking immediately of romance and music and soft dark shadows. Then, as she felt herself flushing under Ross's continued scrutiny, she asked, "Do you especially like to dance?"

"Not really, and I'm not very good at it, either," Ross admitted. "But it's an excuse to hold you close once more—"

Their waiter, showing a monumentally poor sense of timing, suddenly reappeared, carrying an ice bucket and corkscrew. Ross released Tessa's hand, and she wondered if the soft sound she heard was her own sigh or Ross's.

The waiter made a production of opening their wine, then he poured the first sample for Ross's approval.

Ross sipped slowly. He nodded at Tessa, then at the waiter. He had just set down his wineglass when a great commotion arose outside the staid, quiet restaurant. Hoarse shouts and piercing screams, accompanied by vehement Spanish curses suddenly reverberated through the room.

"What—" Tessa began. Then one phrase, repeated over and over again between the bursts of passionate curses and machine-gun Spanish, gradually impinged on her consciousness. *El toro.*

For a split second Tessa's startled gaze met Ross's equally startled one. Then each reacted in characteristic fashion. Tessa dived spontaneously beneath the table, just as Ross snatched up his camera in one swift, economical move and lunged for the front door.

Hiding under the table, while comforting, was still about as practical as a child cowering under the covers to escape the bogeyman. Or so Tessa decided when her churning, terrified emotions finally allowed her the chance to pause and think. Before, she'd simply been reciting prayers by rote, every prayer she'd ever been taught, and since she had once attended a convent school staffed by devout nuns the number of prayers Tessa had memorized was extensive.

But when she'd finished saying all of them she was forced to think once again, and the first thought to enter her head was how ridiculous her present position was.

If the particular mad bull that was loose right now decided to come crashing in here, a small round table and a starched white tablecloth weren't going to stop him. In fact, they would just make it easier for him to gore, stomp, crush or maim her.

Cowering and shivering, Tessa played out several dark scenarios in her mind, with herself cast as the victim. Then as the terrible moments crept by, one after another, she found herself worrying about Ross. What if he was the one being gored, stomped, crushed or maimed?

He certainly didn't warrant her concern—not when he should have been right here beside her. Why, he ought to have held Tessa in his strong arms, fanned her with a menu, since she felt distinctly faint, and whispered that he was going to take care of her and keep her safe and well.

As the fantasy faded, Tessa clamped down hard on her lower lip. So when did I turn all girlish and feminine? she wondered ironically. Then she summoned up the courage to crawl out from beneath the table. While Ross's presence might have been comforting, she really couldn't expect any man to be willingly trampled on her behalf. That was carrying chivalry a bit far. On the other hand, she hadn't expected him to abandon her, either.

Since Ross still hadn't come back to see about her, maybe she'd better go see about him, Tessa thought, standing up on still shaky legs. There might be other injured people, as well. After all, she was a doctor.

At the moment, however, Tessa was quite willing to forget her Hippocratic oath if it meant facing a huge maddened bull.

She stepped out on trembling feet, and one toe bumped a cold wet bottle. Distracted, Tessa glanced down and saw that it was the wine Ross had ordered to accompany their dinner. The bottle was very nearly empty now, its expensive contents having trickled out during the confusion. Still, as Tessa hefted it she estimated that there was at least one good gulp left. She was wrong about that. Providentially, there were two—as she discovered when she upended the bottle and its hastily gulped contents hit her stomach.

Their waiter was nowhere to be seen, nor were most of the other employees and patrons of the restaurant. When Tessa had last glimpsed the man he had been pale, perspiring and screaming. Wisely he had run off toward the kitchen, just as Ross had sped away.

Tessa dropped the empty wine bottle and crept timidly to the restaurant door. She didn't open it since she could peer out through two shattered insets that had once been panes of thick amber glass. Lord, that bull's horns must be sharp, Tessa thought, stepping carefully over all the glass.

Only a deserted street could be seen through the new "windows." Sighing, Tessa began to recite her prayers again as she turned the doorknob and warily stepped outside.

Now she could take in the whole scene at a glance: the lopsided truck that had obviously been headed for the bullring, bearing a huge, spirited participant for tomorrow's corrida.

Most of the shrieks, screams and cries had dwindled as the people still hovering on the edge of the street were shocked into complete silence. A few continued to shout warnings and comments and with the words *"loco gringo"* prominent among them, Tessa knew Ross was nearby.

The glare of an exploding flashbulb soon told her his exact location. Tessa turned and then gasped, clutching the door behind her in sheer horror.

Ross stood boldly in the middle of the deserted street, clicking off photographs of the snorting, bellowing bull that looked, to Tessa's terrified eyes, as big as a runaway locomotive. No, bigger. The bull's wickedly sharp horns glinted in the fading light and were already lowered for his next charge.

"Ross!" Tessa shrieked. "Get out of the way. He'll kill you!"

Ross gave no sign of having heard her—or anyone else. Calmly, methodically, deliberately he continued to get one shot after another. Then, as the bull began his charge, Tessa, stricken, gasped a single word. "Run!"

She didn't even realize that she was running herself, dashing blindly down the sidewalk toward Ross with her heart in her throat and her eyes riveted on the terrifying spectacle before her.

As the bull charged, Ross did an even more rash and incredible thing: he dropped down on one knee to shoot up from that angle. One flash, two, three...and the bull was practically upon him.

Tessa heard herself screaming like a madwoman. "Run, Ross!"

As Ross leaped—too late—for the relative safety of the sidewalk Tessa yearned to look away. But she couldn't. Paralyzed and speechless, she could only listen to the awful, thundering hooves and watch in horror as the big black bull bore down on the crazy man she loved.

In that awful moment, when time seemed suspended, when each second seemed to last a minute and every minute felt like an hour, Tessa knew that she'd made the consummate mistake of her life. She had fallen in love with a man who was probably a half minute from death.

"No!" she heard herself whimper as the bull's dangerous horns hooked Ross under his armpit. Then he was tossed up in the air over the bull's head and slammed down into the dust of the street. He landed limply, like a rag doll, and Tessa felt certain he was dead—his neck broken, his spine severed or his skull crushed. But as the bull turned and whirled, snorting, pawing and positioning himself for his next charge, Ross recovered miraculously and half scrambled, half crawled toward the sidewalk.

He stood up, even if a trifle crookedly and snatched Tessa by the arm. She awoke belatedly to the fact that she'd actually been racing single-mindedly toward him, heedless of any danger to herself. Clearly loving Ross had driven *her* crazy, too.

Ross pulled them inside a nearby store where several people already cowered behind the counters. Panting and laughing, he slammed the heavy door behind them. Then, his handsome face grimy and his new blue shirt ripped beyond repair, Ross sagged against the door.

"You—" Tessa began in a trembling voice, then discovered that her vocal cords simply refused to produce another sound.

"Wow, how about that, sweetheart?" Ross exclaimed in sheer delight. "I'll bet I've got at least one really great picture. Why, I can already see the caption on it now: 'El Toro Resists His Fate'!"

Blood streamed from a shallow cut at Ross's hairline, but he apparently didn't notice or feel it. Exuberantly he caught Tessa about the waist, swung her around and kissed her.

For just a moment time stopped for her once again. As silent sobs of relief tore at her chest, Tessa gripped Ross's strong, wide shoulders and felt the tenderness of his incredibly warm, soft mouth on hers. It tasted like nectar so she yielded, briefly, just because she was so grateful that they were both still alive.

Then, as Ross set Tessa back on her feet, the bright red blood trickling down his face told her he had scant right to be among the living. If he had been a cat, this latest stunt of his would have consumed three or four of his nine lives.

This, in addition to all those times gone before.

Silent tears began to trickle down Tessa's face until she was sniffling audibly.

Ross's elated expression changed immediately. "Oh, sweetheart, don't," he urged as Tessa almost strangled on a sob she was trying to muffle. "Look, Tessa, everything's all right . . ."

His voice lapped over her like a warm bath, but Tessa was having none of it. She reacted swiftly, without thought. Her arm simply drew back of its own volition, and she stopped Ross's soothing, *stupid* verbal flow by slapping him. There! Let that wipe the smug, self-satisfied look off his beautiful face.

She hit Ross just as hard as she possibly could. So hard that Tessa saw his head jerk back and the livid imprint of her hand appear immediately on his cheek. So hard that she felt like examining her own burning, throbbing palm, afraid that she might have raised blood blisters.

"I am not amused or entertained by you," she gasped, dashing the tears from her face.

The shocked, aghast look in Ross's eyes was gradually replaced by an ironic gaze. He shook his head as if to clear it. "Wow, that I can believe," he muttered.

"I think you ought to be committed to an institution for the criminally insane," Tessa went on, her voice gathering heat although she still spoke through cold, pinched lips. Since her palm continued to throb and burn she had the satisfaction of knowing Ross's face was still stinging, too.

"Yeah, I can sure see how you feel."

"No, you don't," Tessa heard herself saying, "and that's the difference in us, Ross. You give lip service to my feelings, but that's all it is. You don't really care about anything or anyone—yourself included. All you care about is shooting just one more great photo. By the way, you're bleeding."

"I am? Where? All I can feel is my face hurting where you slugged me."

But Tessa had turned away, not intending to ever speak to him again. Let Ross find that cut for himself. As for her, all she wanted was to take a taxi back to the hotel just as soon as that very dangerous bull had been rounded up and removed from the Juárez street.

A wail of police sirens told Tessa that help was on the way at last.

One thing about Tessa, she was certainly no hypocrite, Ross thought ruefully. She had always stated her opinions openly and honestly, so a man certainly knew where he stood with her. Why, she had just about as much subtlety as a paving brick—which, incidentally, was what it felt like she'd hit him with. Ross might have admired Tessa to an even greater extent except that for fully ten minutes after she'd landed that unexpectedly strong blow from one small dainty hand, his face still smarted.

In fact, Ross was becoming uncomfortably aware of several other aches and pains, the result of being cut by the bull's horns and flung over the top of the animal's head. Nor had it helped his condition to come down in a heap on a hard-packed earthen street.

Finally Tessa had decided to staunch the blood dripping from the cut at his hairline, tsk-tsking all the while. Ross didn't have the heart to tell her that he considered this a mere scratch compared to the cumulative total of his newly acquired injuries.

Merely getting Tessa calmed down and into the same car with him had been no small thing. All the time that the *pol-*

icía and the *vaqueros* and about two hundred macho male volunteers had been chasing the black bull up and down the street, trying to corral it, Tessa had alternately cried or snubbed Ross.

Finally, when the black bull gave up and allowed itself to be herded back into the broken-down truck, Tessa gave up, too.

"Look, you don't have to eat dinner with me, dance with me or even speak to me," Ross said to her earnestly. "But please, let's get in the same car and go back to the hotel. I promised Aunt Fay I'd take care of you and, believe me, Juárez can get plenty wild when the sun goes down."

"Oh? I suppose it hasn't been wild so far?" Tessa inquired coolly.

"Sweetheart, please—" Ross started pleading, only to see Tessa burst into tears all over again.

"I am not your sweetheart," she declared emphatically, but she climbed into the car that Ross had already brought around.

Did Tessa want to be his sweetheart and despaired because she didn't think he meant it—or couldn't she allow herself to be involved with him? Ross wondered as he guided the rental car back through the busy streets. Was that the reason for her surprising and uncharacteristic flood of tears?

Ross couldn't really believe she loved him—anyway, that simply wouldn't be a good idea at all. He and Tessa were too utterly, intrinsically different, he had to agree with her about that. But before they said goodbye for the last time, Ross wanted to hold her, dance with her and acquire a few more warm memories of the lady doctor.

Now, as Tessa began to recover from her own emotional storm she had a number of ideas all her own. "Ross, you have to be checked over immediately for injuries," she began.

He grinned into the darkness of the car. "Okay," he said agreeably and wondered if she was the one who would do this checking.

"You also need a tetanus shot for that cut on your forehead. I know it's bled freely, but you got dirt in it and I don't believe in taking chances, especially with foreign microbes," she went on.

"All right," Ross said again.

"You ought to go to bed quite early, too."

"Oh?" he inquired, braking for a stop sign. Immediately his fertile imagination pictured himself lying in bed with Tessa draped across his chest while his fingers played over the smooth planes of her face and delicate curves of her body. Although it wasn't a good idea for them to get that close, Ross still felt dazzled by the possibility.

"I want your reflexes tested, too," Tessa continued firmly. "You looked like you blacked out temporarily when you hit the ground."

And so would you, Ross thought silently, if you'd been tossed about by a two-ton bull.

"You could easily have a concussion," Tessa predicted darkly. "Does your head ache at all?"

"No," Ross lied.

"Then you probably don't." She sounded so relieved that Ross felt a trifle guilty for having misled her. On the other hand, Tessa would never stop fussing and hovering if she thought he was really hurt. That was just the doctor coming out in her.

"My stomach does feel unsettled," Ross volunteered. It was certainly unsettled all right, by outright healthy hunger. God, he was starving.

"Oh? Well, I think I'd better give you..."

You're a wretch, Ross Stanton, he said to himself as he listened to Tessa making worried plans for his care. In fact, you're an outright lying and deceitful cad. The best thing you can do for this sweet, caring and concerned lady is simply to let her go.

Yes, that was definitely the decent thing to do.

Except that just thinking about it made Ross feel suddenly sick at heart. Also, he'd be a fool to miss this opportunity to get to know Tessa better.

Tessa was still talking when Ross stopped again. He turned to her swiftly, cupping her lovely, intelligent face in his large hands. Then, before she could utter a protest or even make a sound, Ross kissed those delicious lips of hers just once more, kissed them fervently and hungrily.

When he released her, Tessa looked stunned. Stunned and speechless. Of course, he couldn't see her too clearly with only the dashboard light for illumination. Still, her eyes looked like mysterious pools of crystal water and Ross wanted nothing more than to sink into the softness of her arms, her bed, her body, and stay there until he died.

"What was that kiss for?" she whispered.

"Thanks for caring, Tessa."

Chapter Eight

The night was a star-studded masterpiece. The lemon-yellow moon was nearly full and kept gliding in and out of frothy clouds. The stars looked huge, much closer to the earth than Tessa had ever seen them, and they shone with the peculiar clarity special to stars in the desert.

For Tessa nightfall also turned the ordinarily threatening world into sheer magic. Ross's arms were strong and tight about her and delightfully romantic music swept over the patio. Since the mariachi band had been inside while they were eating and was now on the patio, it almost seemed as if the musicians were following them, Tessa thought dreamily.

But before she let herself be swept away completely by the mood, the music and the man, Tessa forced herself to do a swift mental review. Had she really thought of everything? she wondered, worrying lest some medical matter had escaped her.

If anything should happen to Ross through her own negligence, Tessa knew she could never forgive herself.

As soon as they had returned to the Arroyo Grande Hotel Tessa had rushed Ross straight into the office of the hotel doctor. Then, not content with the man's competent examination of Ross, Tessa had insisted on double-checking everything herself. So she had also peered into Ross's eyes, checked his balance and tested his reflexes. She had verified his blood pressure and counted his pulse for herself. Then she had fussed a little over the bandage the doctor applied to the cut on Ross's forehead. By the time the patient doctor had filled a syringe to give Ross the tetanus injection Tessa had insisted he receive, Dr. Martinez had simply extended it to Tessa with a resigned air since she clearly didn't trust anyone else to treat Ross.

After that, Tessa had insisted Ross sit down and rest for a while. Since the main dining room was closed by then, they had drifted into the hotel's picturesque cantina where he'd had to plead before she permitted him even one glass of sangria. Of course, she should never have allowed that, Tessa thought disapprovingly, although Ross really didn't show any signs of concussion or serious injury. Probably his kiss earlier had softened her brain. Now Tessa regretted that she'd let the atmosphere and especially the man get to her.

The cantina was a pleasant place, decorated in warm earth tones, and accented by muted blue floor tiles and hanging baskets of ivy. It was cozy, inviting and practically deserted, except for the musicians onstage playing their rousing Spanish-style music.

To compensate for the dinner they'd missed, Tessa and Ross had shared a large Mexican pizza with a tortilla crust that was brown and crisp.

Sometime after they finished eating, the rhythmic music grew softer, more lush and romantic.

"Come dance with me," Ross urged, taking Tessa by the hand.

He led her out onto one of the patios for which the hotel was famous and there, under a night full of bright winking stars, with music surrounding them and the water from a merrily splashing fountain trilling its own accompaniment, Ross whirled Tessa around and around before blissfully catching her close.

She allowed herself to relax in the circle of his arms and move with him, slowly and dreamily, her head pressed against his chest, listening to the strong regular beat of his heart. As Ross drew her even closer Tessa could touch and stroke the crisp curls at the nape of his neck, could breathe his intoxicating aroma and let his powerful leg muscles guide her steps just as surely as his hands.

Despite Ross's reservations about his own dancing ability, Tessa decided he was practically an expert. Or was that simply because the two of them glided together so instinctively and intuitively? "I've never found it as easy to dance with anyone as you," he whispered.

Tessa had never found it quite so easy or natural, either. Moving, dipping, swaying, twirling, the love songs poured over them until mutual desire stirred—naturally, perhaps inevitably.

I want him so, Tessa thought, pressing ever closer to his strong lean body, feeling its magical appeal to her senses. No one has ever affected me the way Ross does. Oh, I know we don't have any future together, but surely, we can share tonight.

And possibly tomorrow night, too? she thought wistfully, already hungry for more than just one time with Ross. Then Tessa froze, swallowing hard. Suddenly, as if he'd read her mind, Ross stopped dancing in midsong.

"Let's walk around the hotel," he suggested softly. "We've hardly seen the grounds, and the landscaping is famous."

Tessa nodded, feeling relieved yet disappointed, too. No, he hadn't been able to read her mind. She had wanted Ross to make a strong romantic move, and yet just thinking of it and the inevitable decision she'd have to make, frightened her, too. However natural making love with Ross might be, it could never be a casual occurrence, and Tessa feared for the safety of her heart.

They strolled all around the hotel, then walked along the bed of the stream from which Arroyo Grande derived its name. Amazingly, the music continued to follow them and Tessa was totally charmed as the mariachi band continued to spin out one soulful love song after another.

Yes, the night was magical and enchanted. Tessa and Ross moved down a stone walk bordered with flowering citrus trees that wafted a tangy perfume into the air. They passed lavish fountains with pink and green Spanish tiles and walked alongside beds of extravagant flowers. Once Ross stopped and plucked an especially large scarlet flower, which he tucked into Tessa's hair over her ear.

He knows all of the gentle and seductive little gestures, she found herself thinking involuntarily. Then Tessa glanced over her shoulder and saw that the mariachi band really was following them. Oh yes, Ross definitely knew how to lead a woman along the garden path in more ways than one.

A lacy white garden bench glowed in the moonlight. Ross took Tessa to it, then drew her down beside him. For a moment he let his lips simply nuzzle her chin and glide across her cheek until her pounding heart longed for the moment when he'd actually kiss her.

His lips had no sooner touched hers when the band began yet another song heavy with emotional overtones. *"Te quiero,"* the lead singer wailed. "I love you."

"Wait here," Ross muttered to Tessa. Then he arose, his hand reaching for his wallet and disappointment stung Tessa again. So the music really had been prearranged and must now be paid for. What she wanted to think was magic had actually been stage-managed. She'd been in danger of being seduced by an enchantment brought about by cold hard cash.

By the time Ross returned, Tessa had risen from the bench and walked a short way down the path. Her emotions were in turmoil again, just as they had been when she'd seen Ross in the middle of the street, taking pictures while the irate bull charged straight at him.

As the thought of their profound differences resurfaced, Tessa winced just a little when Ross touched her shoulder. He turned her around to face him, his lips pressed against her throat, a hot kiss that filled her with fervid longing. She'd either better decide to go along with him or make an excuse right now.

"Ross, I—I'm really very tired," Tessa heard herself murmuring. "It's been a long day."

"Yes, it has," he agreed sympathetically, but sighed as he released her.

Now regrets filled Tessa once again. She was sorry she was standing here without his arms around her. Sorry she'd said anything to interrupt the mood even if it was coming from a manufactured and manipulative magic. But most of all, she was sorry she was just so—so damned ambivalent about this man.

Okay, I'm a crashing coward, Tessa thought bitterly. I don't know how to take a chance without counting the cost and I don't know how to love and then let go gracefully. I guess that's why I'm thirty-two years old with nothing in my past except one very lukewarm affair.

Then she felt Ross's strong hands squeeze her waist gently. "Do we really need two hotel rooms?" he asked in a voice that beguiled and seduced. "I'd like to stay with you, Tessa, even if I just hold you while you sleep."

She felt wrenched. No, she felt absolutely torn asunder. But stronger than the persuasion in his voice was the warning crashing through her mind. "Yes, Ross, we do need two hotel rooms," Tessa replied evenly. Because if we had only one we wouldn't be doing much sleeping, she thought.

Besides, Ross needed to rest. Anyone tossed over the horns of a bull ought to tuck in early for sleep, not love-making.

"Okay," he replied pleasantly. "I'll go find somebody who has a darkroom and get my pictures developed."

Why, he didn't even sound disappointed. Tessa was rendered speechless once again. Then fury flooded her, a fury so intense she didn't dare trust herself to speak. In fact, she didn't even trust herself to look at Ross again or bid him good-night.

All she could do was either slap him again or flounce away, hurrying toward her room just as fast as she could. This time she chose the latter course.

"Tessa," she heard Ross call, perplexed, from behind her.

"Tessa!" he said again in astonishment and, last, with a surprised question in his voice: "Tessa?"

She hoped all of his film came out blank. She hoped he'd broken his precious camera when he'd landed on all fours in the dusty Juárez street. She further hoped that one day he married the biggest witch in the western hemisphere and that all of their children were born with low, hairy foreheads and six fingers and toes.

Oh, she'd been right about that man from the very beginning, Tessa thought passionately, tearing the scarlet flower out of her hair. Ross Stanton was absolutely, hopelessly incorrigible and unrepentant. She'd been crazy to have ever harbored even one single serious thought about him.

And as to falling for him headlong, the way she'd done, I ought to have my head examined, Tessa told herself, gritting her teeth.

Of course, I've always had miserable luck with men, Tessa reflected as she stomped around her luxurious hotel room. I remember the first dance I ever attended in junior high school when Harold Mahoney gave a whole new and ghastly meaning to the phrase "blind date." Then there was my junior year at St. Mary's...

By the time Tessa had finished ripping off her clothes and savagely brushing her hair, she'd progressed through the men she'd known in college and medical school until, finally and inevitably, she brooded again over Cary Steward. Shallow! Selfish! Glib and gutless! she accused and stomped around the room again.

Then, keeping up her head of steam, Tessa railed against her brother Glenn for several minutes as she pulled on her baggy old pajamas. But, finally, she was reduced to simply cursing men in general—and Ross Stanton in particular— and trying not to care about him so much, oh, so desperately much.

A new and poignant loneliness assailed her. Just knowing that the scamp had the room next door made her miss him and yearn for him all over again. You are disgusting, she told herself sternly.

"I can't help it," her heart cried back. "I'm in love."

Like any woman, Tessa had often wondered what it would feel like to love deeply and care as much and more for another person's welfare as she cared for her own. Now she almost wished she didn't know, because she kept having this insane desire to go rushing out of her room and burst into Ross's.

But she had too much pride and common sense to follow the impulses egging her on. Any emotions arising from waves of hunger and longing were suspect.

Still, this was certainly a waste of a perfectly delightful night, Tessa thought almost desperately as she crawled into her enormous bed and gave her pillow a savage punch.

First she tried sleeping on her right side, then on her left. She tried to fall asleep on her back or flat on her stomach. Next she counted sheep. Then she tried recalling prescriptions, trying to remember all the various drugs that began with the letter *A*, then *B* and so on.

In the midst of *E*—at one-thirty in the morning—Tessa gave up on sleeping and climbed out of bed. Her brain still refused to settle down and permit her body the rest it needed.

Physical activity, Tessa diagnosed for herself. I need to run or ride a bike or—

Suddenly she dashed out onto her darkened balcony; it overlooked a kidney-shaped swimming pool. Although the pool was completely deserted at this late hour, its lights still blazed welcomingly.

A swim, Tessa thought, darting back inside her room to tear off her pajamas. Yes, a swim would be perfect. It was just what she needed to calm herself down and work off the tension that had accumulated as a result of her busy, eventful day and her frustrating night.

She had brought a swimsuit with her, the same suit she'd packed when she'd left Washington under the delusion that staying with Aunt Fay was akin to being at a dude ranch. Now Tessa pulled on the suit and thrust her feet into sandals. Then she snatched up a couple of the hotel's thick towels as well as her room key and darted out into the deserted hall.

A little uneasiness prickled at the back of Tessa's neck when she walked through the darkened empty gardens and into the fenced pool area. This late at night she certainly did feel alone. But she so badly needed to get in the water that Tessa ignored her sense of foreboding. Surely a hotel as modern as this one was patrolled regularly by security personnel.

Although swimming was not really one of Tessa's talents, at least she knew the rudiments of staying afloat. The cool water felt refreshing, and she paddled doggedly from one end of the pool to the other. Going back and forth, arm over arm, Tessa found herself reflecting on how the first architect to design a so-called kidney-shaped pool had probably flunked out of medical school.

When Tessa's nervous energy was finally spent, and she felt good and exhausted, she turned over on her back. For a time she simply floated, letting the water lap over her. She looked up for a moment at the bright, twinkling stars and studied the fat moon. If only she were still young and naive enough to wish upon a star! I'd wish, oh, I'd wish the evening with Ross hadn't ended as it did. Then Tessa closed her eyes and continued to float—until the sound of sandals slapping on stone brought her up sharply, startled and splashing.

Oh Lord, I completely forgot that a person is never, ever supposed to swim alone, Tessa thought, dashing the water out of her frightened eyes and trying to peer past the citrus trees and the shadows they cast. But, of course, you swam with another person in case you got a cramp. What should you do if you attracted an attacker instead?

The footsteps drew closer just as her vision cleared. Then, to Tessa's vast relief, she saw Ross.

"Hi," he called out blithely and walked over to the side of the pool closest to her. "Looks like you're having fun." His voice sounded wistful.

Tessa's heart continued to bang against her breast a mile a minute, but she told herself that this was sweet relief rather than keen anticipation. "Yes, it is pleasant," she admitted and was confounded to discover herself automatically swimming toward him.

Ross had changed out of his torn shirt and dark navy slacks. Now he wore a pair of tan shorts, a white polo shirt and casual sandals. As he crouched down on the apron of the pool, the better to talk with her, his gaze was solicitous.

"Couldn't you sleep?" he asked and Tessa, now treading water by the edge of the pool, replied with a silent shake of her head. "I couldn't, either," Ross said and shot her a look of rueful understanding.

"Weren't you able to find a darkroom?" Tessa couldn't resist asking him. Of course, she'd never been able to resist poking a sore tooth with her tongue, either.

"Yeah, I found one. Fifty dollars gets you anything in this town. I've printed my photographs."

Ross stopped abruptly, as if sensing that this particular topic was a minefield.

"And?" Tessa went on insistently, apparently determined to rub her own nose in the source of her misery. "Weren't your pictures any good?"

Ross shrugged. "I don't know. I think so—I mailed 'em off, anyway. Frankly, I kept wishing the whole time that I hadn't screwed things up with you." In the moonlight his handsome face looked doleful.

Tessa's head told her this was just a line intended to soften her up, but her heart hung on his words, anyway. "Oh?" she inquired evenly, feeling her pulse racing even faster.

"I stood outside your door for maybe five minutes after I got back," Ross went on sheepishly. "But I didn't hear anything so I finally left. I didn't figure you'd appreciate my waking you up."

"No, I wouldn't have," Tessa said shortly. "Of course, since I wasn't asleep, anyway, it wouldn't have mattered."

"I didn't want to make you any madder," Ross confessed. "Not that you don't have damned good reason to be. That's what I thought about when I was back in my own room. I kept rehashing everything that happened today. I

brought you here to have a good time—and I'm sorry you
haven't."

"Oh, it hasn't been all bad, Ross," Tessa heard herself
reassuring him. "Sort of fifty-fifty."

"That bad, huh?" His face grew even more doleful. "I
was hoping you'd say sixty-forty."

Tessa relented. "Oh, maybe it was, Ross," she agreed.
"Everything was fine until the bull got loose."

This man had the most amazing effect on her, making her
forgive him for positively unforgivable things. Brother
Glenn had always said Tessa could carry a grudge forever,
but of course, Ross had already proved he was the exception to Tessa's every rule.

"Finally I got out of bed," Ross continued. "I was sitting on my balcony, feeling lonely and sorry about everything, when I saw you coming down here. Believe me, Tessa,
that was one of the nicest sights of my life."

Tessa drew herself up indignantly. "Ross Stanton, have
you been watching me like some Peeping Tom?" she demanded.

"No! Well...yes, just for a few minutes, Tessa. You
looked so beautiful in that bathing suit, swimming, who
could resist? Then I started thinking maybe you'd speak to
me again, so I threw on some clothes and stopped by the all-
night grill to pick up a couple of things. By the time I came
through the garden I was just hoping you hadn't already
finished swimming and disappeared like a mermaid."

"What things did you get from the grill?" Tessa asked,
already gliding toward the steps at the shallow end of the
pool.

"Just a few things to eat. See, another thing I felt rotten
about was that I didn't even feed you a decent dinner. So I
brought some fruit and wine, some *buñuelos* and *burros*—"

"What?" Tessa asked as she came up from the pool, dripping and wet as a duck.

"*Buñuelos* and *burros*? They're Mexican sweets." Ross was waiting with both of Tessa's towels spread wide to enfold her. He wrapped the towels swiftly around her suddenly shivering body, then he took Tessa—towels, wet bathing suit and shivering skin—into his tight embrace. His warm cheek rested on her cold wet one and his hands made gentle stroking motions against her back. "Just come over here, sweetheart, and let me ply you with goodies," he whispered.

By then Ross had quite a good grip on her and, a moment later, he was sprawled in a poolside chair with Tessa cradled in his lap. It felt wonderful to be near to him again after she'd felt so lonely and missed him so much.

"Here, try a *buñuelo*," Ross coaxed and a tasty hot chip generously dusted with cinnamon, spices and sugar slipped past Tessa's lips.

"Good!" she exclaimed.

"Now, let's see what this is," Ross said, unfolding another delicacy to take a peek. "Oh, I can't see it, but it smells like a fresh peach *burro*. Here, Tessa, take a taste of this."

He had cared enough to come after her. That was all that really mattered to Tessa as she sat in his lap and let him feed her. They traded bites back and forth and drank directly from a bottle of sparkling fruit wine, since Ross had forgotten to get any glasses. Then Ross passed out fresh cherries and figs.

This is really quite a sensual experience, Tessa thought at about the same time she discovered that she was no longer sitting on Ross's knees, but had allowed herself to slump back, relaxing in the circle of his arms. In this position it was almost impossible to ignore his heady appeal to her senses or the warmth and desirability of his long, lean, all-male body. Her head, damp though it was, rested on his shoulder and, as Tessa and Ross gradually began to forget about food, one of his hands slipped beneath the towels to caress her hip and draw her nearer still.

With his other hand Ross brought Tessa's fingers up to his lips. He kissed them, then turned her hand over and pressed his warm full lips to her palm. Her response was so acute that her hand actually trembled in reaction.

"You taste of cinnamon and sugar," Ross whispered and began to slowly lick each one of Tessa's fingers. "Mmm, I wonder if your mouth tastes the same."

He displayed an almost uncanny understanding of her. Soon the desire to simply press herself against him grew so compelling that Tessa distrusted her ability to resist. In a minute Ross was going to kiss her, really kiss her, so Tessa knew she had to speak quickly now or forget what she planned to say.

"This is never going to work out with us, Ross," she warned. "We're congenital opposites."

"Yes, I know," he agreed. But his voice was a seductive croon that belied the seriousness of their words. "We'll have to forget all about each other as soon as this weekend's over," he added. "Still, I want to thank you once more for saving my life."

"Which time?" Tessa couldn't resist asking.

Then his lips covered hers, powerfully, yet also with an all-encompassing tenderness. Suddenly Tessa could understand why sheltered Victorian maidens had once swooned at very intense kisses. But, of course, she wanted more, far more from Ross than any innocent, sheltered maiden could ever have comprehended. Indeed, Tessa's entire body was now alive, clamoring and quivering with its urgent need of him.

"You're thanking me quite nicely," she assured Ross and allowed his kiss to part her lips until she felt his tongue.

"What you're saying to me is more than 'you're welcome,'" Ross groaned, making Tessa aware of his own instinctive male reaction.

Still, tenderness continued to temper his passion at every step. Slowly he stood up, gently setting Tessa on her feet before he drew her close again—so close that she could intimately feel his own fierce need of her.

Immediately she felt an equally fierce yet purely feminine response. Instinctively Tessa gripped Ross's shoulders, pressing herself to him and fitting her soft body to his lean hard contours. Excitement surged through her like adrenaline.

Slowly Ross ran his hands up and down the skin of her bare arms until Tessa stepped closer, letting his chest crush her breasts. She allowed his mouth, caressing and never still, to absorb hers until pleasure burned through them. Dimly Tessa heard their gasps and sighs. She didn't know why this man should be the one to unleash a tidal wave of passion within her cautious, studious self. She knew only that this passion, this veritable torrent that swept her to him, was now being fully unleashed.

"Come with me," Ross said simply and Tessa nodded.

Then they were walking back toward their hotel, skirting the lobby and entering by a side door. It seemed to Tessa that an eternity passed before they were comfortably alone again, now in a cozy elevator, and she could read the desire being telegraphed by Ross's passion-darkened eyes. They swayed together, kissing hungrily once again, until they were aroused by the jerk of the elevator when it stopped at their floor.

Tessa's room was closest. She whipped out her key and Ross opened the door as soon as it was unlocked.

A lamp burning on a nightstand was their only illumination as Ross drew Tessa to the bed. He dropped down first, then reached up with both arms to pull her on top of him.

As her scantily clad body descended to his they were suddenly kissing avidly, even wildly.

All the love that Tessa felt for Ross poured out now in fierce physical expression. She bent over him, seeking his lips again and again. "You taste like cinnamon and sugar, too," she managed to murmur.

"Come taste some more," he invited, and their mouths meshed again in a flaming kiss that went on and on until Tessa began to feel giddy, almost faint.

She could see that Ross was similarly affected. Now that she was able to glimpse his eyes she saw a rampant hunger for her that was glowing white-hot. His choked whispers against her bare skin only confirmed his desire. Still, Ross's passion never overcame his concern for Tessa, and his all-consuming tenderness absolutely melted her like a lighted candle.

Slowly Ross began to peel down the damp bathing suit that clung to her body. "You're just the way I dreamed, Tessa, only more beautiful," he swore. His lips found the soft hollow of her throat before he drew back to admire her newly bared breasts. "You're so soft, so—so perfect. God, I never want to hurt you."

"You won't, you can't," Tessa whispered, knowing she was more aroused than she'd ever been in her life. Yes, she was ready for Ross and she wanted him to make love to her.

As he slipped the bathing suit below her waist and tugged it over the curve of her hips, Tessa was pushing up Ross's white polo shirt. She let her fingers wander beneath the cottony cloth, running her fingers through his thick golden chest hair.

Her own touch clearly inflamed him. "Sweetheart," he crooned.

Suddenly Ross was in a hurry and Tessa was, too. She bent over him again, seeking his hot lips, until he rolled her over and dispensed with her bathing suit once and for all.

His polo shirt followed, mussing the thick golden hair on his head, and the sound of his zipper sliding down told Tessa that his tan shorts were coming off next. As that garment disappeared somewhere below Tessa's feet, she took his full weight and felt the delicious, totally male marvel that was Ross Stanton for the first time. Tessa heard herself moan as he kissed her throat. Simultaneously his hands roamed over her breasts, stroking and gently kneading. Gradually his hands dipped daringly lower and his mouth moved downward. Where a moment before a thumb had tantalized her sensitive nipples, now his tongue caressed them.

"Tessa, I've never wanted a woman the way I want you," Ross blurted out.

With his words, Tessa wound her arms around his waist, imprisoning him deftly with her bare legs in a position that seemed wholly natural. Then she felt the sudden plunging motion of Ross's body and heard her own ecstatic whimper of delight.

Nothing in her life could compare to her total surrender of herself to him or his to her. She had never experienced anything resembling this spontaneous yielding on her part and the graceful rhythmic motions that delighted her so on his. Almost instantly Ross took Tessa aloft, leading her toward a thrilling crest until their bed became a lake of fire, bubbling and seething, rising and falling. As she lay beneath him, pinned by the movements of the strong body atop her, Tessa paradoxically felt more free and abandoned than she ever had before, for never had she really dared to trust sensation, except with him.

She tried to stifle her enthralled cry, pressing her lips on Ross's shoulder to silence herself and thinking, no, it's too soon. I don't want it to end.

But it didn't end, neither for him nor for her. They were simply too hungry for each other to reach any quick and simple resolution. Within seconds after her first release

Tessa could feel the heat waves rising and washing over her once more, and this response, too, was entirely new and unique.

She lost all track of time, all awareness of where she was. She forgot to count the number of times that Ross made her cry out in ecstasy before she heard his own wild, joyous gasps. She knew only that being with Ross was music and magic and paradise.

There weren't nearly enough hours in the night. Not enough to hold each other and whisper, to make love as many times as they wished, to rest and to sleep.

"You're every dream I ever had," Ross said softly, looking down at Tessa as the first gentle rays of dawn began to streak the eastern sky.

"Ross—"

He didn't let her finish. Instead he drew her close for another lingering, passionate kiss. "Every single, solitary dream," he vowed, "is you."

"And you are all of mine," she answered and buried her face in his shoulder. The skin there, which she'd tasted earlier, was deliciously salty. How, she wondered, had he divined all of her fantasies and made each one come true?

Beware this treacherous afterglow, her practical mind tried to warn her. But she wasn't going to listen to sanity and reason on such a perfect night, especially not when Ross was kissing her all over again and she could feel his clear intent.

With an eager murmur Tessa sought to roll beneath him, but instead, Ross guided her over him. Then the waves of passion began to crash again as she set their rhythm and Ross moved powerfully beneath her until she collapsed, spent and sated.

This time the afterglow led them straight down into sleep. Deep, dreamless, refreshing sleep. Held fast in each other's arms neither of them awoke or even stirred again until it was well past noon.

"Smile, Tessa," Ross coaxed. His finger was poised on the shutter, waiting for that rare but engaging smile of hers to emerge.

"Ross Stanton, you've taken dozens of pictures of me, and I'll have none of you. It isn't fair." The way Tessa crinkled her nose at him was adorable, too, Ross thought, so he snatched two quick shots in succession before Tessa flounced away, pretending to be angry.

"I'm not as photogenic as you," he argued, following her down an especially attractive Juárez street that she'd chosen at random. Ross grinned when he saw Tessa looking around curiously, peering over the attractive whitewashed walls to see the stately houses beyond with their many balconies. Yes, too many balconies, the well-traveled Ross observed, his knowing grin widening. While every country had different traditions, some things never changed.

"Why don't you take a few pictures here on this picturesque street?" Tessa asked.

"Because I don't get too many requests for Cathouse Row," Ross replied candidly.

Tessa swung around, gasping in shock. "What?" Her beautiful blue eyes were wide with consternation and those luscious lips that Ross had spent half of last night kissing opened in a surprised O.

"You're kidding me, aren't you?" she demanded.

"Heck, no," Ross said truthfully. "By dusk all these balconies will be filled with pretty, uh, ladies of the night. They'll be calling out offers and prices to the gringos below."

"Why did you ever let me come down here?" Tessa wailed in dismay.

"Heck, sweetheart, you acted as if you liked it!"

"I did not," she cried indignantly, putting her hands defiantly on her hips.

Ross grabbed another shot of Tessa then, making sure that one of the grand houses with its balconies was clearly evident over one of her shoulders.

If they were simply two very ordinary people, that shot in their photo album would surely become one to joke about, Ross reflected. "Tessa on Cathouse Row" he would carefully label it and she would pretend to be upset and distressed. "Of course you can't let the children see it, Ross. Why, I'd *die* of embarrassment!" And forty years after their Mexican honeymoon they'd still start laughing together anytime they glanced at that particular picture.

Abruptly Ross jerked up, aware of the strange direction his thoughts had taken. Why, he had never imagined being married to someone before.

How ironic, too, that his mental slip had occurred when he was with Tessa, a woman with whom he was not at all compatible.

Oh, wasn't he? Images suddenly drenched Ross's mind until his body began to grow uncomfortably overheated. Okay, so he and Tessa were certainly compatible in the physical sense—and enthusiastically so. In fact, just looking at the curve of her cheek, the curl of her hair or the hint of a womanly breast beneath her loose shirt could start Ross's hormones churning.

But mentally and emotionally the two of them were miles apart, so this weekend, wonderful though it was, had not even a hint of a future to it. Why, once he'd returned Tessa to Aunt Fay's cottage in Progresso Ross would be on his footloose way once again and Tessa could go back to a sterile, refrigerated lab.

Briefly Ross tried to imagine her there, wearing a severe white lab coat, her lively dark hair sternly slicked back.

Sensible shoes on her feet, a dark drab skirt. Would she also wear glasses? he wondered.

Ross stopped, momentarily frustrated. He just couldn't visualize his vibrant, passionate Tessa in that mode at all. Too many flaming memories from last night kept intruding and now his eyes fastened on the gentle feminine sway of her slender yet rounded hips.

Ross ran down the middle of the deserted street to catch up with Tessa, then swung her around to face him. He kissed her then, bending his long frame down to her much shorter one. Kissed her until their lips began to burn, kissed her until they had to stop.

"Where are you going in such a hurry, Dr. Fitzgerald?" he demanded and heard a surprisingly husky timbre to his voice.

"To hunt up some nice, safe landmarks," she retorted, "like a cathedral, or maybe a straw market."

And there it was again, the unlikely leap of his imagination and the incongruous image. Ross, who hadn't set foot in a church since childhood unless he was expected to photograph it, suddenly imagined himself standing in one with Tessa at his side. There were flowers and music and she wore a long dress....

Ross shook his head to clear it. He was certainly having weird flights of fancy today, probably the result of physical bliss last night. Or maybe getting dropped on his head by the bull was to blame. Still, he was having trouble keeping even the simplest of facts straight.

For instance, the only reason Ross was taking photographs of Tessa now was because, once the weekend was over, he had vowed never to see her again.

Chapter Nine

I guess this is it, Ross," Tessa sighed when the road sign pointing to Progresso finally appeared.

"Don't be in such a hurry to get rid of me," Ross snapped, displaying the sort of ill humor Tessa hadn't seen from him before—no, not even when he was at his sickest.

Astounded, she turned to stare at Ross's suddenly stern profile, which also happened to be manly, devastatingly handsome and completely lovable to boot. Oh God, what in the world is wrong with me? Tessa thought. Aloud she demanded, "What in the world is wrong with *you*?"

"I think your farewells are just a little premature," Ross flared. "In case you forgot, I'm planning to see Aunt Fay, spend the night and leave early in the morning. I'm afraid you can't rush me out of your life until then."

"Ross, I am not trying to rush you out of my life," Tessa replied patiently. "You're the one who's been in a breakneck hurry to get away from me."

"I have not," he barked.

"You have, too," Tessa contradicted. "You've been driving seventy miles an hour all the way across New Mexico. You could have gotten a speeding ticket or killed us both."

"Make up your mind, Tessa. Which jolly alternative is it going to be—mere doom or outright death?"

"How dare you!"

Tessa heard herself screaming like a fishwife and then she saw confusion and misery flood Ross's deep aquamarine eyes.

"I—I'm sorry," she stammered at the very moment that he said, "I didn't mean to yell at you."

Abruptly Ross headed the car onto the shoulder of the road. He cut the motor and stretched out his arms to Tessa. She fell against him almost frantically and for several minutes they clung together like lost children.

Then Ross began to smooth her hair back from her forehead. He framed her face in his hands and kissed her forehead, temples and eyelids. His lips were so warm and their touch so tender that Tessa felt a lump rise up in her throat again. To hear herself sniffle was even more infuriating. She'd never been a woman who cried easily or wore her emotions on her sleeve. A professional demeanor had always come naturally to her, not weak and silly tears. But all that had certainly changed since she'd met Ross.

He always made her so aware of being a woman, coaxing feminine responses and reactions from her that Tessa would have scoffed at before, believing herself impervious to them.

If only he'd been a little less virile. If only he'd been a lot less tender. Then she wouldn't be an emotional basket case about his leaving her, Tessa thought. But, of course, if he were less virile and less tender he wouldn't be Ross, the man she loved.

With her face pressed into the warmth of his neck, her nose gratefully inhaling his clean delightful scent, Tessa tried desperately to bring them back to reason. "We agreed—"

"Yes, we sure did, sweetheart."

"I mean, it's not like either of us is ever going to change."

"No, of course not. We're not kids. Our personalities are fixed."

"We've each practiced our professions for quite a number of years," Tessa went on. How reasonable her voice sounded. How rational and sensible she was being. But looking down she saw that her hands were curved almost like talons, gripping Ross's shoulders as if afraid to let go.

He turned and kissed her once more, one of those encompassing embraces that wiped everything else out of her mind and made her think only of sprawling across a bed with him, of drawing him down closer and ever deeper....

"Let's go see Aunt Fay," Ross sighed and Tessa forced herself to pull away.

He turned the car off the interstate and headed onto the narrow dirt road that led to Progresso.

They were greeted with delight by Aunt Fay, who had been watching for them eagerly. Apparently she had enjoyed her own weekend with the Sandovals almost as much as Tessa and Ross had enjoyed theirs. Unfortunately, she must have also gone hog-wild and eaten everything in sight, Tessa surmised when she checked her aunt's blood pressure and found it elevated. Yes, Aunt Fay had obviously been off her salt-free diet, but Tessa just didn't have the heart to scold her as she ordinarily would have. Instead, she went off to make up beds, leaving Ross to give Fay a considerably abridged version of the way he and Tessa had spent their long weekend.

Tessa found fresh sheets and began fixing both the bed in Aunt Fay's guest room as well as the lumpy sofa. As she worked she stifled her sigh of longing. But she and Ross simply couldn't sleep together here. Not with Aunt Fay right down the hall.

"Oh, Tessa, I forgot to tell you sooner," Aunt Fay suddenly shouted. "Glenn called."

"Glenn!" Tessa dropped the sheets and dashed back to the door of her aunt's room. "Do you mean it was my own negligent brother, Glenn Fitzgerald?" she asked suspiciously. "It wasn't a lackey, or a secretary, or even Evie—"

"Nope. It was himself in fine voice. He was sorry he missed you, but said he'd call back again in a few days."

Tessa returned to her chores, although she longed to kick the wall in frustration. She knew all about Glenn's promises to call. Why, she'd be lucky if he got back to her in two weeks—no, make that three.

She'd just finished with the beds when Ross came down the hall to announce that Aunt Fay was retiring for the night. "Actually she dozed off while I was telling her about our walking tour through Juárez," he said, grinning.

"Oh." Tessa swallowed and made herself look away from that keen light flaring in Ross's eyes. "Look, I, uh, made up the bed in the guest room for you, Ross. I'll take the sofa."

He stared at her incredulously, his thick blond eyebrows knitting together, consternation tightening his face. "The hell you say."

"Ross, please don't be difficult," Tessa begged. "We can't stay together tonight."

"Why the hell not?" he demanded. "It's certainly our last chance."

"Aunt Fay—"

"Sleeps like a log and snores like a lumberjack," Ross interrupted heatedly. "She's also a little deaf. Anyway, I have the distinct impression that she highly approves of you and me getting together—"

"Well, I wouldn't be comfortable cutting up under her roof," Tessa flared, her own overwrought nerves simply snapping.

"'Cutting up?' My God, you have the most antiquated notions and vocabulary for a young person," Ross flared right back.

"I don't care to discuss either my notions or my vocabulary," Tessa cried. "I just want to go to bed. I'm tired."

Ross's jaw jutted out stubbornly. "You take the bed. I'll be fine on the sofa." His words halted Tessa's protests. "No, I insist."

She followed him as he turned toward the living room. "You're the one who has to get up at the crack of dawn to leave."

"I suppose you're not going to be working like a dog, pumping gas, tending the store—all those simple fun chores you enjoy so much," he retorted. "Anyway, I can doze on the plane."

"The plane!" Tessa exclaimed in disbelief.

"I do it all the time. I've been sleeping on planes for years." Ross stared down at her amazed expression. "Oh, don't tell me. I know, you're a scared, finicky flier. Probably stay in the crash position the whole way, don't you?"

"Ross, you're still recuperating—"

"Tessa, in case you hadn't noticed, I am well—completely well. Just stretch out on the sofa with me and I'll be happy to prove it all over again. In fact, I think I could prove it to you all night long."

"There's no reason to be so crude—"

"Sometimes I'm a crude guy." On his way to the living room Ross turned back to stare at her. His own face looked suddenly weary, too, his eyes bewildered with pain. "Oh God, Tessa, here we go sniping at each other again. I guess I'm upset."

Again Tessa felt the wrenching threat of tears. "I know I'm upset," she admitted.

"And tired," he agreed. Suddenly his hand chucked her gently under the chin. "Go to bed, sweetheart."

"You'll wake me up in the morning, Ross, before you—you—"

"I promise."

They headed toward their separate beds, but even with her door closed firmly Tessa couldn't sleep. She ached all over with weariness and impending loss and her mind still kept clicking along a mile a minute, remembering and reliving....

Then she heard Aunt Fay start to snore rhythmically.

Was Ross already asleep? Tessa wondered. Or was he feeling just as sad and frustrated and sexually deprived as she was?

Oh, he'd been right. This was their last night, the final chance they'd ever have to be locked close and warm in each other's arms. Only Tessa Fitzgerald was such an absolutely sickening prude....

Before she could rethink her latest opinion of herself, Tessa jumped up, flung her door open and hurried down the quiet dark hall. Then, in the doorway to the living room, she stopped. In the dimness Ross was merely a huddled figure on the uncomfortable sofa and he appeared to be asleep. Her determination was beginning to wilt when she saw him suddenly move from one side to another, muttering a soft curse under his breath.

Tessa's heart soared. So he couldn't sleep, either. Once again their needs and longings were meshing. She kicked off her pajamas in record time, then padded naked and barefoot to Ross's side.

"Tessa?" Ross whispered hoarsely and then he scrambled up in bed.

"Do you still want me?" she whispered back.

He replied by simply throwing back the sheet in welcome.

With a gasp of relief Tessa dropped into his arms. He wore his undershorts, but they concealed nothing from her as she burrowed against his hard, hair-covered chest. Their mouths crushed together ecstatically and his tongue plunged deep inside even as Tessa felt one insistent knee impatiently starting to edge her thighs apart.

"Just see if I want you," Ross whispered when their mouths parted briefly. Then he had torn off his shorts and was pulling Tessa over him in blatant and hungry need.

She felt as if she were absorbing and inhaling him. He was as necessary to her as air and water, and her body delighted in welcoming him again. His mouth covered hers; his hands deftly and lovingly caressed her breasts. Gradually their eager breaths grew deeper and their movements, so natural and easy at first, turned primitive, wild and wonderful.

Tessa collapsed on Ross's chest just as she felt his arms finally loosening their grip. "Now we can sleep," he said in dreamy satisfaction, and while they still lay in a tangle of arms and legs Tessa felt herself sink into oblivion.

It seemed that she'd scarcely closed her eyes before she felt Ross's lips stroking her cheek ever so gently and his body beginning to stir beneath her. Slowly Tessa forced up her eyelids. This really wasn't the worst day of her life, she assured herself. After all, she and Ross were still healthy and alive, so they had no genuine reason for complaint.

"You slept on top of me like I was a sack of potatoes," Ross said, his voice amused.

"Oh, I'm sorry—I—" Tessa stammered.

"And you felt like a feather, you're so little and light. Did you get enough sleep, sweetheart?"

Slowly Tessa tested her various muscles. "I'm all right," she replied. She actually felt rested and refreshed so, although it was still dark, she knew that she and Ross must have slept for six or seven hours.

"I got kind of carried away last night." Now apology filled Ross's voice. "I hope I didn't hurt you."

"No, not at all. We both got kind of carried away," she assured him.

"Good. There's just barely enough time..." His face a trifle scratchy with new beard, Ross started to kiss Tessa's throat as his hands expertly touched her breasts once more. Immediately Tessa felt them contract to readiness, greedy again and aching with desire as they awaited the expert attentions of his mouth. Soon she guided Ross's golden head downward.

After another few minutes he rolled her over. Now she was looking up, trying to memorize every line, curve and plane of his passion-filled face. Ross kept studying her in just the same way. And this time they couldn't seem to quit loving each other. It just went on and on, until Tessa knew that letting him leave her was going to be the hardest thing she'd ever done.

"Tessa?"

"Yes, Ross?"

"I can never forget this, you know."

She knew. Perhaps it was fortunate there wasn't really time to say more—they'd spent it all making love. Now they both had to fly around frantically, gathering up Ross's possessions. Then they dashed outside and into the thin morning light that was just beginning to stream over the Chiricahua Mountains.

Back into the trunk went Ross's bag, his extra camera and all his other photographic and electronic equipment that had been stored at Aunt Fay's. Ross, still buttoning his shirt over his jeans, sank onto the seat, then drew Tessa through the car door.

Their lips met for one last, tingling kiss. "Why do I feel like hell about leaving you?" Ross muttered, his eyes dark with shadows.

Tessa replied with a silent shake of her head. Once again the uncharacteristic tears were clogging her voice and tightening her throat. She couldn't even tell Ross to please take care of himself—as if he ever would.

"Look, I can call you, can't I?" Ross suddenly blurted. "At least we could stay in touch."

The temptation to simply nod was almost overwhelming. But Tessa made herself shake her head again.

"You're saying that isn't wise?" he demanded.

She nodded emphatically.

"You intend to just forget me, right? And you think I should forget you?" Ross went on, but now icy sparks were starting to light the depths of his eyes, turning them to green glass.

Tessa nodded even more vehemently.

"You think you can do it, Tessa? Just shelve everything we've had—everything we've been to each other? That's right, nod your head off. My God, I wonder why I'm surprised. I always knew you had ice water in your veins!"

With that crack, Tessa shot up and banged his car door shut. She caught one last glimpse of Ross's flushed and furious face, then his camera appeared and a flashbulb exploded in front of her.

That ended Tessa's silence. "Ross, you overage miscreant!" she screamed.

"Yeah, I can live without you, too," he yelled back. Then the navy-blue compact jumped backward five feet before Ross wrenched the wheel around. The car leaped into the road and he went roaring away.

Tessa stood watching, coughing in the thick dust cloud raised by the car. She waited until the cloud had settled and Ross and his car were just a speck traveling rapidly across the flat desert, headed toward the far horizon. She watched until her eyes began to burn, watched until she saw only a last tiny moving blur—and then Ross Stanton was gone.

"Glenn, you worthless creep," Tessa said accusingly to her brother in a tone filled with cold fury. "First, you lured me out here to this godforsaken hellhole where I've had nothing but rattlesnakes and Gila monsters for company, then you left me stranded here with our poor sick aunt! By God, you're lucky you're almost three thousand miles from here. And that's just how far you'd better stay from me for the rest of your life."

"Good Lord, Tessa, Aunt Fay said you'd been upset, but I sure didn't think—"

"That's right, you've never thought about anyone else in your life, have you, Glenn? All your thoughts are strictly self-serving. Well, you'd better hope that I never get a chance to give the media my sisterly opinion of you. They'd have to print it on asbestos or it would burn up!"

"Tessa, honey, listen to me. I didn't dream things had been—I mean, never in your life have you talked to me this way! Why, if I'd had the least idea—"

"You had the least idea, you jerk. I left at least a dozen messages with everybody on your whole miserable staff."

"And I called you back, honey. Well, I did as soon as I possibly could. You don't know the demands I have on me. Anyway, when I did call back you weren't even there. Aunt Fay said you were in El Paso or San Antonio, someplace like that, with that famous photographer, Ross somebody-or-other. Well, yes, of course, I've heard of him. Who hasn't? So it all sounded fine. I thought you were fine and having a nice time. Aunt Fay said she was fine—"

"Well, she isn't, you—you rotten, lying politician! She's a sick old lady who needs help and money—"

"Why didn't you tell me sooner? I can't read minds. I told you I'd do anything I can for Aunt Fay. Just tell me what and when and how much, Tessa."

"I'll let her tell you, Glenn. I'm all through talking to you. In fact, I never want to talk to you again as long as I live. Did you hear that loud and clear?"

"Tessa, you're my little sister and I've always loved you and cared—"

"Forget it, Glenn."

"Will you talk to Evie, honey, if you won't talk to me?"

"Not unless she's planning to divorce you."

Her rage vented temporarily, Tessa relinquished the phone into Aunt Fay's waiting hand. Then, turning on her heel, Tessa stalked out of the cottage and headed for the store.

For three hours she worked furiously until the store had been dusted, swept and mopped from one end to the other. By then Tessa was drenched with perspiration and exhaustion had replaced her rage.

Luis, Juan and Consuela Sandoval arrived to tiptoe around Tessa, just as they'd been doing all week. I'm acting like a witch, Tessa thought in near despair. I've been making everyone just as miserable as I am.

Leaving the Sandovals in charge of the store, Tessa slunk back to the cottage. She planned to shower, change and then simply close her bedroom door and take a nap. And she would not let herself remember one single thing about Ross. But Aunt Fay was sitting in the living room, lying in wait for her.

"Don't you think you were a little hard on Glenn?" Aunt Fay demanded of her niece.

"Maybe," Tessa conceded, then her wrath swelled anew. "On the other hand, he also deserved every word."

"He's certainly distressed. You know Glenn. He always likes for all the folks around him to be happy and feel good."

"Sorry—but I'm not and I don't," Tessa replied tartly.

"You'll be glad to know that Glenn approves of my hiring the Sandovals to run the store on a permanent basis, starting bright and early tomorrow."

"Wonderful," Tessa said tonelessly.

"Consuela will continue to do the cooking at the café."

"That's good, Aunt Fay." At least this welcome news eased a little of Tessa's ever-present misery.

"Alberta will drive me back and forth to Tucson for physical therapy treatments. And I'm to send all the bills to Glenn's accountant," Aunt Fay finished triumphantly.

"Well!" Tessa sank down on the sofa and stared across at her aunt. "That really is good news, isn't it? Frankly, I'm surprised that everything worked out so easily."

Aunt Fay winked at her niece. "You got Glenn all softened up for me."

Tessa tried to make herself look chagrined.

"Also, I didn't inform Glenn that he really isn't the person you're maddest at," Aunt Fay continued.

Tessa didn't even try to reply to that.

"You know that you're mad at Ross, of course, for actually driving away and leaving you," her aunt went on softly. "But do you know that you're mad at yourself, too, for letting him go?"

Startled, Tessa looked up again. "But, Aunt Fay, I had no choice. Ross Stanton and I are complete opposites. Why, we'd never be compatible, not even if we—"

"Oh, fiddle," her aunt interrupted and rose, leaning heavily on her walker. At the door she stopped and glanced back at her disconsolate niece.

"All right, Miss Tessa, you're free to go back home now. But if you've got even a lick of horse sense, what you'll do is go running straight after that man."

"I can't! He and I both agreed—"

"Or else," Aunt Fay went on regally, "you're an even bigger damn fool than I think you are."

A knock on his door interrupted Ross's reverie. "Come in," he called and heard the door swing open.

"'allo, Ross."

"Oh, hello, Mrs. Couvillion," Ross said absently from the depths of the big armchair. He barely glanced up at his roly-poly Cajun landlady, who was carrying a stack of snowy, sweet-smelling laundry in her arms. He merely sighed, then returned to studying the various photographs he had posted on his wall. "Clean towels and sheets, huh?"

"I ever bring you dirty ones, *cher*? Do I ever dip 'em in swamp slime or hang 'em on nettles and poison ivy to dry?" Mrs. Couvillion inquired with heavy irony.

"That's lovely, Mrs. Couvillion. Just drop them on the bed or someplace. Anyplace."

"'ey, Ross, you still not feelin' any better? And you put up more pitchers."

Something about this conversation wasn't going quite right, Ross realized. Also, he'd completely forgotten his manners for correctly receiving older women. Belatedly he got out of his chair.

"I—I'm sorry, Mrs. Couvillion," he said to the plump black-haired woman who now regarded him with outright dismay. "I don't think I quite understood what you said."

"*Cher,* you haven't heard a t'ing I say all week. All you do, sit right here and mope—"

"I'm going back into the swamp to do some picture-taking tomorrow," Ross said hastily. "I'll be looking for the ivory-billed woodpecker again. Meant to do it sooner, but . . ." His words died away with his shrug so he forced himself to continue. "I think I'll turn in early so I can start out at dawn."

"Ross, *cher,* this is Saturday. Saturday night, 'member? What you do on Saturday night for years is go down on th' bayou to Pogue's. Eat *boudin, tasso, andouille* and crack-lings. Dance to Cajun band wit' my niece Marie or my niece Emmeline and drink home brew or red-eye. Else you go to Kacoo's, eat jambalaya, gumbo, an' *à l'étouffée.* Drink plum wine and dance wit' my cousin Angelina or my cousin Aimée—"

"Predictable so-and-so, aren't I?" Ross said heavily.

"You go out dancin' tonight, *cher*?" Mrs. Couvillion asked Ross ominously.

Ross gave an elaborate shrug. "No, I don't think—"

"This pretty witch-woman got you hexed!" Mrs. Couvillion's very solid arm shot out, her index finger pointing accusingly at the numerous photographs of Tessa that now hung on Ross's wall. "Who's she?"

"Oh no." Ross laughed awkwardly. "That's just Tes—Actually, she's Dr. Fitzgerald."

"Oh." Mrs. Couvillion's attitude underwent an immediate and startling transformation. "That th' nice lady called me 'bout you? 'Fraid you'd die."

"Actually—" Ross cleared his throat "—we're just casual friends."

"Uh-huh. Sevente'n pictures hang on t'is wall of casual friend."

"Are there that many?" Ross said, surprised. "I didn't know I took—well, she is photogenic, don't you think, Mrs. Couvillion?"

"Real casual friend, 'ey Ross?"

Mrs. Couvillion's plump finger had now zeroed in on Ross's final shot of a sleepy, still-tousled Tessa wearing pajamas.

"Oh, er, that was the morning I left. She helped me carry out..." Ross's sentence trailed off, the way a lot of his sentences did these days. "We've said goodbye," he finished painfully.

"I t'ink you say hello again soon. *Mais oui?*"

"*Mais non!*" Ross turned away, his voice final. "That woman's a typical doctor. A fussbudget and a worrywart! Why, she'd make my life hell on earth, nagging me to wear sunscreen, wear a straw hat, watch out for snakes, 'gators, mosquitoes—"

"'bout time."

"You women are all alike," Ross said wryly. "And you clever little devils sure stick together, too."

"Ah'm not gettin' insulted." Mrs. Couvillion shook her head vigorously, then pointed to Ross's breast. "You building a new shrine."

"Does this mean you're going to dismantle the old one?" Ross asked hopefully.

"*Cher,* I wouldn't do that," Mrs. Couvillion assured him. Then, on her way out of the room, she deliberately stopped at the door and looked back over her fat little shoulder. "Ross, you call pretty witch-lady-doctor." It was an order.

"I can't—"

"Or I call her. Invite her to mebbe come see me, eat fresh seafood bisque, dance with my nephew Roland or my nephew Gabriel—"

"You wouldn't," Ross said, appalled.

"Ha!"

On that note Mrs. Couvillion left, slamming the door explosively behind her.

Chapter Ten

Tessa found Washington sweltering in the midst of a relentless heat wave. Why, it's practically as hot here as it was in Arizona, she thought resentfully when the morning temperature grew high enough to drive her in from her pleasant, plant-bordered patio.

The plants didn't look very good, either, she thought, having examined them critically. Several were wilting and yellowed. See if she ever hired that wretched neighbor kid to tend them next time. The little thief had obviously not bothered to do his job. Tessa overcompensated by repotting everything and then drenching the plants with water.

Her comfortable spacious apartment, the place she'd dreamed of returning to, suddenly didn't suit her very well, after all. Had she always tolerated noises coming through the walls? It was outrageous that she had to listen to bathtubs filling, dishwashers churning and toilets flushing. How had she ever managed to tune out all of that before? Tessa wondered, wandering aimlessly through the neat rooms.

If only she could go back to work, she thought yearningly at least a dozen times a day. Work had always been Tessa's antidote to problems, heartaches or hard times. When each of her parents had died and later, after Cary had moved out, Tessa's work had proved her salvation. But now, since she didn't have it to fall back on, she found herself straightening picture frames, dusting already immaculate surfaces or rearranging the books in her library just to stay busy. Previously she'd shelved her books alphabetically by title. But she'd noticed recently that she had a tendency to forget the titles of her favorite novels. Better to organize them by author, Tessa thought, and managed to spend one whole day working on her shelves. Why not? She certainly had nothing else to do.

Tessa had, of course, checked in promptly with Dr. Corman on her return. "I've been following some promising leads, Tessa," her fellow scientist and friend assured her.

"Really? Where?" she asked him eagerly.

"There's a small college in Northern California that might support our work. A similar situation might be developing in the south, but that one's still iffy. I hope you'll consider California. I know, of course, that your close relatives live in this area, but—"

"Oh, I'd consider a move," Tessa said rapidly. "I'll consider anything at this point."

Dr. Corman hesitated. "Tessa, you might want to start looking on your own," he suggested.

For a moment Tessa was stunned. Although she rarely called Dr. Corman by his given name, preferring to keep to a proper professional relationship, she now blurted it out unconsciously in her concern. "Michael, you're not trying to get rid of me, are you?"

"Of course not, Tessa. Why, I'm shocked that you could even think of that after our years together and our collaborative research projects."

At least Michael Corman sounded sincere, Tessa thought and felt momentarily gratified.

"I just didn't want your loyalty to me to prevent you from checking into other offers," he went on.

"Forgive me, Dr. Corman," Tessa said abjectly. "I'm not used to being unemployed. I think I'm going a little crazy."

He chuckled warmly. "I know my wife swears I am. But let me promise you, Tessa, that if you can just hold out a little longer I certainly will want you to have a prominent place on any research team I head."

"I can hold out—and I will—because I want to be on that team," Tessa reassured him. At that moment she was grateful that, unlike Cary and many other doctors she knew, she hadn't always lived to the limit of her salary. As a result she had quite a substantial sum in conservative investments.

"It's really such a dratted shame that we've been reduced to this," her former boss fretted. "You know, those militant animal rights people who saw our laboratory shut down aren't even rational. They don't want to hear about all the diseases medical science has conquered through animal research and development of vaccines—the onetime killers like polio, smallpox and cholera."

Ross would listen. Ross is reasonable and rational, a little voice whispered in Tessa's head. But then her chest began to hurt, as if her heart had been squeezed tight, the way any thought of him always affected her.

"Right," was all she could manage to say to Dr. Corman's complaints, and even that took an effort.

Later that day, with the apartment cleaned to Tessa's satisfaction, she invaded the local public library seeking information on Northern California. She came home burdened with books, which she tried to read, only to recall Ross's telling her about how he had grown up in the Golden State.

Ross. Finally Tessa let her head drop onto her arm and allowed herself to think about him. She even decided it was okay to cry, except that her many tears and all of her emotions still seemed to be in deep freeze, hanging like slabs in her oh-so-heavy-feeling chest.

She had never hurt like this about anyone before. Of course, she'd never really been in love before, either—not that she'd ever admit as much to Ross or anyone else. No, not even if torturers were threatening to tear out her tongue! It was too humiliating. Careful, precise and professional Tessa Fitzgerald crazy about that death-defying daredevil with the lady-killer smile? Why, if any of her friends and colleagues ever heard about it, they would think she ought to be committed. Talk about a total mismatch!

But to herself Tessa could admit the truth. Yes, she was head over heels in love, fool that she was, and even knowing that it had all ended didn't help her to deal with a life that didn't include Ross.

Where was he? she found herself wondering desperately. Had he gone back to Louisiana and the lonely, wild wetlands there to risk another snakebite? Or was he leaping out of planes somewhere over Nepal, Afghanistan or Peru?

He could be anywhere.

Of course, I could phone his landlady and find out, Tessa thought. For that matter I might phone Stan and Linda in Richmond....

Tessa's head drooped even lower over her books. Oh God, what am I thinking about? A single tear trickled down her cheeks and splashed on the open page.

She wished that she really did have ice water in her veins. Then it wouldn't hurt so much to breathe, to think, to remember. Instead Tessa felt as if she'd been throttled or maybe worked over by experts employing brass knuckles. Now that she'd finally let down her guard and allowed herself to think again of Ross she ached worse than she had during a bout with flu last winter.

The magic of belonging to him swept back over Tessa in waves. His tenderness had disarmed her from the beginning. And Ross had made love to her so perfectly, so beautifully, yet without any of the sex manual expertise that marked a man only interested in conquests. No, it was as if Ross had celebrated her own particular uniqueness, making her receptive to the passion that drove him until Tessa had met and matched him every step of the way.

I wish I didn't know what it was like to make love with Ross, Tessa thought desperately. If she just had never known that particular splendor, then surely it wouldn't be so difficult now to reclaim her own heart.

But did she really, sincerely wish she'd missed such splendor? her heart inquired of her bemused and weary mind. No, of course not. To have experienced that sense of totally belonging to him, of being joined mind, heart and body, that was surely worth whatever it had cost her. But, oh, the price was high.

At least she was now one of the group of women who had experienced the ultimate in physical love. Tessa no longer had to wonder about what she might have missed. There was nothing else. In loving Ross she had reached the final, exquisite fulfillment.

Except, perhaps, if I had his baby....

Being childless had never bothered her before. Now she didn't know why, but she suddenly felt empty, barren and bereft. Being unmarried had never particularly bothered Tessa, either, but now it worried her a great deal. She didn't want to live the rest of her life like this, in an impersonal, overpriced apartment where she had to listen to the sounds of other people's telephones and blenders, their washing machines and garbage disposals. She wanted her own home, her own family. She wanted to hear the comforting sound of her husband's electric razor early in the morning. She wanted to listen for the cry of their hungry baby.

Why, I had all these womanly needs and didn't even know it, Tessa marveled and groped for another tissue to dry her wet eyes.

She still hadn't broken down and cried as she should. Steel bands continued to imprison her chest while the hard knot in her throat made it next to impossible to eat. She tossed and turned in bed at night, trying not to think of Ross and finally fell asleep only to dream of him.

How long would all these distressing symptoms continue? Tessa wondered desperately. Had any psychologist ever done a scientific study to research the broken heart? If she just had a timetable that stated when she would recover, then this awful interval between love and the acceptance of its loss would surely be easier to endure. At last, unable to concentrate on either television or her books she made her way again to her wide lonely bed.

Tessa rose early the next morning after another nearly sleepless night. At least she had a midmorning destination, she remembered almost gratefully as she pulled on her good clothes for a change. During her hiatus from work Tessa knew she should take care of all those annoying appointments that even professionals tended to put off—chores like going to the dentist and having her automobile serviced.

This morning it was her teeth. Silently Tessa endured the scratch, scrape, polish and floss routine as the dentist and her assistant discussed a current long-running play which they had both seen and thought would interest Tessa. But its plot sounded far too dark and gloomy to tempt her into purchasing tickets.

In fact, right now might be a very good time to simply let her brain atrophy while she wallowed in good escapist yarns and bright brainless movies. Once Tessa had paid her bill and fled the office with a mouth that felt sore and acutely sensitive, she stopped at the first newsstand she saw.

She had just scooped up a half dozen paperback novels, promising stock characters and hair-raising adventures, when she passed a rack of newspapers on her way to the checkout stand. On the first page of the local newspaper was one of those photographs designed to set weary commuters chuckling.

This one featured a bull charging madly through an area of tasteful shops and stalls, scattering people in its wake. In the background was a familiar-looking bullring. Even before Tessa snatched up the paper in trembling hands she had recognized the scene. As she burst into long overdue tears and proceeded to make a public spectacle of herself, she read the caption, "El Toro Resists His Fate", and the credit line "By Ross Stanton."

Tessa continued to cry as she paid for five copies of the newspaper. She cried all the way home and then she curled up in her favorite recliner in the den and cried some more, until the photograph before her grew smudged and soggy.

Damn it, the man was really good. Only a truly expert photographer could have captured the bull's satisfaction at having escaped from the old, lopsided truck or the lugubrious expressions on the faces of those fleeing his sharp horns and wicked heels. Briefly Tessa admired Ross's skills, then she settled down into steady weeping. At last the bands around her chest began to ease enough for her to draw a deep breath and the perpetual knot in her throat that kept her from eating disappeared momentarily.

Less than three weeks had passed since she'd seen him last. Had time ever passed so slowly and painfully? Had she ever felt quite so lost and bereft? Would she ever, ever see Ross again?

Tessa carried one copy of the newspaper off to bed with her and stretched out with a cold wet cloth over her eyes. She had no appetite, no energy, no enthusiasm. She had lost an astonishing amount of weight. In fact, she felt so rotten overall that she was sure she was coming down with a virus at the least or experiencing the early symptoms of a truly dire disease at the worst. Wearily she reached for the pad and pen she kept by her bedside and scribbled a note to herself. Tomorrow she must call her internist and request a thorough physical examination, complete with X rays and every lab test ever devised.

Just at that moment her telephone rang.

Startled, Tessa jumped, then pounced on the receiver even though she knew it was just a casual friend or chance acquaintance. Maybe it was Aunt Fay or Glenn. Come to think of it, she really *hoped* it was Glenn. She needed somebody to snarl at.

"Hello?" she whispered, her heart pounding as it always did whenever the phone rang.

"Tessa, is that you? You don't sound like yourself, sweetheart."

Her eyes closed, her breath eased effortlessly out of her chest and she gripped the telephone with fingers of steel lest she drop it or miss one single word. Oh, thank you, thank you, thank you, God! she thought.

"Ross, you don't sound like yourself, either. You sound so gruff," she said shakily.

"No, I don't," he denied even more gruffly. Then, as Tessa waited, breath bated, she heard his sigh. "Look, why don't you give up and come see me?"

"Well, I—I don't know about that," Tessa stammered, thunderstruck.

"Great! I've made plane reservations for you, Washington to New Orleans, for tomorrow morning. But I ought to warn you that you'll absolutely hate it here."

"Oh?" Tessa asked eagerly. She reached over the foot of her bed to tear open a bureau drawer and start choosing clothes to pack.

"Yeah. The Atchafalaya Basin is a terrible place to visit this time of year. It's hot and steamy, and it rains every afternoon. Heat like nothing you've ever felt, not even in Arizona. The whole place crawls with snakes and 'gators and mosquitoes. Gnats and flies try to eat you alive. Motel accommodations are strictly third-rate and the nearby restaurants are greasy spoons. You'll hate every single minute. Well, are you coming?"

"How could I possibly say no?" Tessa asked faintly, spilling underwear across her bed in a heap as she reached for another drawer.

"Boy, that's a relief," Ross admitted. "I thought sure you'd tell me to drop dead."

Momentarily Tessa stopped her mad emptying of dresser drawers. "Do you really want me to come, Ross?" she asked, rocking back on her heels.

"That's a profound understatement, Tessa."

Now she could hear a familiar buoyancy and eagerness returning to his voice. The mental image of him flashed through her mind, and suddenly Tessa felt weak with yearning to be held tightly in his warm strong arms.

"Same here, Ross," she admitted, too.

"You've actually missed me, sweetheart?" Ross sounded amazed.

"I've had my moments—and almost all of them have been those kinds of moments," Tessa said, yielding.

"I can't wait to see you," he said huskily. "Okay, here are your flights. Got a pencil handy?"

"Certainly. I always stay prepared, remember? That definitely includes keeping a pad and pen right here by the bed."

"I should have known."

Never had Tessa packed clothes quite so rapidly, pausing only to eat an enormous TV dinner. Then, between bites of a peanut butter and jelly sandwich, she assembled her emergency medical kit. To the standard remedies that she carried with her everywhere—aspirin, antacid, antiseptic, airsickness pills, antibiotics and antihistamines—Tessa prudently tossed in a few things designed specifically for life in the tropics. Let Ross tease her; she still believed in being prepared for everything.

As she wolfed down a piece of cheesecake she hesitated over an assortment of vitamins. In Tessa's opinion their therapeutic worth had yet to be decisively proven, but of course, with the sort of diet Ross probably lived on—"Oh, what the hell?" Tessa muttered and tossed in all her vitamins, in proper alphabetic sequence.

Then she dashed out to the automatic bank teller to get a couple of hundred dollars in cash. She also detoured through a fast-food restaurant for a strawberry milk shake and some chocolate chip cookies. Good Lord, I've been starving to death and didn't even know it, she thought, driving away with a lap full of food and her pockets brimming with money.

Then she saw the store that advertised men's hats and, providentially, it was still open.

Tessa had rarely felt quite so energetic or so sublimely happy, either when, back home once again, she phoned that nice neighborhood kid to come water her plants during her absence. Then she called Dr. Corman and Glenn to give them her temporary address and phone number. "Oh, I'll probably be there for a couple of weeks," Tessa said vaguely in response to Dr. Corman's questions.

"Southern Louisiana in June?" he asked, appalled. He had once lived in New Orleans, Tessa recalled. "My goodness, but the weather will be dreadfully hot."

"God, why would anyone ever want to visit the Cajun country?" exclaimed Glenn. "I got stationed at Fort Polk while I was in the army, remember? Talk about two years I definitely prefer to forget! Why, the voters oughta elect me to Congress just for patriotic loyalty, 'cause if ever a guy had reason to go A.W.O.L.—either Antarctica or Guam would have been a thousand laugh fun fest after Fort Polk without air-conditioning. And those Cajuns are damned funny folks, Tessa. Real snobbish and standoffish. Believe me, they hate outsiders. And they speak this fractured French no university language department ever heard of and eat the sort of creepy, crawly things any red-blooded American guy would get his gun after and shoot as varmints—"

"Thank you for sharing those fond memories, Glenn," Tessa said equably, finishing off her evening's fare with a simple glass of milk.

"Listen, you'd better make damned sure you've got a round-trip plane ticket, 'cause you're gonna want to leave again exactly ten seconds after you hit the airport tarmac—"

With Glenn's recommendations to guide her Tessa, not surprisingly, fell in love with Louisiana from the air.

She had intended to read during her flight. In fact, she had packed the brand-new issue of the *Journal of American Medicine* specifically because it carried an article entitled, "Death-Defying Acts and Their Correlation to Current Mortality Statistics in the United States." Despite the inflated title, Tessa thought the article was probably relevant to people like Ross. But she soon discovered that she was entirely too excited about seeing him to concentrate on his ultimate demise. So the magazine went back into her briefcase and Tessa returned to the window.

From this vantage point she could follow the loops and curves of the wide, muddy-brown Mississippi as it wended its way toward the Gulf, creating a swath of lush green delta on either side. As the plane banked steeply, preparing to land at New Orleans International Airport, Tessa found herself over a very large body of water that surely wasn't the Gulf—oh no, not with all of those black trees sticking straight up out of it.

"What's that?" Tessa said excitedly to one of her seat-mates, a Mrs. LeBlanc of New Orleans, who had already informed Tessa that she was of Cajun descent. Mrs. Le-Blanc not only spoke perfect English, but she was quite friendly as well.

"That's Lake Pontchartrain," she informed Tessa.

"Oh yes! How could I have forgotten?" Tessa said, abashed.

"There's our famous Pontchartrain Causeway that cuts across it. See, it's right here on your Louisiana map." A polished fingernail traced the route for Tessa.

"Your first time to visit Louisiana?" asked a distin-guished white-haired man, turning in the seat directly in front of Tessa. "I'm Armand Trépagnier. I own a French restaurant in Baton Rouge."

"A very good one, too," Mrs. LeBlanc informed Tessa. "It's acquired a national reputation."

"Take my card," Mr. Trépagnier urged Tessa. "Drop by for a drink or a bite to eat. We serve authentic Cajun cui-sine."

Tessa recognized the name of a famous restaurant, and she looked at Mr. Trépagnier with respect as she pocketed his card. "Thank you. I hope I can do that," she said, beaming, then the sign to fasten seat belts flashed on.

So much for snobbish and standoffish Cajuns, Tessa thought. As usual, brother Glenn had been about one hundred eighty degrees off target.

She never even felt the heat and humidity, and barely glimpsed the interior of the airport. As Tessa came hurrying up the stairs and into the arrival lounge, all she could see was the tall smiling man with golden hair and eyes like the Caribbean who stood waiting eagerly for her.

He still wore comfortable, casual-looking clothes, but his carefully creased and pressed khaki slacks and safari jacket had come straight out of a dry cleaner's bag. And his hair was noticeably shorter and neater. Trimmed in my honor? Tessa wondered.

She hurled herself straight into his arms—blindly, without a thought for anything or anyone else. There was just Ross, there was nothing but Ross. She could touch him again. Could hold him and inhale his characteristic aroma and kiss him over and over again, his cheek, his chin, wherever she could reach. She could feel his warm hair curling against her fingers, the brush of his crisp clothes against her bare skin, and the firm hard muscles in his back that her hands kept gripping. Ross was everything that was sunshine—her own treasure, golden and warm.

Then Tessa grew aware of him murmuring her name, of his lips gliding hungrily over her brow, her face, moving steadily closer to her mouth until he was kissing her again after what had seemed an absolute eternity. And it was one of those kisses that mixed tenderness and passion until Tessa didn't know where one ended and the other began, just that she loved both equally because she loved Ross.

"Mama, lookit that man and woman playin' kiss on the mouf," a child suddenly piped up, his voice loud and piercing.

"Don't stare at them, Douglas," his mother reprimanded and, reluctantly, Tessa and Ross pried themselves apart.

Lord, I become a whole different person when I'm with him, Tessa couldn't help thinking. Prim, correct and pre-

cise Dr. Fitzgerald had suddenly changed into an absolute
sex fiend.

She should have been appalled. But, strangely, she rather
liked that woman who acted like a sex fiend.

Laughing, even if a little chagrined, Tessa and Ross
headed into the terminal together. His arm stayed securely
about her waist, her fingers still gripped a handful of his
shirt. Each held on as if, otherwise, the other might somehow manage to slip away again. They hugged on the esca-
lator as they followed the signs that led downstairs to the
baggage carousel.

Tessa felt as if a long agony had suddenly ended in
triumph. Gratefully she savored the feeling, even though she
was fully aware of not knowing when or how the story might
end.

In the covered parking lot, one level below the airport
terminal, Ross teased Tessa about having moved south for
the summer. But he kept smiling as he loaded all of her
suitcases, carryalls and packages into the back of his Blazer.

"Wait a minute, Ross. I brought you a present," Tessa
said, tearing open a hatbox. "See!"

"Hmm, a straw hat. How very, uh, thoughtful of you,
Tessa."

"I know. You hate it and you'll probably never wear it.
But I still wanted you to have one," she said, a trifle de-
flated now that she was face-to-face with his open dismay.

"I love the idea—you thinking about me," Ross said
diplomatically. He kissed Tessa again and then dropped the
straw hat in the back of the Blazer, too.

It was a raffish-looking vehicle and Ross apologized for
its appearance. Dented bumpers and numerous rust spots
attested to the rough, rugged life to which he'd subjected it.
But the Blazer was also sparkling clean, Tessa noticed,
without a speck of mud or a single strand of weed or grass
detectable either inside or out. She very much doubted that

this was its usual condition, either. Touched that Ross had slicked up the vehicle for her, she clambered up into the passenger's seat. Ross joined her swiftly, sliding under the steering wheel, then he turned and reached for Tessa again.

"I can't believe how I've missed you," he muttered and Tessa, remembering that she'd felt the same about Ross, simply dissolved against him.

Their kisses were beginning to escalate toward a closed-circuit, adults-only entertainment when a yellow school bus bearing a load of kids pulled into the garage and stopped at a nearby parking slot.

"I see about forty little monsters," Tessa whispered in Ross's ear, then she eased away from him and started smoothing down the skirt in which she'd traveled, but which had now climbed, courtesy of Ross's impetuous hands, almost to her hips.

"I see 'em, too," he muttered. "What do you want to bet they all have voices like Douglas?" Then he pressed one last hungry kiss on Tessa's lips before reaching out to button her blouse and tuck in his own wildly rumpled shirt.

The children, a rowdy crew, were shepherded by two nuns who wore navy jumpers and plain white veils. One of them looked at Tessa and Ross suspiciously, as if they might be potential child molesters.

"Hello, Sisters," Ross called out genially, but Tessa, smoothing her tousled hair that Ross's long fingers had been playing with, couldn't help flushing a little. Now she'd been caught parking, necking and petting like a teenager. The nun nearest to Ross grinned at his greeting, but the one closest to Tessa threw her a grim look, obviously branding her a shameless hussy. Worst of all, Tessa didn't care. Tomorrow, of course, she'd revert to type, but today she felt giddy and lighthearted, young and carefree.

"Where are we going?" she asked Ross as he put the Blazer into reverse and backed out carefully to avoid brushing any kids.

"I'd like to take you straight to bed with me," Ross admitted with a grin. "But it's only fair to show you New Orleans."

"Yes, I do want to see it," Tessa agreed and then they were off.

They did all of the typical tourists-in-New-Orleans things. They bought rich pralines and ate them as they rode the one streetcar still in operation all the way out St. Charles Avenue to the end of the line at Audubon Park. Then they rode it back.

After that, they strolled down Canal Street while Ross described for Tessa how colorful and exciting it was in early spring when the vast Mardi Gras floats moved along the parade route and perfectly ordinary people indulged in carefree dancing.

Next, they turned into the Vieux Carré, better known as the French Quarter, and zigzagged up and down all the narrow, world-famous streets: Rampart, Burgundy and Bourbon. They admired the iron grillwork and the heavy wooden doors of the dwellings, even the weather-faded shutters on century-old apartment houses.

They passed clubs and taverns where Dixieland jazz drifted out of open doors, wending their way gradually toward the old French Market.

Along the way, Ross swept Tessa into Pat O'Brien's to drink a Hurricane in the cool secluded courtyard. An hour later they lunched in yet another colorful New Orleans courtyard, at the Court of the Two Sisters where Ross identified the lush tropical foliage for Tessa as banana palms, elephant ears and palmettos. Here she tasted her first crawfish *à l'étouffée* and rolled her eyes heavenward in sheer ecstasy.

Lunch consisted of so many courses that Tessa, even on her present eating binge, left feeling stuffed. But who cared? Anyway, they were getting a lot of exercise. They walked through the old city, visiting bookstores and antique shops, admiring southern fashions in exclusive boutiques and strolling along Pirate's Alley and around Jackson Square where they watched the sidewalk artists at work.

At last, when their feet were worn out from walking and they were beginning to feel burdened by Tessa's impulsive purchases of a few souvenirs for Glenn, Evie and Aunt Fay, she and Ross climbed the steps built up over the grassy levee to the walk that overlooked the Mississippi. A couple of paddle-wheelers were docked nearby and Tessa exclaimed over the old vessels as well as remarking on the oceangoing liners docked next to them.

Then Ross swung Tessa around so that she was looking down, and she blinked, unable to believe the phenomenon that confronted her.

To her astonishment the city's cathedral lay considerably lower than the Mississippi River with its numerous docked vessels. Obviously the picturesque levee was an absolute necessity, restraining a great tidal wave of water. "Why, the river is higher than the land!" she blurted.

"Yes," Ross agreed. "New Orleans, in fact, most of south Louisiana, depends on its system of levees to keep from being flooded. There's water everywhere, not just in Pontchartrain and the Mississippi, but in bayous, lakes, marshes and canals. There's a saying that Louisiana can't make up its mind whether it wants to be land or water." Ross stopped to draw a breath and his arm, still about Tessa's waist, gave her a gentle squeeze. "Now there's one last bit of New Orleans that can't be missed—café au lait and *beignets.*"

"What are *beignets*? Not more food, I hope," Tessa exclaimed. "Ross, I can't eat another bite."

Beignets proved to be light fluffy doughnuts, deep-fried, then liberally dusted with warm powdered sugar. They were the most delicious and addictive things in the world, Tessa discovered when she sat across from Ross at a small round table. She warily sampled just one, only to wind up eating three of the six that Ross had ordered. Their perfect accompaniment was café au lait, made from a strong dark coffee combined with hot milk.

"I never want to eat again," Tessa swore, trying futilely to dust off the powdered sugar that covered her lips, chin, hands and lap.

Ross leaned over their small table and dropped a light kiss on Tessa's mouth, a kiss made even sweeter by the powdered sugar dusting his lips.

"Let's go," he said softly.

The sun was just beginning its descent when Ross headed the Blazer out of New Orleans and turned west. Tessa realized with a thrill of anticipation that it would soon be nightfall and then she would be in Ross's arms again.

Nothing's really been settled, you know, Tessa's mind prodded her. He's still Reckless Ross, world-famous photographer, who'll lay his life on the line for a unique and dramatic photograph. And you're still a life-loving doctor who can't accept that.

But right now she was too weary from travel and exercise, too full of food, and too thrilled to be with Ross once again to worry about any of that . . . yet.

Chapter Eleven

I am not going to fight with Ross, Tessa vowed. Absolutely no fights, no matter how distressed I am. He's a grown man. He doesn't need me to nag him constantly. He'd resent that, and who could blame him? But, oh, how I wish he'd put on sunscreen, insect repellent and his new straw hat.

Determined to think of something else, Tessa looked all around at the strange new world of the bayou. Heaven knew there was plenty to see and she actually found it rather appealing.

Bald cypress trees were draped with lacy streamers of gray Spanish moss that swayed gently in the breeze. On the bank an immense live oak spread its venerable arms wide, and birds chattered amid its strands of trailing moss while squirrels scampered up and down its ghostly branches. Amazed, Tessa followed Ross's lead as they paddled into a scene straight out of a child's storybook or an adult's fantasy world. Everything here was exotic, languid, almost unreal. Perhaps even surreal.

The labyrinthine bayous that ran this way and that fairly teemed with life—plants, fish, insects and long-legged water birds. There were also furred animals that scampered away quickly as the humans drew nearer, invading the wild, natural world.

"Look, Tessa!" As he had many times already, Ross pointed out a special sight. This time it was blue geese crowded onto a sandspit. Alongside them, a sleepy alligator trod water. Alarmed by Ross's cry, the geese flew away with a great fluttering of wings. Tessa watched the sedentary alligator with its deceptively benign grin, which, to her untrained eye, resembled a newly fallen log floating downstream in the bayou's dark, brackish water.

"The dawn of creation looked like this, didn't it, Ross?" Tessa heard herself saying in a strangely hushed and awed voice. No wonder the Atchafalaya Swamp had attracted wildlife specialists and environmental biologists from all over the world. It was an absolute wonder.

"Sure did, sweetheart. The first time I ever saw this place and all the birds and animals here, I knew I'd have to live nearby," Ross called back over his shoulder. Then surprise filled his eyes. "Why, you actually *like* this primeval stew."

"I'm still collecting first impressions," Tessa said prudently and tried not to notice just how damp with sweat Ross's broad shoulders were becoming. He was dressed as she was, in shorts and a light shirt, but where she wore sandals, his feet and legs were encased in knee-high rubber waders, and they were bound to be hot.

Ross laughed again at Tessa's noncommittal answer and his joyous noise sent more birds flying up off the limb of a nearby water bush.

"I am kind of amazed," Tessa confessed and watched a drop of perspiration trail down Ross's lean bronzed arm.

"Primeval stew" was a very good description of their surroundings, she thought as she spied more reptilian life than she'd ever imagined existing. Frogs leaped agilely out of the way of their paddles and lizards, their color changing adroitly according to the foliage nearby, scooted up and down leaves and branches. Turtles sunned on sandbars and half-submerged trunks of trees. Sleepy alligators sank and disappeared below the waterline as the boat drew nearer, apparently not wanting to wage a territorial war. A fat brown cottonmouth slithered past, vanishing completely in a floating garden of lavender water hyacinths.

In this steaming torpid world where sunshine bounced off billions of leaves and lush strands of grass, the light created was an eerie kind of yellowish-green haze. Yes, from just such light and relentless heat life must have been formed at the beginnings of time. The process of creation still teemed all around them. Tessa could almost feel the animals and insects, birds and reptiles mating and multiplying feverishly. The very air thrummed with their passionate voices and the endless chorus of whistles, chirps and croaks grew steadily louder the deeper and farther she and Ross went into the mysterious and almost impenetrable swampland.

Tessa's own body gave a sudden involuntary throb, as if it recognized and remembered the rhythm, the sighs and cries. Her gaze fastened again on Ross's back and shoulders. Tessa could still feel those strong muscles moving rhythmically under her hands, even quivering at the last as he'd claimed her as his own. His lovemaking had been so thrilling that she had been lost to everything except him and the excitement of her own feelings, her own response to such blatant, sexy maleness.

Last night they had shared a dreamy sort of lovemaking. As soon as they'd reached Ross's plain, yet scrupulously clean motel cabin, he had urged Tessa to take her shower while he struggled in unaided with all of her bags, cases and recent purchases. Tessa had emerged wet, weary and yawning.

The sound of his shower had lulled her to sleep, her eyelids too heavy to stay open.

"Tessa?"

She had come half awake to Ross's soft voice, a voice gentle and amused by her drowsiness. With a great effort Tessa had made her hands move, finding the welcome nakedness of his lean hard body. Then she and Ross had simply melted together and no sooner had their tender, languid movements ended when Tessa had tumbled headlong into a deep sound sleep.

But early this morning it had all happened quite differently. Tessa had wakened gradually to find herself curled up in a ball like a cat with Ross's long, strong frame wrapped around her protectively. Even his hands rested on top of hers. Suddenly Tessa had felt sheer sensuous delight in lying in his arms, sharing his bed, being warmed and protected by his body all through the dark hours of the night. She had turned, studying his peacefully sleeping face and marveling anew at the straightness of his nose and the thickness of his golden eyelashes. To her, Ross seemed the handsomest man who had ever walked the earth. Deliberately Tessa had pressed her lips to his, kissing him awake, until Ross's hands began gliding gently up and down, caressing her body with, apparently, the same sort of wonder that she'd felt for him.

Suddenly, too, Tessa had been seized by a raw physical hunger, a need to totally belong to this glorious male creature. In his arms, lying beneath his hands, she had felt as ferocious and wild as any swamp creature—for this, surely, was their very own mating season.

So Tessa had sought Ross more aggressively than ever before. She had urged him on, both with her whispers and the movements of her hands and body, caressing him until he gasped. Then he had joined them in just the way she'd wanted, his hard deep thrusts making her tremble, cry out, even beg, until she was twisting in his arms, coming half off the bed in her eagerness to meet his body with her own, and still begging for more, more, more....

Rapture had shaken them simultaneously. Exhausted and awed they'd rested in each other's arms, exchanging gentle grateful kisses until the faint rays of dawn began edging the darkness from the room. Then their passion built once again—still ferocious and not quite tamed. But in the moments that followed passion a matching closeness was born, and Tessa sensed the joy of being one with Ross and utterly at peace.

Now, as she gazed around at the wildness of this land that was more than half water, she thought its subtly emanating vibration of life must have affected her as well. She still wanted Ross so, even though her immediate physical need for him was sated. Now, she simply wanted to be close to him and follow him wherever he went. She wanted to be held against his heart and rest for hours in his arms. It would probably take a lot of nights and an astonishing amount of lovemaking and cuddling before her persistent desire for this golden-haired man who'd so completely stolen her heart slackened.

Once again Tessa felt the same kind of protectiveness toward Ross that she'd felt when he had been desperately ill and she had cared for him—the same sort of protectiveness that he had unconsciously manifested last night by curling himself around her. She felt an overwhelming need to watch out for him and—yes, to watch over him, too, keeping him safe from dangers both seen and unseen.

Now the beautiful golden hair that curled down his neck was turning wet, too. Oh, the hell with it, Tessa thought. I have to say something to him or explode.

"Ross," she called, pulling in her paddle.

"Yes, sweetheart?" The face he turned back to Tessa was flushed both from heat and perspiration.

Just as she'd feared. "Please stop a minute and take off your shirt," Tessa coaxed. "It's also time to put on that straw hat I brought you."

She didn't actually see Ross crinkle his nose with disdain, but she knew he wanted to. "Tessa darling, I'm quite all right," he said with elaborate patience. "Anyway, we're almost there. The island's just around the bend."

Tessa glanced ahead, wondering if the scurrying animals whose domain she and Ross had dared invade were resentful of them. She couldn't begin to guess exactly where "the bend" might be, but the realization that she was now hopelessly and completely lost among all the twisting and meandering bayous was worse.

"Ross, I mean it," Tessa said, her voice quite steady, even implacable. "I want you to stop now and rest for several minutes. Take off your shirt to get more air circulation and I'll sponge your back before I rub on sunscreen. Kick off those waders, too. And you ought to take a big drink of water—"

"Nag, nag, nag," he complained, his tone humorous, if slightly barbed. "If you really want to help me quit playing doctor and learn to be a better oarsman—"

"You mean an oars*woman*, of course."

"Hey, how about paddle person?" he suggested. "Look, sweetheart, we're going to be there in a twinkle. Really."

"I know your 'twinkles' and I'm not buying them. I really want you to stop, Ross," Tessa commanded, feeling her lips quivering just a trifle. "Please!"

He obeyed with an audible sigh, swinging his long legs and then the rest of his body around on the seat to confront her. Tessa couldn't miss the grim set of his mouth.

"You know, I wouldn't even consider stopping if I were here all by myself, the way I usually am," he asserted.

Tessa heard the warning that Ross hadn't voiced: you're not here to protect me all the time.

She decided to answer his unspoken phrase. "Ross, I know I can't control what you do when you're out here all alone," she said placatingly. "But I happen to have a strong sense of self-preservation, even if you don't."

"Meaning?" His eyes were sparkling with amusement again. He tugged his white sleeveless shirt over his head and dropped it on the seat beside him.

Tessa decided to go ahead and hit him with the truth— even hit him hard. "Ross, if you keeled over right here and now, if you had another sunstroke and died, why I'd certainly die, too. I'm hopelessly lost in these bayous. Have you thought about that? About how I could never find my way out of this swamp?"

His busy hands stilled. Abruptly his eyes deepened, turning a darker blue. "No, I really hadn't thought about that, Tessa," Ross had the grace to admit.

"I didn't think you had," she allowed. "Okay, if you'll just present me again with your big beautiful back—" Tessa began uncorking the bottle of sunscreen she'd brought.

"Wait a minute." Ross looked at her steadily. "When you first made this pitch to me in Arizona, I just thought you were trying to scare some sense into me."

"You know, I had the distinct feeling I wasn't really getting through to you," Tessa said wryly.

"But you're really dead serious about this, right? I'm more likely to have a sunstroke than other people?"

"Yes." Tessa returned Ross's level look with one that matched it. "Having had one stroke, your chance of another has increased markedly. Overall, your risk factor is still low, of course—especially as long as you have a really superb doctor sharing the boat with you."

"Okay. But say I up and bought the farm right now, or, I guess it's more accurate to say that if I went belly-up into the swamp muck—"

"Oh, God, Ross, don't even talk like that," Tessa blurted, shivering with superstitious apprehension. "I can't stand for you to be morbid."

"I'm not being morbid. I'm trying to be practical and realistic for a change," he insisted. But, to Tessa's relief, his lips were twitching wickedly once more. "Anyway, don't do anything formal. Just kick me out of the boat and sink me over there by the palmetto—"

"Ross," Tessa wailed and her hands flew up to her stricken face.

"What I'm trying to say, sweetheart, is that I've been a selfish swine and I'm sorry."

"No, you're not," Tessa cried vehemently. "A swine, I mean."

"Yes, I am, if I've endangered your life in any way. My God, are those tears?" Ross asked, startled. "Look, Tessa, don't worry. You won't be stranded here all alone, I swear. I'll drink something and take a salt pill and rest for a few minutes. Hell, if you insist, I'll even put on the damned straw hat."

Tessa managed to blink back her tears, but now her nose had started to run so she groped around futilely for a tissue among the many items piled in the boat. "I'm not really worried about being stranded out here all alone," she mumbled. "In fact, if anything happened to you I think I'd almost rather be."

"Why, Tessa," Ross exclaimed, his voice softer than she had ever heard it.

"Look, sweetheart, you're putting me on, aren't you?" he pressed.

One reason she loved him so much, Tessa thought, was his absolute lack of conceit. Women tripped all over their feet just trying to get a look from Ross Stanton. Tessa had watched it happen at breakfast that very morning, when two lovely waitresses had hovered over Ross's coffee cup like it was the Holy Grail and refilled it constantly just to be the recipient of his blinding smile.

"No, I wasn't putting you on," Tessa said and now she had to resort to the childish technique of rubbing her nose on her shirtsleeve.

"You mean, you really do care that much?" Ross looked as amazed as he was dubious.

"Well, I care at least a little," Tessa allowed inadequately, rubbing her nose again.

Ross gave a great whoop of delighted laughter and suddenly lunged for her.

"Are you crazy?" Tessa screeched, moving back out of his reach as rapidly as she dared. "You're going to upset this boat and dump us in the bayou! Anyway, I don't want you to touch me right now, not with my nose running—"

"I don't care about getting dumped in the bayou and I don't care if your nose runs," he said, even as he delved into his shirt pocket and came up with a clean handkerchief that he passed to Tessa. "All I care about right now is that you care—"

Then Ross stopped, electrified by a sudden sound. All Tessa heard was the now-familiar flap and flutter of wings, followed by a strange bird cry directly overhead. It sounded like, "Trent, trent."

"Oh, no," Ross yelped. "Hellfire and damnation! Oh, my God, I can't believe this."

The sudden change in his mood, the howl of anguished disbelief followed by a blast of vehement oaths left Tessa nonplussed. One minute he'd been trying to hug her, the next he'd glanced up and undergone the rapid mood change of a madman. Now, his face positively purple with fury, Ross was standing straight up in the boat and it was rocking dangerously as he waved a fist at the sky and continued to curse steadily, using blistering language.

"What on earth?" Tessa choked out, gripping the sides of the aluminum boat with both hands.

Ross sank back down heavily. "I just missed grabbing a shot of the ivory-billed woodpecker," he sighed in exasperation. "Again. That was it flying overhead, making its little mocking cry. Yeah, I just screwed up and missed getting a shot of the stupid bird *again*!"

Tessa had to admit that Ross's favorite island looked enchanting. At an abrupt bend in the bayou they came to the wider, deeper Atchafalaya River and in its midst stood an island that was higher than the river's banks. Snowy egrets waded in the shallows on long spindly legs and their white forms were reflected in the still, black water.

As they paddled closer to the island, Tessa could see that it was dominated by tall, spreading live oaks that cast huge shadows. Beneath the trees, along the sandy shore, rose a dense stand of bamboo, the straight stalks giving the terrain a tropical Asian atmosphere.

No sooner had they splashed to shore, dragging their boat onto the land, when large yellow butterflies fluttered low over the water. Disturbed by Tessa and Ross's presence, they rose as one, a cloud rapidly drifting out of sight. In their place came a pair of large dragonflies. One alighted upon the boat as soon as it was beached.

A delightful breeze dispersed the usual mosquitoes, and the long shadows cast by the oak trees made the island feel ten degrees cooler than the swamp. Ross set their picnic paraphernalia under the trees, draped his binoculars around his neck where his ever-present camera already dangled and then held out a welcoming hand to Tessa. "Come see my version of paradise," he invited her.

She clung to his large warm hand while they explored the island. It seemed big to Tessa, although certain areas were clearly impenetrable, due to natural barriers of bamboo and buttonbush.

The middle of the island contained a small cypress-ringed pond and Ross led Tessa toward it. Lonely-looking black crows sat quietly upon dead stumps at the edge of the water and birds fluttered low. The water itself was sparkling and bluish-green. Almost the same color as Ross's eyes, Tessa thought.

"There's an old legend that says pirate gold is buried on this island somewhere," Ross told her.

"Really? Have you ever hunted for it?" Tessa asked him curiously.

"Not yet. I probably will one day when I'm an old man with a limited income. But, right now, while my photographs still pay off, I'm sticking to what I do best. Anyway, I don't come to this island to work. I come to rest," he said.

Tessa raised a skeptical eyebrow and pointed at the camera and binoculars around his neck.

"Oh, these are just for the ivory-billed woodpecker—if the stupid bird ever shows itself again."

"How long have you been hunting it?" Tessa asked.

"Three years," Ross said grimly, following a faint path down to the edge of the placid pond. "It's led me a merry chase, too."

"Three years!" Tessa exclaimed and started to laugh. "You've been hunting a supposedly extinct bird for three whole years!"

"Well, hell, it's a very shy bird," he protested. "Also, mankind has nearly killed it off completely by cutting down all the virgin timber it requires. Now the birds' forest has been replaced with soybean fields. So no wonder the woodpecker isn't too fond of people."

"Why does the bird need virgin timber?" Tessa asked, thinking it was the first time she'd ever found herself concerned about any bird's habitat.

"Because in a natural forest, there are always plenty of old and dying trees," Ross explained, "and this particular bird pecks away at them to get out wood-boring beetles that are only found in old trees. That's how it survives and the way it feeds its young."

"Oh." Tessa pondered for a moment. "It's really quite a complex natural chain, isn't it?"

"You bet. Destroy the forest, you destroy all the beetles and the ivory-billed woodpecker dies off with them. Naturalists thought for several years that the ivory-billed was extinct. Articles were written about its tragic loss. Then some naturalists claimed to have spotted a pair in a rain forest in Puerto Rico, but they don't have pictures to prove it. That happened about the same time my friend Émile saw ours."

"But you're still not sure?" Tessa persisted.

"I'm sure. It's not extinct, it just wants the whole world to think so—and it wants Ross Stanton to be buffaloed! Oh, go ahead and laugh," he said resignedly to Tessa. "Everybody else does. Here I am, a highly paid wildlife photographer and I'm always outwitted by one stupid bird. I'm beginning to think it's a jinx.''

Tessa bent over double laughing. "How about an albatross?" she gasped.

"I'll find that ivory-billed woodpecker one day," Ross vowed. "Just wait and see. And then I may really shoot it, with a gun, I mean. God knows I want to!"

"No, you don't. You want to photograph it for posterity, but you can't—" Tessa stopped, laughing again.

"Hey, anytime you want to pull yourself together, we can see the rest of the island."

Tessa managed to control her mirth and they continued walking along the water's edge where Ross pointed out an alligator turtle, named for the prehistoric-looking ridges on its back. A short distance from the turtle he spied what he called a South American friend blundering around in a thicket. It proved to be a gray nine-banded armadillo, the first one Tessa had ever seen.

"You're really in luck," Ross enthused. "Most first-timers don't see such a variety of animals, especially one like an armadillo. They're usually nocturnal prowlers."

"Is it, uh, harmless?" Tessa inquired, taking a strategic backward step that placed Ross safely between herself and the rooting, snuffling creature.

"Sure is, sweetheart. Unless you annoy him by trying to pick him up or turn him on his back. He's got some mighty powerful paws that he uses for digging, so you could get scratched," Ross informed her.

"I don't intend to pick him up," Tessa assured Ross.

"Actually there aren't many dangerous animals in the Atchafalaya. Oh, the occasional bobcat might scare a novice—"

"Bobcat!" Tessa cried.

"—but they'll just run away. They're loners. And all that a swamp bear ever really wants—"

"Swamp bear?" Tessa interrupted in deepening horror.

"A black bear, actually, and he's only interested in eating. His preferred diet is anthills, honeycombs and blackberries. Catfish, too, if he can catch them. I'm much too big for a swamp bear to fool with, but of course, one might think that you're a tasty little tidbit."

By then, Tessa had flung herself into Ross's arms, colliding a trifle painfully with his camera and binoculars. Then, as he dipped his golden head down to kiss her and his arms closed around her, she realized that it wasn't by accident that she'd landed here.

"Ross Stanton, you planned this very maneuver," Tessa cried accusingly.

"Who, me?" he said, feigning innocence. But the truth was revealed by the mischievous glint in his eyes and the softness of his half-parted lips that covered hers so readily.

When the sun reached its zenith, Tessa and Ross retreated beneath the trees to eat the picnic lunch that Mrs. Couvillion had packed for them.

Tessa had met Ross's landlady earlier that morning and had concealed a knowing grin both at Mrs. Couvillion's appearance and her overpowering curiosity. Tessa didn't believe for one moment that the dark-haired Cajun woman was usually fully dressed, with makeup and an elaborate coiffure, at six-thirty in the morning. Especially since Mrs. Couvillion's husband was still unshaven, yawning and wearing his undershirt as he sat sipping a cup of thick black coffee.

While Mrs. Couvillion looked Tessa over carefully Ross had explained that they'd grabbed a quick breakfast at the local truck stop. To Tessa the Cajun landlady had been pleasant, although she was clearly still reserving judgment where this Yankee lady doctor was concerned.

But there was no mistaking the look that fifty-five-year-old Mrs. Couvillion trained on Ross. She adored him, just as most women did, but she was a realist. She was also a long-married woman, fond of her husband and used to his company. Still, she would carefully inspect any woman that Ross invited to St. Clément, and should his lady fail Mrs. Couvillion's exacting standards, woe betide her!

Now, Ross opened the picnic cooler eagerly. They were seated on a fallen log whose bark scratched lightly at the backs of Tessa's bare legs. Her navy shorts and bright yellow shirt were growing progressively dirtier as the day wore on, but for once she didn't care. Ross had pulled his white shirt back on to deflect the sun's rays, but had kicked off the hot-looking waders.

"Po' boys!" Ross exclaimed with delight, drawing out long, foil-wrapped packages.

"What are they?" Tessa said, feeling her stomach rumble hungrily.

"A Louisiana sandwich. Just try it," Ross urged, peeling back the foil to show off crusty French bread. Then he pressed the whole package into Tessa's hands. "Iced tea?"

"Please," she said and found a full quart jar deposited at her feet. Another had been packed for Ross and both held clear sun tea delightfully flavored with lemon and fresh mint. Gratefully Tessa took one long refreshing gulp.

Then she bit down on her sandwich and found the French bread the most delicious she'd ever tasted. But packed within it, half-smothered with mayonnaise, lettuce and tomatoes, lay myriad crawfish, fried golden brown. Their smell was so appealing that Tessa's mouth fairly watered. Still, she wondered if they dared eat the seafood and glanced worriedly over at Ross.

He was munching heartily on his own sandwich, obviously unconcerned. Reluctantly Tessa decided to go ahead and broach the subject. "Ross?" she began hesitantly.

He raised his eyebrows, his mouth too full to speak.

"Ross, seafood and mayonnaise both spoil awfully quickly. Do you really think it's, uh, safe for us to eat these? I know I may sound fussy, but food poisoning really isn't a bit of fun."

Why do I sound so apologetic? Tessa thought as she watched Ross stare at her in amazement. The weather here is hotter than Hades and the concern I have just voiced is reasonable. A worse thought suddenly occurred to her. What if Ross's casual nonchalance was catching? Maybe if she stayed around him very long, she'd get to where she did crazy things, too, like popping food into her mouth without a thought for when and how it was prepared.

Ross swallowed his bite of sandwich, grinned at Tessa ruefully and then reached for her hand which he guided to the top of the sturdy red hamper. "Sweet worrywart, this is called a cooler because it keeps food chilled for long periods of time," he said gently.

Tessa continued to fret. "Yes, but we don't know exactly when Mrs. Couvillion cooked these crawfish. Or when they were caught."

"Caught and cooked this morning, definitely," Ross said, his voice starting to sound a little flat. "Claude Couvillion checks his traps around six every morning."

"But Ross—" Tessa spoke up spiritedly, refusing to let herself be intimidated.

"Look, Tessa, the Cajuns have survived in southern Louisiana for more than two hundred years and they haven't done it by polishing themselves off with food poisoning. Go ahead and live dangerously for once. Take a taste!" His tone was one of carefully controlled patience.

Tessa took a breath, then bit down through the crunchy bread, tasting a crawfish so delectable that she had to silently admit that Ross must be right. This particular shellfish had been alive and swimming a very short time ago. Reassured, she began to eat hungrily, dipping into the slaw and potato salad that was included and eyeing the chocolate-iced brownies. Surely food had never tasted quite so good.

She glanced up to see Ross watching her. A quizzical little half smile played on those perfectly molded lips of his. "Okay?" he asked.

Tessa nodded since her own mouth was full now.

"Anyway, I'm sure you have a quick cure for food poisoning in that big ominous-looking bag you insist on toting everywhere. What's in it, anyway, besides sunscreen and insect repellent? What are those two hundred different pills for?"

"You'll just laugh," Tessa said, licking her fingers lest a single delicious crumb escape her.

"Probably. You laughed at me over the ivory-billed woodpecker. Turnabout's fair play." Ross's face wore a whimsical expression. "Seriously, what do you have in there?"

"Tablets to purify drinking water. A tourniquet, bandages and a snakebite kit. There's an oral drug to administer if either of us start having malaria symptoms—"

"Malaria!" Ross exclaimed in alarm.

"Well, you're the one who told me all about the mosquitoes and how they'd be humming up a storm at dusk. I'm just carrying a standard tropical medicine kit," Tessa finished.

She read outright dismay in Ross's eyes and in the slow gradual shake of his head. "You know, every time I start, well, letting down my guard around you, Tessa, I find out something like this. Then I get reminded all over again that you and I really are awfully unalike. For instance, where were you twenty years ago?"

"Me? In a convent school in Baltimore. Where were you?"

"Naked in a redwood hot tub at a California commune. Seriously. Stan and Bambi lived there for a while. You see, all the time you were learning to truss everything up and tuck it in tight, I was learning to let it all hang out. No wonder we're so different."

The rest of Tessa's appetite faded. She looked away from Ross's eyes and began brushing crumbs from her hands. "I think incompatible sums it up neatly, Ross."

He shook his head slowly, sadly. "I shouldn't have brought you to Louisiana, Tessa. I knew we were too different—knew you'd learn to hate this place. I don't know what possessed me—" Abruptly he stopped. "Yes, I do. I felt so miserable without you I figured being with you again was worth putting up with your thousand-and-one anxieties."

"Anxieties!" Tessa began heatedly.

"I apologize. Maybe I should say your numerous professional concerns." His eyes met hers steadily now, looking green and ominous. "Well, at least we're not sexually incompatible. Last night, this morning, the way I feel right now just looking at you . . ."

"I'd like to set you straight on another point, Ross. I don't hate it here," Tessa said. She heard her voice trembling as her heart, which suddenly felt jeopardized, raced away madly. For a moment she'd thought Ross was about to end it all, to renounce her forever and send her back home. "I really don't know why I don't because I generally do dislike the great outdoors. Maybe it's because I've never been exposed to nature very much. Maybe I'm just a city dweller at heart. You were honest with me and I want to be equally honest. So, frankly, I'm as surprised as you that this swamp kind of appeals to me. I think it's dangerous, but it's also grand and glorious, too, with a wild primitive beauty. It . . . this may sound crazy, but it sort of calls to me—"

The rest of her sentence got lost as Tessa found herself hauled up abruptly and crushed against Ross's chest. This time his binoculars bumped her temple.

"You're going to knock me unconscious if you don't take those things off," she complained, but already she had wrapped her arms tightly around his strong hard waist.

"Yes, ma'am." Ross pulled the straps over his head and then he folded Tessa close.

His broad chest smelled of the sun. The golden hairs in the open V of his shirt were soft and silky. Instinctively Tessa burrowed her face into that warm shield.

"Ross, what's going to happen to us?" she whispered.

"I don't know, Tessa." He sounded just as baffled as she felt. "But at least we've got a couple of weeks together. Let's make the most of them."

Because they may be all we'll ever have. Ross hadn't really said that, but Tessa heard its echo, anyway. "Good idea," she agreed, her voice muffled against his chest. She felt him rub his chin on the crown of her head before he dropped a passionate kiss there.

"Tessa, do you know what I want right now?" Ross asked and then his lips trailed downward to kiss her ear before beginning a blazing path toward her throat. His body, tightening with intent, moved against hers.

"I think I have a pretty good idea," she replied, hugging him even closer.

"Yes, we definitely are compatible in a few special ways," Ross murmured against Tessa's lips. Then his own ground against hers and together they sank into the soft, sun-warmed grass.

Chapter Twelve

It was a perfect fortnight, but it sped past much too quickly. Tessa and Ross had their differences, but they certainly agreed on that.

During the magic thirteen days that followed their only disagreements were light and trivial. It was as though, having stated their respective positions that day in the swamp, they resolved their differences by not resolving them. Silently they had each determined that neither would expect more from the other than what was already there. After that, they simply relaxed and had fun.

During the early mornings, the coolest time of the day, they usually went deep into the swamp. Tessa grew to anticipate the peace and solitude she found there. She even grew accustomed to all the animal sights and sounds and actually relished being outside beneath a canopy of mossy trees, scanning with binoculars to help Ross in his search for the elusive ivory-billed woodpecker.

She learned quite a lot of other things, too—things that once she wouldn't have given a hang about, but which seemed fascinating when Ross related them. For instance, the extensive growth that looked, to a casual glance, like green pond scum was actually duckweed, a very tiny living plant. That the diamondback water snake wasn't really poisonous, despite its resemblance to more vicious and deadly vipers. And that more exotic and entrancing birds lived deep in these wetlands than she had ever dreamed existed on earth. The yellow-crowned night heron was an ordinary, even familiar one here, but the male painted bunting was extremely rare, as well as being one of America's most beautiful birds with its bright plumage.

The wild orange bobcat, when Tessa finally saw one, merely looked like an overgrown house cat. Spying them, he slunk away quickly. An even rarer black swamp bear who had his snout caught in a swarming beehive when Tessa and Ross happened on him was a comical sight. As the bees began to sting him, he danced up and down in a torment he'd brought on himself. The sight was so funny that Tessa and Ross both laughed until they nearly fell out of their boat and Ross's camera began to click.

Tessa learned further that Ross Stanton was regarded as one of the kindest, friendliest men in the Atchafalaya Basin, judging by all the friends he had. Trappers, alligator hunters, fishermen and elderly ''widow women'' living in quaint houses built on stilts all seemed to know Ross and he knew all of them by name, too, Cajuns, French-speaking blacks, Choctaw or Houma Indians and Creoles.

But they didn't spend all their time in the swamp. There was also a number of beautiful and famous places in the nearby area and Ross made sure that Tessa didn't miss a one. They toured the famous jungle gardens and bird sanctuary on Avery Island. They drove around a genuine salt mine, looked at a sugar processing mill and spent an hour at the only Tabasco sauce factory in the world, without which, Ross told Tessa solemnly, all the Bloody Marys in bars from Mongolia to Argentina would cease to exist.

Ross also kept Tessa busy sampling the famous local cuisine. She sighed with delight over gumbo, jambalaya and bisques. She went into raptures over turtle soup, rich with sherry, and oysters served à la Rockefeller. She steadfastly ignored the alarming caloric contents of pecan pie, rich rice and bread puddings, soufflés, sponge cakes and meringues, and she quickly learned to adore both the smell and taste of Louisiana's dark-roast coffees, either with or without chicory.

On Saturday night Ross took her to a *fais dodo* which, Tessa soon discovered, was a local St. Clément dance featuring Cajun music. After Tessa and Ross had danced a couple of numbers together, Tessa was quickly in demand. Soon she found herself partnered with Émile Arceneaux, then with a whole slew of Mrs. Couvillion's nephews and cousins.

"Get me out of here," Tessa finally whispered to Ross and saw from his smile that he was ready to leave, too.

And every night she slept in Ross's arms.

"'ey, *chérie,* you stayin' with Ross a while longer?"

"I don't know, Mrs. Couvillion," Tessa admitted. "We really haven't discussed it."

An hour earlier Ross had taken his Blazer into town to buy gas and have the oil changed. Tessa, feeling lazy, had just now emerged from his cabin and encountered Mrs. Couvillion. As the landlady stared at the younger woman in surprise, Tessa went on more slowly, groping for words to explain her feelings. "You see, I came down here so precipitously that we've just been taking things day by day."

"I don' understan' that 'precipitous,'" Mrs. Couvillion said flatly. "But I understan' men and women. You better marry Ross quick and make him settle down before he hurts himself real bad taking his pitchers, mebbe even dies."

"And just how do I make a grown man do anything?" Tessa mused aloud. "Even assuming I wanted to?"

"Cry. Scream and carry on. T'row somethin' at him. T'reaten to shoot yourself. Mebbe even shoot at him!" Mrs. Couvillion spoke carefully, but from the expression in her eyes Tessa could tell she thought she was dealing with an absolute idiot. Why, imagine Tessa not even knowing that! Didn't Yankee women learn any wiles with which to control men?

"Oh," said Tessa noncommittally.

"Then tell him he's got you too upset to climb in the bedstead wi' him and have fun shakin' the sheets. You've got a sweet man really loves you, that works eve'y time," Mrs. Couvillion advised.

I do have a sweet man, Tessa thought with a sigh. And he acts like he's as much in love with me as I am with him. So the hell of it is Mrs. Couvillion's probably right. Her way just might work, at least for a while. But what happens when Ross wakes up from love's sweet dream and goes back to making his own decisions and doing what, as a mature man, *he* really wants to do?

Just at that moment Ross's Blazer whizzed into the parking area. He slammed on the brakes, stuck his camera out the window and grabbed a shot of Tessa and Mrs. Couvillion. Then he grinned roguishly and saluted them with a piece of red and white stick candy that protruded from the corner of his mouth.

Scratch "mature," Tessa thought, repressing a sigh as she walked over to the vehicle. Unfortunately for the state of her emotions, Ross also looked absolutely adorable.

He removed the candy stick from his mouth and regarded it fondly. "Old-fashioned peppermint," he announced. "Sometimes this soft kind is hard to find. So I bought a whole gallon jar of it. Want some, Tessa? Mrs. Couvillion?"

The women shook their heads simultaneously. "Too early in the day," Tessa murmured.

"I gotta watch ma figure," said Mrs. Couvillion, then turned quickly. "Hear ma phone ringin' in the office."

Ross regarded her fondly. "Plenty to watch," he remarked to Tessa. "Her figure, that is. Well, sweetheart, what shall we do today?"

"What are you suggesting?" Tessa asked, smiling up at him.

"You want to go fishing?" he asked, climbing out of his Blazer. "Oh, I can see you're not too keen on that. It's just as well. I always feel so sorry for the poor fish that I throw them all back. How about a sight-seeing trip instead? There's a very attractive convent nearby—"

"No offense, but I've already seen plenty of convents," Tessa interrupted and couldn't resist snuggling up under his arm.

"That's okay. I always make the nuns kinda nervous, for some reason. I don't think they're too used to male hormones." Ross bent down and whispered another invitation in her ear. "Want to go back to bed with me?"

That's not a bad idea, Tessa found herself thinking even as she felt her cheeks turn warm. But, goodness, what sort of shameless wanton is he turning me into?

"Tessa, *chérie*!" Mrs. Couvillion's voice stopped Ross as he started to kiss Tessa. "Phone call!"

It was Dr. Corman, who said he had exciting news that he needed to discuss with Tessa immediately. An unusual career opportunity had just been offered to them. Could Tessa please fly back to Washington today?

"Today?" she asked in dismay, then covered the receiver and turned to Ross. "I think I've got a new job at last. But Dr. Corman wants me to come right back. What do you think?"

Ross hesitated for only a second. "It's your career. Do what you think best, Tessa."

"I have to earn a living. I suppose I should go..." Her voice trailed off uncertainly.

"I'll drive you to the airport," Ross said. Both his face and voice were inscrutable.

"Ow-w-w!" Ross howled as Mrs. Couvillion dashed a stream of homemade antiseptic over his cut and bleeding hand.

"Stop yellin', *cher,*" his landlady ordered him, her voice not entirely sympathetic. "You tryin' to kill yourself again?"

"No," Ross said through gritted teeth. "I was trying to change a damned flat tire. Don't pour any—ow-w-w!"

Mrs. Couvillion ignored him heartlessly, and Ross began to curse silently yet steadily. He cursed life, he cursed fate. He especially cursed women, reserving a particular vengeance for all women doctors. Meanwhile his hand felt like it was going up in flames and Mrs. Couvillion acted as if he had deserved the injury. He knew she would say something to him about Tessa in a minute. Holding one's tongue was not exactly a well-known Cajun virtue.

"What's that stuff you're using?" Ross demanded, peering down into the unmarked bottle she held. It looked as dark as stagnant swamp water and reminded him of nothing so much as slime and fungus. The noxious smell, however, absolutely defied description. The nearest Ross

could come was a cross between swamp gas, decaying car-
rion and goat.

"*Ma grand-mère*'s own recipe," Mrs. Couvillion said
with satisfaction.

At least Ross didn't doubt the antiseptic's potency. But as
he looked at his hand, now twitching helplessly, he wondered if those paralyzed fingers would ever move again.

Tessa had flown away less than four hours ago and already his whole world had turned to ashes. "Don't go,"
Ross had suddenly heard himself blurting as Tessa began
walking toward the waiting plane. She'd turned back, her
face happily startled yet expectant.

"What do you mean by that, Ross?" she'd asked gently.

He'd shaken his head. "I don't know," he'd admitted and
heard that strange gruff note in his voice again.

Tessa's blue eyes were still very wide, but as Ross had
watched, a certain wariness, maybe even a certain sadness
crept into them. "Then I think I'd better go," she'd said
flatly—and off she'd flown.

"Why didn't you stop her from goin'?" Mrs. Couvillion
suddenly demanded.

"How could I?" Ross muttered, irritated that his
thoughts were so transparent. "You saw what happened.
That joker she used to work for gives her a call and she
drops me like a hot potato!"

"I didn't hear you askin' for her to stay," Mrs. Couvillion accused.

"No, I didn't!" Ross lied. "Because if you want to know
the truth, I was getting plenty sick of her hanging around."

"Yeah. I noticed."

"It's better that she's gone. With us, it's useless, anyway.
There's nothing left to do now except either break up or—
or—" Ross stopped just in time, biting the inside of his
cheek.

"Marry her, *cher*. Live here in Louisiana wit' your friends. Eat good food, dance to th' fiddle, make love and have beautiful babies," Mrs. Couvillion pressed on. "You'll be happy and live forever."

"Tessa would laugh in my face if I proposed. She'd laugh until her sides caved in. What in the hell could she do here—nag me to death? Why, she's a bright, ambitious lady—"

"You did'n' ask her to marry, did you?"

"Hell, no!" It felt good to Ross to explode in wrath. "And I'm not about to, either. We wouldn't last a month, then we'd be raking over each other's bones in divorce court—"

"Go after her, *cher*," Mrs. Couvillion advised, winding a bandage around Ross's hands.

"I don't want to marry Tessa and I wouldn't go after that contrary wench if she were the last woman on the face of the earth!" Ross roared. Then he turned and stormed toward the door. "Thank you for bandaging my hand. I'll let you know if I'm ever able to use it again."

"What you do now, *cher*?" Mrs. Couvillion inquired.

"Print some new photographs, what else?" Ross snapped.

"So, Tessa, what do you think?" Dr. Corman asked eagerly.

"Why, uh..." Tessa hesitated, rapidly reevaluating what he had just told her. That small college in Northern California had just declared its willingness to provide Dr. Corman with a lab and financial help to support his research. Because he'd already received a small grant several weeks earlier Dr. Corman would be able to take Tessa with him at her previous salary.

"Naturally, all your moving expenses will be paid. Did I mention that?" Dr. Corman added.

"Yes. No. Uh, I don't really know." Nor did Tessa know just why she kept feeling such a strange sense of disappointment or why the lump obstructing her chest and stomach wouldn't go away.

"I must say, you don't seem very enthusiastic, Tessa. Is it because you'll be leaving your family?" Dr. Corman probed.

"No." Tessa drew a deep breath. She had taken the time to carefully review the offer and there was nothing to be said against Northern California, no, not one single thing. She had to commit herself now. "It uh, all sounds wonderful, Dr. Corman. I'm sure we'll both be happy in California and I'll start making my preparations now. Thank you for including me."

"Then why is it, Tessa, that I don't believe a word you're saying?" Dr. Corman asked plaintively.

"Well, I, uh . . ." As she heard herself stammering again, Tessa closed her mouth abruptly. She had never been one to stammer. What on earth was wrong with her?

As if she didn't know.

"I guess I just wish it was Louisiana," she said and heard the sudden passion that echoed in her voice.

"Aha! So we get at the truth at last." Dr. Corman laced his hands together on his small desk and looked at Tessa thoughtfully. "Are you really going to be able to forget him, that particular gentleman in Louisiana?" he asked Tessa quietly.

"I have to, Michael. Even if we weren't completely unsuited, Ross has a—a rather distressing sense of omnipotence and a total disregard for danger. Did you happen to read that article on daredevils in the last issue of the *Journal of American Medicine*?"

"Why, yes. I have it here somewhere." Michael Corman pulled a magazine off a pile stacked near his elbow. "Yes, here it is: 'Death-Defying Acts and Their Correlation to Current Mortality Statistics in the United States.'" Dr. Corman's face crinkled with momentary amusement. "Only another scientist could make an article on trapeze artists and tightrope walkers sound so abysmally dull."

"We are a dull breed, aren't we?" Tessa agreed with a world-weary sigh. "I presume you remember the article's conclusion?"

"Yes. I found it fascinating that a person who has slammed around successfully for years, living like a bat out of hell, is suddenly much more apt to suffer a fatal accident following a happy event, particularly marriage or the birth of a child."

"Would you agree with the researchers' theory that suddenly those risk-takers are hesitating just a moment too long, maybe holding on to life too tightly?" Tessa inquired earnestly. "Do you think that an abrupt infusion of caution into their previously incautious lives is the very thing that ultimately does them in?"

"Frankly, I don't know," Dr. Corman admitted. "The most dangerous thing I've ever done is to drive the Washington freeways. But it all sounds logical. When you care deeply about someone—I especially remember this from my early days of marriage with Mrs. Corman—maintaining that person's happiness suddenly becomes urgently important to you."

"I saw that happen to Ross in Louisiana," Tessa added, her voice restrained as she sought to keep it under control. "He wouldn't stop to rest or use sunscreen for himself. He wouldn't swallow salt tablets or water. He didn't think he needed them. But he'd use them all for me, so I wouldn't be left stranded in the swamp if anything should happen to him."

"Sounds like the man may be in love," Dr. Corman said with a rare smile, then he glanced back at the article in his hand. "Yes, I suspect that when life grows sweet, even people who've ducked danger for years will cling to that trapeze one split second too long. I think then they kill themselves simply trying not to."

"Yes," Tessa returned unsmilingly. "And, of course, if that should be true, then I could be the most dangerous thing that's ever happened to Ross Stanton."

The more times Tessa reread the article, the more sense it made. That realization stayed her hand when she might otherwise have reached for the phone and called Ross. It stopped her from writing him a long loving letter or even flying straight back to Louisiana and saying, "Since you can't quite propose marriage, I'm here to do it."

And that, of course, was just exactly what she wanted to do now. Ross's halfhearted attempt to prevent her from leaving him had at last revealed the truth to Tessa.

She loved him utterly.

She wanted to marry him.

But she absolutely didn't want to be responsible for killing him. No, that was what she positively couldn't bear. As painful as life without Ross might be, at least there would be some consolation in knowing he was still alive somewhere in the world, taking his photographs even as he battled hostile elements, terrain or people.

So obviously the sooner they got over each other, the better off they both would be. This time Tessa was going to be sane and sensible about Ross. After all, she'd been sane and sensible most of her life. Surely those attributes shouldn't be too hard to relearn.

So, instead of phoning, Tessa settled for a polite impersonal greeting card that said, "Thank you for a wonderful time." She signed her name to it and shoved it into the first mailbox she passed, then went home and off to bed early. She skipped dinner. Not surprisingly she'd lost her appetite again. Also not surprisingly she simply lay in bed and couldn't sleep.

At least she finally had work to look forward to and that would occupy her lonely, empty hours. From daybreak next day Tessa stayed busy sorting through her numerous possessions in preparation for the move to California. She had to evaluate what to save, sell or toss.

On the fifth day following her return to Washington, Tessa opened all of her overdue library books and made herself start reading about California. This move certainly promised new horizons to explore, she thought, thumbing through the colorful pages. Automatically she began picking out sites of particular interest. Carmel and the Big Sur area headed her list. Ross had told her how spectacular the scenery was there. The castle of the late newspaper mogul, William Randolph Hearst, was something else Tessa wanted to see because Ross had photographed it. Determinedly she thrust Ross out of her mind, then wondered why she wasn't more excited about her move to the West. Why did she keep feeling like she was being led off to a guillotine?

Because she wanted to be back in Louisiana with him, of course.

Glenn phoned while Tessa sat reading, propped up in bed. He would be in town on the following evening, he informed her, and would like to take her to dinner. Yes, he'd had some recent news of Aunt Fay and she was doing just fine. He'd tell Tessa all about it at dinner tomorrow night.

"I have some news to tell you, too," Tessa said.

"You're getting married!" Glenn exclaimed.

"I certainly am not," Tessa retorted in annoyance. "But I do have a job again."

"That's great, Tessa. Save the details for dinner."

Tessa hung up, feeling even more annoyed. Glenn didn't take her career seriously, she thought. Otherwise he wouldn't always be harping on the subject of marriage, which she could certainly exist quite well without, or at least she sure hoped she could.

Unexpectedly her doorbell rang, rattling every nerve in her body and making her sit bolt upright in bed. Immediately Tessa's heart started pounding berserkly. Of course, it must be someone who had made a mistake, someone who was hunting for another resident's apartment. All of Tessa's friends were much too well-bred to turn up in the evening unannounced.

But a part of Tessa—a yearning, hopeful part—already knew who it was. She leaped out of the bed and jerked a thin robe around her.

By the time she reached her darkened living room and stood before the front door her courage almost failed her. Could she stand to hope and then have those hopes dashed again? "Who is it?" she called, clutching the robe closed over her breasts.

"At this hour who do you think? I got your thank-you card and flew up to tell you what I think about it, which isn't much. Now, will you open this damned door? I'm loaded down with gear," Ross shouted, loudly enough to disturb every neighbor on Tessa's floor.

Tessa's shaking hands loosened their clutch on her robe, and it fell carelessly open as she struggled to unlock the dead bolt, then the burglarproof lock and finally the chain.

Ross swept inside, wearing his best tropical khakis. Both of his arms were loaded with packs of various sizes and his camera and binoculars swung as usual from straps around his neck.

He shed his baggage and faced Tessa, his expression grim. Even in the dim light she could see the blazing blue-green glare of his eyes. "And that card you sent," he continued, "was downright snotty!"

"Ross..." Tessa began uncertainly and watched her hand move, as if by magic, to touch the warm reassuring solidity of his elbow. A Ross who was angry and on the offensive was obviously being buffeted by strong emotions, she knew. Usually, he was such a cheerful, happy, peaceful man.

How could she bear for him to be unhappy, Tessa wondered, even when it was for his own good? Well, she had to deal with it, but seeing Ross sad felt like someone had turned a knife on her and it became hard for her to think, or even breathe.

"Since we seem to be having trouble communicating, I thought maybe we'd do better in person," Ross continued, his voice at its gruffest. But already his hand had reached out to capture hers.

"Ross, I didn't mean to send you a snotty card," Tessa said and heard her voice start to quiver. Oh God, what was she going to do? He was off on some horrible trip somewhere, otherwise an overnight bag would have sufficed— and he was much too tense and tightly wound up for this to be a purely social call.

"I didn't mean to stall at the New Orleans airport, either," he said swiftly. "But, sweetheart, I've never tried before to tell a woman that I wanted her—for always, I mean."

Warmth, like a newly stoked fire, flamed up inside Tessa. Her heart actually turned over and her eyes began to sting as she finally realized the true extent of his feelings. "You love me, Ross? I mean, you actually, truly do?" she couldn't resist asking him.

"I actually, truly do, though I probably need my head examined." Tessa heard him draw an uneven breath. "I flew up here to tell you so." As Ross talked, he swung the camera and binoculars over his head. "So what do you think about that?"

What Tessa thought, for one single splendid moment, was that she had never felt quite so ridiculously happy in her life. Ross really loved her and had finally found the words to tell her so! Then Tessa was afraid she was going to start crying again. God, she was disgusting. She had never known she could be such a tragically dependent, emotion-riddled person, always hanging onto one man's every utterance. She hoped none of her women friends ever, *ever* learned about her wretched fall from independence. She was a disgrace to professional women everywhere.

But I just never knew it could be like this, Tessa thought, loving someone so badly and wanting everything I can't have with him so very, very much.

At least she knew she couldn't have him. She wasn't too far gone for that.

Then, as Ross's hands began to connect with her shoulders, Tessa felt herself being pulled awkwardly yet tenderly against him. "Will you marry me, Tessa?"

Another wave of joy rushed over her, even as her mind gave a scream of pain. She had to decline immediately, she couldn't hesitate. "Of course not," she breathed. "Why, I'd be a widow in a month." Then Tessa did start to cry, and deep, silent sobs shook her until she found herself nestled close to Ross, his large hands stroking her back while his lips moved against her hair.

"Somehow I don't find that too convincing, Tessa, at least not while you're hanging so tight on my neck," Ross laughed.

"Oh, I want to say yes, Ross. I really do want to," Tessa wailed and found a big clean handkerchief being shoved into her hands. Thank God, Ross always came equipped for her tears. She wiped her eyes, then began again more hesitantly. "I don't suppose you'd ever consider another line of work?"

"Are you crazy?" he blurted.

"Probably. But so are you. Well, would you at least consider giving up—"

"Taking my most dangerous photos? Not on your life. In fact, I'm leaving for Brazil in just three days. You wouldn't believe the big bucks they're going to pay me."

His voice was blunt. Honest. At least Reckless Ross was a truthful man, Tessa thought. "Oh," she said flatly and wiped her nose.

So that settled things for her, although Tessa knew that Ross wouldn't really believe she could stand firm in her refusal to marry him. There was definitely a stormy scene brewing on the horizon, but right now, all Tessa could deal with was his suddenly possessive touch and the welcome feel of his hands as they began to move over her.

"You look so lovely," Ross breathed, his voice deepening with desire. One large thumb brushed the lace cup over Tessa's breast, then an inquiring finger slid beneath the spaghetti strap above.

He's rarely stopped to take a look at me in a nightgown, Tessa thought, amused despite her fears for the future. Always in the past, she'd no sooner dropped a nightgown over her head before Ross was tugging it off over her ankles.

Now he stopped to really look at her again. Then he caught her close, allowing his lips to follow his hands across her throat and breasts, and start on a heated downward path. Immediately Tessa's whole body awakened, arching toward Ross, aching for him. She felt dizzied by his touch, his scent.

His mouth, tasting of passion, moved back to cover hers hungrily and Tessa gripped him, wanting him just as much as he so obviously wanted her.

Momentarily Ross paused between kisses. "Five days. It's only been five days and I thought I'd go nuts missing you."

"I know how you felt," she agreed, winding her arms even tighter around his neck.

Then Tessa found herself being slowly led backward to her long, low living-room sofa. Ross stretched her out and began to remove the thin robe that still clung to her shoulders. He peeled away her lacy nightgown next. He buried his warm face in her neck and she felt the slight scratch of his beard and the eager stroking of his hands.

"No fair," Tessa whispered in his ear. "I'm naked and you're not. I want to touch you, too."

A shiver ran over Ross at her words. Swiftly he drew back and began rapidly shedding his clothes. His shirt and undershirt dropped first. Next he carelessly threw down his socks and kicked off his shoes. Tessa heard his zipper hiss, then he dragged slacks and shorts together down over his narrow hips.

He was the most beautiful sight she had ever seen—but, of course, he really was the most beautiful man in the world, Tessa thought dreamily. Ectomorph, the most desired body type. Long limbs and elegantly stylized lines . . .

Then Ross was beside her again, alive and virile, and Tessa wanted him like this—healthy and breathing and near her every single night. She wanted him as her husband, the father of the children she longed to create with him. But there could be no wavering and no compromise on her part, Tessa thought as her hands searched for him avidly. She couldn't agree to accept him, to reluctantly endure his dangerous profession—not as long as who he was and what he did would almost inevitably prove fatal. It was all or nothing now. Tessa loved him passionately, but she had told Ross just exactly how it had to be.

Because, by simply loving her, Ross was now in more danger than he'd ever been in before.

"Tessa, sweetheart, you'd better stop that or I..." Under her touch Ross groaned with pleasure.

"I don't want to stop," Tessa said fiercely, knowing she needed no further arousing. But of course, all Ross had ever had to do was kiss and caress her and then pure instinct took over, readying her for him.

Tonight was no exception. He was a flame that sent searing heat sweeping over her in wave after wave, until she was carried away from everything and everyone else. Only Ross was there, rising and falling with her, murmuring her name. Their lovemaking lasted until Tessa wondered how much pleasure she could possibly endure, only to find even more in the last and highest of those searing waves of fire.

Slowly, very slowly, real life began to ebb back. Tessa found herself shaken and breathless, tears trickling down her face again, but since Ross's face was also damp she couldn't be sure if they were her tears or his. For a moment she closed her eyes again, not wanting to face the real world and all of its appalling problems.

"Tessa, you didn't mean it, did you? About not marrying me?" Ross asked, his lips against her temple.

She'd meant it. Rarely had she ever meant anything more.

"Not yet," Tessa replied urgently. "Don't let's talk just yet, Ross. Let's just lie here and be close to each other and even make love again because, later, I think we're going to have a very bad fight."

Chapter Thirteen

As it turned out, once they sat down to talk next day there really wasn't all that much to fight about. Two very different people, each absolutely unmoving, had reached an inevitable impasse. That meant there was little left to say or do.

"At least we're not descending to name-calling or accusing each other of being selfish," Ross said at last. "I think it's encouraging, Tessa, that we respect each other that much."

Tessa turned away without comment. She was hardpressed to find anything encouraging in today's discussion.

From her viewpoint, that of simply wanting Ross to stay alive, the news of his next expedition couldn't sound worse. He was leaving the day after tomorrow for Brazil where he would team up with a bush pilot named Gene Adams. According to Ross, they had worked together a couple of times before.

Gene would then fly Ross into an area of mountainous and almost impenetrable jungle that still showed up as Unexplored on current maps of the area, along with a chilling notation that the Indians who lived there were hostile. All other would-be explorers, photographers and missionaries who had been dropped into this particular region had disappeared without a trace.

As if all that wasn't enough, Ross planned to parachute from the plane since there weren't any natural landing strips nearby. Then, if the Indians didn't spot him floating down and if he survived the jump and didn't hang himself or his parachute up too badly in the thick trees, Ross would make his way downriver photographing the various birds and animals he met along the way. Ideally, five to ten days later, he was to meet Gene again at a clearing where two rivers intersected—provided, of course, that Gene didn't crash trying to land between the mountains.

It was exactly the sort of thing that Reckless Ross was famous for, but getting him to own up to all the fearsome details had been about as easy as pulling hens' teeth, Tessa reflected.

Aloud she made no negative comments, but she was sure her face said it all.

Obviously Ross read the dismay that Tessa wasn't allowing herself to show, for he came over to her. As she stood with her head down he swung his arms around her, then wrapped her close and tight in a bear hug.

"Hey, I lead a charmed life, remember?" Ross said. Then he brightened as he always did when their mood threatened to turn somber, swinging Tessa around and grinning down at her.

"Okay, charmer," Tessa sighed. "You can go out to dinner with me tonight. My brother Glenn is in town, so you'll get to meet the future congressman."

"Ah, the famous Glenn about whom I once heard so much."

"It was all true, too," Tessa retorted. "And I should tell you that Glenn is pompous, conventional and boring, and I guarantee you two will absolutely detest each other."

"Wonderful. Tomorrow we can drive over to Richmond where you can meet my father and stepmother, Linda. I'm sure you'll hate them both, too."

The evening with Glenn was going to be a disaster, Tessa just knew it. She even wondered what twisted part of her psyche insisted on introducing the two dramatically dissimilar men to one another.

Because I happen to love them both. That's why it's important to me that they meet, Tessa thought.

She expected, at best, an evening of gritted teeth and inane pleasantries, especially once the talk turned to business, as masculine conversations almost inevitably did in her experience. Then when Ross, a dedicated conservationist who longed to see the natural habitats of wildlife and fowl preserved and protected, found himself pitted against Glenn, who encouraged industry in any form in order to lower unemployment, things would get unpleasantly sticky.

"Please don't tell Ross that you favor spreading concrete over all our national parks and leasing them out to free enterprise concession stands," Tessa muttered to Glenn when she opened the door to him.

She had already warned Ross about what was liable to set her brother's hair on fire. "Please don't tell my brother that you favor reintroducing both the wolf and the bison into the industrialized Eastern corridor."

Perhaps her warnings helped. Glenn, at least, seemed duly impressed with Ross's various prizes and awards, having heard about them from Aunt Fay.

"How is that dear lady?" Ross inquired, a genuine affection for Aunt Fay revealing itself at the mention of Glenn's favorite aunt.

"Why, she sounds just like her old self again, and she said to be sure and give you and Tessa her love. You really impressed her, Ross...."

At dinner in a posh Washington restaurant Tessa sat back and watched in astonishment as the two men talked away like each was the other's best friend.

The evening with Stan and Linda was going to be a disaster, Ross just knew it. Stan would make his usual cracks attacking the medical profession, reserving especially scathing remarks for research scientists like Tessa.

Then Linda would inquire if Tessa was a vegetarian and, on learning that she wasn't, Linda would go into her hour-long "Flesh-is-impossible-to-digest-and-your-stomach-will-be-ruined" routine.

Ross, in fact, felt so nervous about the upcoming meeting that he had even called ahead from Washington, using a pay phone while Tessa thought he was out buying more film for Brazil. "Look, Stan," he began, cutting through his father's pleasantries. "You and Linda may not like what Tessa stands for, but please remember that she did save my life."

"And we are all certainly very grateful to her for that," Stan assured his son.

"So if you could just skip the usual philosophical debate about whether or not white mice have souls—wait a minute, Stan. Just who do you mean by all?" Ross asked warily.

"Why, your other stepmothers will be here, too. Kiki, Deby and Bambi were all quite distraught when they found out you were near death's door in Arizona. Linda and I had called them immediately, of course, and they came over to wait with us. You know how very close we all are. So your stepmothers naturally want to meet Tessa.''

''Yeah, sure,'' Ross muttered disconsolately and hung up. What would be worse, for Tessa to be exposed to Stan and Linda on their respective soapboxes or to have her welcomed into what looked like a polygamist's big, happy family? Ross groaned aloud, contrasting Stan's five marriages and three divorces to Tessa's very staid and conservative upbringing.

But to his surprise, Tessa actually seemed to enjoy meeting Linda, Stan and the former participants of what Ross privately labelled ''Stan's harem.''

''Oh, Ross will look just like you in a few years,'' she exclaimed spontaneously on shaking Stan's hand. Nor did Tessa even flinch when Linda, a chronic hugger who still looked like a refugee from the sixties with her floor-length dress and long straight hair, folded her in an embrace.

Tessa also apparently liked Ross's three blond exstepmothers. She seemed especially drawn to Kiki and, more than once during the evening, Ross saw their two heads close together as they whispered about something they both clearly considered important.

Because Stan and Linda wouldn't eat restaurant food, believing that it was too loaded with sodium and preservatives to be fit for human consumption, Ross had braced himself for some awful casserole full of tofu and laced with weeds and seeds—and, of course, there was one. However, Bambi had brought a bucket of fried chicken and Kiki a dish of scalloped potatoes while Deby, the best cook of all, had prepared a scrumptiously rich chocolate dessert, so there was no need for anyone to go hungry. A fresh green salad and Stan's homemade wine were both excellent. So all Ross had to do was sit back and let Stan and the women chatter away while the dinner passed quite painlessly.

But matters turned serious after Ross's three ex-stepmothers were hugged farewell by Linda and Stan and the door had closed behind them.

When Stan said, "Look, we need to talk to Tessa," the topic wasn't at all what Ross was dreading.

"Yes, I need another doctor's opinion," Linda said in her soft, little-girl's voice. "You see, I've been feeling really lousy for the last couple of months, so I finally saw a medical doctor earlier this week. He ran some lab tests and we got the results today...."

Adult onset diabetes. Those words scared the living hell out of Ross and, when he glanced over at his father, he could see that the handsome, graying Stan wasn't even trying to conceal his deep concern. Stan had already been widowed once. Now that he was happily married again, after striking out three times, he was desperately worried about the health of his young wife.

Tessa was wonderful to them, Ross thought. First she asked a whole string of questions that revealed her genuine interest in Linda's condition, then she made a number of recommendations, suggesting first that Linda should be more precisely evaluated by an endocrinologist. It was entirely possible that Linda would be able to control the diabetes with diet, weight loss and exercise. If not, there were a number of effective oral medications available. No, it would probably not come to insulin shots if the facts as stated by Linda and Stan were correct. Adult onset diabetes was not nearly so serious as juvenile diabetes, Tessa added, continuing to soothe them.

"Juvenile diabetes is my own special area of expertise," Tessa informed Stan and Linda. "I understand that you're opposed to medical research, but I'd like to explain why I believe that mine is essential. I'm trying to learn more about the mechanism of nerve damage, which often leads to a loss of feeling in the legs and feet of diabetics. Sometimes this nerve loss problem even necessitates the amputation of toes and, occasionally, feet and legs...."

Quietly Tessa talked on, explaining her work, which involved studying this nerve loss syndrome in diabetic mice and rats in the hope of later being able to apply the newly gained knowledge to help threatened human beings. While Ross was convinced of Tessa's sincerity, he still couldn't help noticing the dubious looks passing between Stan and Linda. But at least the old boy wasn't yelling with his customary militancy, Ross noted.

"I see no reason why we can't agree to disagree, and still be friends," Stan said diplomatically at the last, holding out his hand to Tessa.

Then, as Ross watched in complete surprise, Tessa took it, and at the door, when Linda and Stan both reached for her, she actually hugged them back.

No one had gotten killed! Ross could still scarcely believe it. But a quick glance at his watch told him his last hours with Tessa were winding down fast. So he leaned on the gas as he headed Tessa's small sports car back to Washington. It was a responsive little devil, and Ross was having quite a lot of fun gradually opening it up to full throttle—until Dr. Spoilsport slowed him down.

"Where's the fire?" Tessa asked, and Ross reluctantly touched the brakes.

He didn't have the heart to tell her just how early he was leaving tomorrow morning or that he wanted to get back in time to make love to her. Later, if Tessa got as mad as Ross thought she would be, tonight just might be their very last time.

* * *

Someone was kissing the backs of her ankles, then the same warm lips glided up to the backs of her knees. And she knew just who that someone was. Tessa smiled and opened her eyelids a smidgen, but they still felt so heavy that she snuggled even closer to the mattress. It was much too early to get up just yet. There was scant light in the room and that was artificial because all the windows were still black as pitch.

Anyway, Tessa felt too replete to move, her well-satisfied body limp and relaxed. Surely Ross wasn't interested in *more* lovemaking, she thought with a little inner chuckle. After last night and the ecstatic heights they'd scaled together, he was surely starting something he wouldn't be able to finish.

Should she tease him and tell him so? The little inner chuckle became a soft outer one as his lips now feathered up over her hip, then moved abruptly to her shoulder, her temple, her brow.

"That's right, sweetheart, keep smiling," he whispered. "I'll be back in touch just as soon as I can."

Tessa was so sleepy that his words didn't register immediately. "Mmm-hmm," she said, then dropped right back to sleep, only to jerk awake not ten seconds later.

"Ross!" she screamed, sitting up in bed and pushing the hair out of her eyes.

"Bye," he called back to her glibly. She heard him opening the front door.

"Ross!" Tessa's second cry was even louder as she jumped up and went running after him.

The front door slammed just as she rounded the corner. Tessa dashed over to it and flung it open. Ross was already standing by the elevator, wearing his tropical khakis and carrying his gear. "You wretch," Tessa screamed again. "You told me you were leaving around ten."

The elevator door opened. Ross tossed his gear inside, stuck a foot in the door to prevent it from closing and then turned back to Tessa.

"Don't go," she pleaded. "Oh, Ross, something really awful could happen to you on such a wild, ill-conceived—"

"I love you, worrywart. And we'll get married just as soon as I get back."

"The hell we will, Ross Stanton. I'll never marry you!"

Even Ross looked a bit taken aback by Tessa's ferocity. She saw him hesitate, then he swallowed hard. "Tessa, is that a final and definite no?"

No? How could she say no? Why, she'd never been able to say no to Ross, at least not for long. Why did she think this particular no would stick, either?

"No," Tessa sighed, her rage fading as she came to her senses. "I mean that's not a definite and final no. Oh, Ross, please come back. We'll get married now—today!"

"I've got a little errand to run first. Hey, don't dress like that for anyone else but me."

Belatedly Tessa glanced down and realized for the first time that she was stark naked. She noticed further, that various apartment doors were starting to be opened as a result of her screams. As the elevator closed behind Ross, Tessa slunk back inside her own apartment.

I never even told him I loved him, she thought, sagging against her front door.

Well, yes, she had, in a way but she wondered if Ross would ever notice in all of the excitement over his latest jaunt. He had made fresh coffee in the kitchen and left half a pot for her. Tessa slopped some into a mug with dangerously shaking hands. It was just as well that Ross had walked out of her life. Take a look at the wreck he'd already made of her. Why, she'd been willing to beg and plead, to abandon her scruples and lower her standards—to do virtually anything to keep him safe by her side. But none of it nor all of it had proved to be enough.

Now Tessa certainly didn't relish waiting out the next several days. She'd had a bad feeling about this trip from the beginning, a really bad feeling. Nor was she the only one who had. Apparently Mrs. Couvillion was on Tessa's wavelength for she'd said in St. Clément that Ross might hurt himself if Tessa didn't manage to stop him.

Last night Kiki had expressed the very same reservations. "Ross has been going on these harebrained jaunts long enough. He's already made a small fortune, so he can't possibly need the money. I think he's hooked on the excitement and the pride of being known as the best. But he's pushed too hard and too long. Frankly I'm afraid his luck's going to run out. Oh, Tessa, stop him if you can."

But she hadn't been able to. She'd failed. She couldn't stop Ross with logic, and she couldn't stop him with her first proud refusal to marry a man who gambled with his life. Why, she hadn't even been able to stop him with her last desperate cries.

I've been a stupid fool, that's what I've been, Tessa thought bitterly. Because she had been loath to do anything really sneaky, rotten and low-down, anything that preyed on Ross's emotions or manipulated him through his love for her or actually threatened him with the loss of her love, she had let him go walking out of here on the most perilous assignment of his life. And she was probably going to spend the rest of her life regretting it, too.

The delicious premium coffee now tasted like so much hemlock. Tessa slammed the mug into the kitchen sink so hard that it cracked. Then she crept back to bed, to hug the pillow on which Ross's golden head had rested, a pillow that still carried his scent, and tried to bargain with God. First she said her entire repertoire of prayers, then she started making rash, impulsive promises that all ended the same way:

"Just send Ross back safely and I swear I'll never let him get into trouble again."

On this occasion, at least, Tessa was just too plain scared to cry.

Dr. Corman's phone call interrupted her promise of a medical missionary practice and donation of her worldly goods to the poor if God would please—

As usual, Dr. Corman came right to the point. "How strange that you should have mentioned Louisiana the other day," he said thoughtfully. "There's a job for you there, in New Orleans, if you'd like to consider it, Tessa."

Then, while Tessa listened incredulously, Dr. Corman explained that a former colleague of his, knowing of his and Tessa's predicament, had phoned to offer them positions. Dr. Corman had already rejected Louisiana for himself since he preferred to go to California. However, one job in New Orleans, which included a part-time clinical practice with diabetic children, as well as research, just might suit Tessa.

"Yes, I believe it would," she said, casting a somewhat awed eye upward.

"I was afraid you'd say that, my dear." Regret vibrated in Dr. Corman's voice. Then he added hastily, "But, of course, you have to do what's right for you. And somehow, Tessa, I think you've chosen what's right."

"Yes. If—if Ross just comes back alive from Brazil, then I want to marry him," Tessa heard herself saying.

So, finally, it had come down to simply this. She just had to be with him for every single day she possibly could, even if she did disapprove of his life-style and even if she became a widow almost before she'd had a chance to be his wife.

"All right, Tessa," Dr. Corman sighed. "I'll set up an interview for you in New Orleans."

"Thank you, Michael," she whispered and hung up, thinking that Dr. Corman made a highly unlikely, but effective archangel.

It was a fine fair morning bright with golden sunshine and as Ross climbed into Gene Adams's small bush plane he felt ready to take on anything and anyone.

Hey, it's going to be all right, he told Tessa silently, as if she could pick up his thoughts and feel more reassured.

"Ready to go, Ross?" Gene yelled over the sound of the plane's engines.

From the small cargo area, where Ross sat all strung up in his bulky parachute, he grinned and flashed Gene a confident thumbs-up sign.

Yes, he was ready, as ready as he'd ever be. Three days ago he'd flown down to Belém and he and Gene had been busy ever since, poring over maps and handling all of the last-minute details. Then they had made the preliminary hop to their jumping-off place—a town so tiny it barely showed up on the map.

At least the place had a halfway decent hotel with a pleasant watering hole, so, for the past two evenings, Ross and Gene had unwound over a beer. *Just one, Tessa.* Gene, another relaxed, easygoing, laid-back type was always good company. He and Ross had laughed and talked, reminiscing about previous photographic treks they'd worked on and swapping inflated lies about what they'd been doing meanwhile. It was all very manly and full of gusto. *And I swear I didn't see a single woman I would have touched with a ten-foot pole, Tessa.*

Every night, right at ten, Ross and Gene had drained the last drops of beer and had bidden each other good-night, because consummate professionals always did their partying after the job was complete, not before.

You probably won't believe me, sweetheart, but it's the truth.

As a result, Ross and Gene were both bright-eyed and bushy-tailed this morning. The plane taxied down the dirt runway where Gene swung it around deftly. He revved the engine and up they went. Ross, glancing out occasionally through his own tiny window, began his customary last-minute check of his cameras and other photographic equipment.

Much of his stuff, of course, had been left back at the hotel to await his return. Also, Ross had, of course, checked daily on the contents of his one priceless pack that would come floating down from the sky with him. It was priceless because where Ross was going there would be no photography shops and no anything else. So he'd better damned well have everything he needed with him and all of it in perfect working order.

Ross had checked his pack again first thing this morning, making sure no thieves had broken into his room during the night and that no curious hotel maid had gone poking around, either.

Everything had been fine, then and now. So at last it was time for his final ritual. Rapidly Ross began ripping open his gold boxes of film, then he opened the small black cartridges that contained the film as well. He had never forgotten being deep in the dangerous bush of New Guinea and discovering to his horror that two spools of 35-mm film had somehow been wound backward at the film factory. Leo at *American Geographic* had definitely been less than happy to have to express Ross a few inexpensive cartons of film and refinance the whole trip for him.

On the other hand, Ross didn't like to rip open boxes of film for checking a minute too soon, either, because even with today's less than fragile product there were still the hazards of light, water and sticky human hands.

Swiftly Ross checked the first six boxes. Perfect, he thought with pleasure. Only two more to go.

The seventh didn't open as readily as the others had. Frowning, Ross slipped a fingernail under the carton and pulled.

It opened then, but the canister also failed to fall out as smoothly as it should have. What the hell? Ross thought, shaking it impatiently.

Then the canister dropped into his lap, along with a small stick-em note that landed upside down. Ross turned it around and read it quickly. Even with Tessa's physician's scrawl to contend with, this particular message was easy to decipher.

"I love you."

As he clutched that simple message Ross forgot all about checking the remaining boxes. Tessa had never told him before that she loved him. Of course, he knew that she did, but still, seeing those words in black and white made a lump rise in his chest even as he laughed out loud and then he felt . . . well, he didn't exactly know. Good. No, better than good. What Ross felt now was something warm, something that reminded him of home.

Suddenly an old memory flashed into his mind. He had been just a kid, about eight years old, when he'd opened his brown lunch sack at school one day and had found a special treat. It was a cupcake with vanilla frosting and on the top his mother had spelled out, "I love you," in small tasty chocolate letters.

Ross had licked her words off quickly, lest someone else see them and hoot, but a similar feeling of love and warmth and home had engulfed him then. He knew at the time that baking cupcakes for him had taken a special effort on his mother's part because she hadn't been very well lately—although Ross hadn't yet started to suspect how really sick she was.

Life had changed irrevocably after his mother had died, Ross remembered. Changed both for Stan and for himself. And somehow life had never quite felt the same again, even though he'd later been blessed with four dear stepmothers who'd all loved him, spoiled him outrageously and still took pains to stay in touch.

Life had been even worse for Stan, Ross realized. Oh sure, Stan was finally happy again with Linda, but even that relationship, at best, was a rather quirky one.

Now, as Ross looked down at the note he held, the powerful realization swept over him that without Tessa he would be just as lost as his father had been. Sure, there might be other women someday, but there would never be one to replace this very special and beloved woman.

And Tessa obviously felt the same way about him. Why, she'd said it quite a number of times and in a lot of different ways. By fussing over him and worrying about him. By loving him at night in that no-holds-barred way that swept him up into heart-stopping rapture.

She had told him so in the Atchafalaya, when Ross had first thought she was just worried about being stranded and lost should he inconveniently drop dead. What was it Tessa had said? "If anything happened to you, I think I'd rather be left here."

He'd heard her. He'd understood her words. And yet somehow he *still* hadn't really gotten it. Not completely. Not until right now.

Suddenly Ross found himself looking out the window once again, at the jagged, rocky mountains and the deep green of the jungle far below. It was going to be hot down there—very hot. And Tessa had told him to avoid being out alone in extreme heat since he was more susceptible now to sunstroke.

The memory of her stricken face as he'd seen it last rose up before him now. The way she'd looked just before he'd leaped into that elevator. By now, if he knew Tessa—and Ross thought he did—she would be worried sick, her easily inflamed imagination working overtime. She would worry about whether he'd wear sunscreen, or take salt pills, or do any one of a dozen other things. Because she loved him she worried. Consequently, she'd be suffering plenty as a result.

Was that what a man did to someone who really, truly loved him? Was that what a real *man* did to someone he loved? Why, loving someone always meant you had responsibilities.

Anyway, how long could he count on Tessa to put up with such worry and suffering? Not very long, Ross suspected, because Tessa was no masochist. She'd get fed up with him eventually. The next time she told him no she might even mean it.

He glanced back out of the window, assessing the situation below coolly and realistically. *You know, I really could get hurt down there,* Ross admitted to himself. *I don't feel like it will happen—I still think I'm equal to the challenge—but I might be wrong. I could break a leg on the jump, or encounter an animal, snake or Indian I can't handle. Why, I might even have another sunstroke.*

It had been one thing to go slamming around the globe when he was young, single and not involved with any special woman. Yes, it had been one thing when he'd had no reason to doubt his stamina and health. Then it had been worth a few risks and injuries to be Ross Stanton, wildlife photographer par excellence, who snapped the pictures nobody else could have gotten in a million years.

He'd made money, too. He'd won a hundred photography awards, including that Pulitzer. Yes, he'd had a hell of a good time and he sure didn't regret a minute of it.

But, right now, I want to live more than I ever have before, Ross thought. *Yeah, I sure don't want to mess this one up, because I want to marry Tessa and live with her and a flock of kids for the rest of my life. And I want to photograph that ivory-billed woodpecker, because I know the stupid bird is still alive and well and hiding out in the Atchafalaya. Why, I'll bet Tessa would come with me into the swamp to look for it. She actually liked it there.*

"Three minutes, Ross, till we hit the drop zone," Gene called back over his shoulder.

Casually Ross stood up and began shrugging out of his parachute. "Turn around," he shouted up to Gene, his voice steady and matter-of-fact. "I'm not going to make this jump. Let some other hotshot go for it."

Gene swung his head around in disbelief, staring in consternation. "Ross, are you kidding? My God, you're serious, aren't you?"

"Damn right," said Ross cheerfully as the parachute fell free. Suddenly it felt like another burden had just dropped off him as well. Maybe the burden of being Reckless Ross had grown a lot heavier than he'd thought.

"Leo at *American Geographic* is going to have your hide," Gene warned.

"Oh, he'll get over it. I've taken too many great pictures for Leo to hold a grudge. And I'll take some more. Why, I'm going to hand him the ivory-billed woodpecker in living color, home in Louisiana and drilling its little beak off getting beetles out of a tree.''

"You're a great guy, Ross, but you're such a dreamer."

"Hey, Gene, I'm going to get married, too. You want to come to a big Cajun wedding?''

"Hell, no.'' Gene shuddered. "Marriage could be catching.''

Tessa was packing to fly to New Orleans when her telephone rang for the second time in less than ten minutes.

The first call had come from a Dr. Jerry Meyers at the New Orleans Institute for Endocrinology. "Michael Corman told me all about you, Dr. Fitzgerald,'' Dr. Meyers said without preamble. "And anyone that he recommends so highly is certainly someone I'm eager to interview. When can you come down?''

Why, I'm going to be a shoo-in for this job, Tessa thought, feeling pleasantly surprised for the first time in days.

Since Dr. Meyers didn't mince words, she didn't either. "I'll be happy to come immediately,'' she offered.

"Good! I'm anxious to get the position filled.''

So, once again, Tessa's suitcases lay on her bed and she was hastily tossing things into them. At least updating her résumé and running lots of errands had kept her from going crazy worrying about Ross. He was probably crawling his way through a tangle of jungle right now, she thought, trying to avoid primitive Indians with spears or blow darts or machetes or something....

Her phone rang again. Tessa scooped it up, then listened incredulously. "Dr. Tessa Fitzgerald has a call from the Caribbean,'' announced an operator with a faintly British accent.

"This is Dr. Fitzgerald," Tessa said while her heart pounded frantically and her hands began to sweat. It had to be Ross. But how could it be Ross? Anyway, why would he be calling from the Caribbean?

Oh, God, if you'll just keep him safe I'll do anything! Heal the sick and feed the poor and help the homeless. . . .

"Tessa? Sweetheart, is that you?"

She sagged against the wall, suddenly almost too weak from relief to stand. "Of course it's me," Tessa cried, feeling positively giddy.

"Good! For a minute there I thought I was talking to Mother Teresa in Calcutta."

"What in the world are you doing in the Caribbean, Ross Stanton?" Tessa demanded. Then her knees buckled, and she had to sit down abruptly on the floor.

"I'm in Trinidad. I just flew in from Brazil. Early tomorrow morning I'll be on a direct flight back to the States."

"Why did you leave Brazil?" Tessa demanded, clutching the receiver with both hands.

Then, when Ross told her in a few crisp, well-chosen words, she started crying. "I don't believe you," Tessa said and kept on saying it. "I don't believe you." But the reason she also kept on crying was because a part of her did believe him.

"But—but how do you plan to make a living, Ross?" she asked at last.

"I'll open a studio in New Orleans. Take pictures at Mardi Gras. Otherwise I'll shoot brides and kids. I sure know the first bride I want to photograph."

"You're awfully sure of yourself."

"That's right," Ross continued. "But you'll have to put up with my swamp pictures. I intend to go to St. Clément on the weekends. I guess we'll have to build a place over there, because I want to specialize in photographs of that region. The birds and animals. The people who live there and the very unique way they live—"

"You don't really mean it. You're not ready to settle down, are you?" Tessa said dubiously, then she started crying again. She could tell from Ross's voice that he really meant it.

"Look, lady, you just be at New Orleans International Airport at noon tomorrow and you can see for yourself."

At 12:10 p.m. on the following day Tessa paced restlessly up and down by the gate where Ross's flight was scheduled to arrive at any minute. It had already touched down and was taxiing in from the runway.

What on earth will I do if he's had another change of heart? Tessa thought. *Oh, what if he's not on that flight?*

Finally, a few long minutes later, the plane stopped at the gate.

Or what if Ross thinks he means it now, but misses the excitement in a month or two?

Tessa puzzled over that one for a moment, then craned her neck and stood on tiptoe, trying to peer through the crowd. Passengers were coming off the plane, but she still didn't see Ross.

Listen, where that man is concerned I'm all through being good and noble and straightforward. If I ever get my hands on him again I will never let go! Tessa swore fiercely. *And if Ross ever tries to leave me again or do anything rash and reckless I will scream and cry and throw things! I will threaten to shoot myself—I may even shoot him—and I'll tell him if he doesn't behave that I'll never, ever make love with him again or—*

"Hey, sweetheart! First thing I'm going to teach you is how to relax and take life loose and easy."

Why, he was here, actually *here*, and he'd obviously watched her pace and worry, fret and fume and bite her fingernails to the quick, since he was laughing.

"Ross," Tessa heard herself gasp. She'd been looking everywhere for him, how had she missed seeing him? Especially since he was such a handsome, wonderful-looking man.

He swooped her up, kissed her hungrily and enthusiastically, his lips warm and tender, and she clung to him for dear life. Oh, yes, it really was going to be such a beautiful life, she thought when, finally, their eager lips parted for just a second.

Then, gazing up at Ross, Tessa understood why she hadn't recognized him immediately. And she knew, too, that everything really was going to be all right.

He was wearing a straw hat.

*   *   *   *   *

FOUR UNIQUE SERIES
FOR EVERY WOMAN YOU ARE..

Silhouette Romance

Love, at its most tender, provocative,
emotional... in stories that will make you laugh and
cry while bringing you the magic of falling in love.

6 titles
per month

Silhouette Special Edition

Sophisticated, substantial and packed with
emotion, these powerful novels of life and love will
capture your imagination and steal your heart.

6 titles
per month

Silhouette Desire

Open the door to romance and passion. Humorous,
emotional, compelling—yet always a believable
and sensuous story—Silhouette Desire never
fails to deliver on the promise of love.

6 titles
per month

Silhouette Intimate Moments

Enter a world of excitement, of romance
heightened by suspense, adventure and the
passions every woman dreams of. Let us
sweep you away.

4 titles
per month

SILG-1R

Silhouette Special Edition

COMING NEXT MONTH

AVAILABLE THIS MONTH:

ATTRACTIVE, SPACE SAVING BOOK RACK

Display your most prized novels on this handsome and sturdy book rack. The hand-rubbed walnut finish will blend into your library decor with quiet elegance, providing a practical organizer for your favorite hard-or soft-covered books.

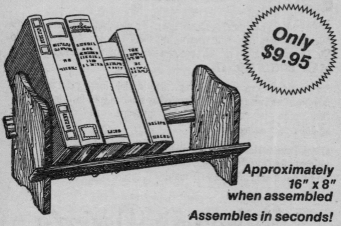

Only $9.95

Approximately 16" x 8" when assembled

Assembles in seconds!

To order, rush your name, address and zip code, along with a check or money order for $10.70* ($9.95 plus 75¢ postage and handling) payable to *Silhouette Books.*

Silhouette Books
Book Rack Offer
901 Fuhrmann Blvd.
P.O. Box 1396
Buffalo, NY 14269-1396

Offer not available in Canada.

BKR-2A

*New York and Iowa residents add appropriate sales tax.

Silhouette Desire®

1989
IS THE YEAR
OF THE MAN!

What makes a romance? A special man, of course, and Silhouette Desire celebrates that fact with *twelve* of them! From Mr. January to Mr. December, every month spotlights the Silhouette Desire hero—our **MAN OF THE MONTH.**

Sexy, macho, charming, irritating...irresistible! Nothing can stop these men from sweeping you away. Created by some of your favorite authors, each man is custom-made for pleasure—*reading* pleasure—so don't miss a single one.

Diana Palmer kicks off the new year, and you can look forward to magnificent men from **Joan Hohl, Jennifer Greene** and many, many more. So get out there and find your man!

Silhouette Desire's

MAN OF THE MONTH...